S. LEGEND

TRISTAN

S Legend Fiction

ALSO BY S. LEGEND

XAVIER'S SCHOOL OF DISCIPLINE

TRISTAN II: A BRAT'S TALE

TRISTAN II: A BRAT'S TALE THE NOVELLA

SLegend Fiction

www.mockingbirdpublications.com

ISBN 978-0-9920246-4-2 (pbk)

ISBN 978-0-9920246-6-6 (epub)

Edited by K. J. Stevens

Cover art by M.A.Sambre

Cover Design by Chiara Monaco

Love is merely a madness; and, I tell you, deserves as well a dark house and a whip as madmen do; and the reason why they are not so punish'd and cured is that the lunacy is so ordinary that the whippers are in love too.

— William Shakespeare, As You Like it

"If I must fall. Let me fall. I promise I will rise again."
~S. Legend
This book is for everyone who believes in me. And for those who don't too.

CONTENTS

CHAPTER 1

*H*i. I'm Tristan Kanes. At least I was once upon a time. Tomorrow, who knows who I'm going to be?

But I digress. I'm getting ahead of myself as usual. I'll back up a bit. I thought it would be a good idea to attempt to run away from my destiny, but destiny tends to follow a person.

I've reached the upper ridges of Markaytia's North Wood and I've been gone for several hours. Lucca will come after me soon. I creep to the edge of the plateau and look out to her, to Markaytia. Tomorrow, I'm to marry an Elven Prince. I know it sounds luxurious, every boy's dream and all, but it isn't that simple.

I must give up my entire life for this man.

It's not long until I hear footsteps I recognize behind me. I'm certain of whom it is, I don't even turn to look, until the tree branch pokes into my back.

He wants to fight me today, does he? I jump up with lightning speed, conditioned from the day I could stand on two feet and because I always take reconnaissance of my surroundings, I know there is a stick for me to use against him, two feet away. I snatch it up and take a defensive stance against my assassin. I strike, slice, slash, pierce, and segment his pathetic battle strategy—well, pathetic against mine, my cousin is a formidable swordsman—I outsmart him at every turn with my dexterous footwork and accomplished foresight.

We've fought in many battles, since the time we were fifteen and trained together from almost the moment we sprang from the womb—it's in our blood. Peace is a warrior's mission, yet in succeeding, he renders himself useless. It makes him no less driven to battle. Peace is a fleeting season, even for Markaytia and I sense that this season of peace has had its turn and war is on the horizon. Either way, everywhere is dangerous now and the people need protection. War will continue to happen whether I want it to or not and when it does, I want to be the one leading the troops.

Now to convince my husband-to-be of that.

"You see, Tristan? You'll make a great Warlord someday," he says, not caring how miserably he's failing.

"You know the truth as well as I do, Lucca. I'll never succeed my father as warlord."

He knows this is a sore spot for me, but of course Lucca pushes me, as usual. He hates my brooding. *Enough with this game.* I draw the real sword I have at my hip (the one I'm not supposed to have) and cleave his fake one in two. "There. You lose."

"Did I? Got your mind off things for a moment." That damn, pompous tone of his leaks right into his expression. I can't deny he's right. It did feel good to move like that—my dark hair whipped with the snap of my movements, my nimble muscles contracting powerfully to move my sword in any arc I desired.

"Okay you did—but it doesn't change anything."

"You're not still sore about it are you? It's not like you're the first royal to have a marriage arranged for him," he teases.

I scowl at him.

Arranged marriage. *Why is my father so old fashioned?* Especially when he and Papa married because they love each other. I wanted to fall in love someday. Perhaps on the battlefield like them. I would be warlord and he would be my second.

"Come. If we are going to misbehave today, let's do it in style. I have a place I've been meaning to show you."

Even my father, Markaytia's current warlord, doesn't leave the palace without an armed guard. It's certainly not a good idea for his son and the Crown Prince of Markaytia to do so either, but Lucca and I do it often. It's far too cumbersome having several members of the guard along on every outing.

I follow behind him, not caring where he'll take me so long as it's far away. Maybe Lucca and I can run away together. He'd do it for me if I asked him, but I would never ask that. He'll be king someday. The people of Markaytia need him.

"Here we are," he says, gesturing to the small lake nestled in the summit of the hilltop. Trees mingle around the perimeter, and open in the right places for the sun to glisten off the water. The place is alive with character, pristine enchantment mixed with naïve innocence, holding secrets from times long turned. There's an eerie aura in the air that prickles my skin, one that suggests we are not the only ones to find this place, but we are of a select few. The

3

water is not the usual aqua, it swirls with blues and purples. It bubbles and boils and steam rises from the surface.

"Lucca, how did you find this?" I whisper not wanting to disrupt the tranquility of this place.

"Let's just say it involved a horse, a deranged ironsmith, and his daughter," he says winking.

Knowing him, he and said ironsmith's daughter have fucked in this mystical pool. I shake my head at him, jealous more than anything. We both peel off our clothes and jump into the water splashing at each other.

The water is lovely and warm. I dip under, drench my long, black hair, resurface, and sweep it off my face. Lucca closes his eyes as he lazily floats on his back and I stare not too directly at the bright sun.

"You don't have to worry you know," he says.

I flick a little water toward him. "And why is that, exactly?"

"When I am king, I shall simply order you to come back."

I roll my eyes. Now he's just being ridiculous. "Somehow, I don't think that applies to betrothals."

"I'll buy you back if I must, then."

He's making me sound like cattle but I know he doesn't mean it that way. "If it were about money, I wouldn't be in this predicament in the first place."

Distress mars his beautiful features. It's as desperate a face as I've ever seen on my dear, sweet cousin, and it tugs at my heart. In a flash, he throws himself on top of me, clinging to my torso, and sobs.

"I know. I know the truth well—I'm never to see you again. How will I live without you?"

I smooth his wet blond hair off his face and kiss his fore-

4

head. "You'll do fine Lucca. You'll go onto achieve great things."

"Do you think he'll let you visit?"

"He might," I say, forcing a smile to filter through my doubt. Appeased, Lucca leans back and floats away from me again, exposing himself to the sun.

I remember the day I was called to the Great Hall alone which set off all kinds of warning bells. Lucca and I were attached at the hip then and were usually called to the Hall together. In hindsight I think it was because my uncle, King Amarail Kanes, knew Lucca would react poorly when he heard the news.

I walked into the hall with my stomach already churning and when I saw that my father and uncle were not alone, it plummeted like it had been shoved in ice-cold water.

That was when I saw *him* for the first time.

The power of his features came from what wasn't there, rather than what was. The man was devoid of imperfections; not one thing about his face or his body hinted to a deficiency. There was no weakness in his impenetrable demeanor—the man was used to winning and getting what he wanted. His cold purple eyes knew no warmth or sunshine, and sat as sentinels atop the high bridge of his patrician nose, complementing the supercilious manner that surrounded him. Without a smile on his face, he looked cruel, and stony. At the same time, there was no darkness in him whatever. Gold hair flowed long over silver robes that were open to reveal porcelain white skin; unmarred, and solid. The breezy, pretty robes did nothing to diminish the restrained force of his chest and abdomen muscles—he seemed to dominate the effeminate attire, as if he'd already defeated it. Not a body built for fieldwork, but for blood—*war*.

My cock stirred for him and made it impossible to deny that I was attracted to this ice mountain of a man—I blushed. This was not the place I wanted to have an erection. I shifted my eyes away from the prince, down to my boots, placing my hands over my crotch.

"King Vilsarion, Prince Corrik. This is Tristan, my son," Father introduced me.

"Welcome," I said giving a deep bow to each using the Markaytian etiquette Papa taught me, then I took my place beside Papa.

"Tristan," my uncle said. "We are honored to announce that we have reached an alliance with Mortouge."

I smiled my best smile. *Absolutely, bloody fantastic!* The Elves didn't align themselves with just anyone and knowing what I knew of the recent unrest in the North Eastern Plains, since we helped them a while back, I knew it was best to have as many strong alliances as possible, if the Kanes were to maintain our hold of Dragon's Rock. For the first time in millennia, we had to take extra measures to protect Markaytia's crown city.

"That is excellent, Sire." I turned to the Elven King. "I've been named as successor to my father at my coming-of-age ceremony, and as future warlord, I will look forward to dealings with your warlord. We Markaytians could learn from your teachings. I've read much about your weapons—I know you forge the best ones," I gushed.

I wage for peace, but war is inevitable and the prospect of fighting alongside an Elf was exciting. All I knew of Elves at the time was of their weapons and great wars. I had little interest in their other qualities. The Elves are a beautiful, mysterious race, but I didn't see much use getting involved in their politics or anything else about them since they were also a private race who didn't often allow outsiders into their grand kingdom.

I didn't expect the Elven king to frown at my words. The smile on his face lit up the room before, and especially standing next to his grouchy-looking son, the contrast was far-reaching. I turned to look at Papa, confused, and he took a sharp breath, ready to cry. Father stepped between us, his dark eyes pinned me in place.

Uncle continued. "The alliance will be sealed with a marriage, Tristan. You to Prince Corrik."

The displeasure must have been plain on my face, though I tried for the life of me to hide it.

"This is the opportunity of a lifetime, Tristan," Uncle continued, trying to sell me on the idea while complimenting the Elven royals. "You will get to move to Mortouge. It will be, so lovely. You are lucky."

How could Uncle give me away and try to convince me how wonderful it would be? He knows how much I love Markaytia. Worse. He knows of the struggles and hardship I endured to earn the honor of being named future warlord at my coming-of-age ceremony by my father.

If he wasn't the king and my uncle, I would have told him to stuff it, but as it were I couldn't do that. I respected him too much even if he'd momentarily gone insane. I listened with rising dread and tried not to smash anything.

"You will follow Elven law," he rambled on.

Obviously.

He said other stuff too, but I stopped listening. When the initial shock wore off, I cut him off to ask, "But how will I become warlord if I move to Mortouge, Uncle?" I already knew the answer to this, but I wanted him to say, in front of everyone, I wanted everyone to know what I was giving up.

When Uncle's smile vanished, I wished I'd kept my mouth shut, but it was too late, and my words brought him to what he'd been avoiding. "No, Tristan. You will never succeed your father as warlord of Markaytia, I'm afraid."

I looked over at Father, hoping he would say something contrary to this whole debacle of me marrying the Ice Prince, but his face lacked emotion. It was the same face I'd endured through my youth, unyielding to anything that stood in the way of the kingdom he'd sworn to protect. Marrying Prince Corrik was a chance to obtain something no other land had: the protection of the Elves of Mortouge. Which did bring to mind, *why us?* Whatever their reason, this arrangement was of great value. Markaytia would be undisputed and it was the greatest gift I could give to Markaytia and to Dragon's Rock.

More than what I could give as Warlord.

No matter how much I was attracted to the Prince when I first set eyes on him, I hated him for choosing me. Of course, it wasn't unusual for members of the royal family to have to submit to an arranged marriage, I just thought that if it happened, I would remain in Markaytia with two feet firmly planted in Dragon's Rock.

I thought Uncle would never stop speaking. I stood there, fuming, wanting his speech to end, but it went on and on. *By the Gods!* I couldn't look at anything, or anyone, fearing I would end up saying something I would regret later. When he finally finished speaking, the Elven Prince came over to me. I froze.

Like it or not, this man was going to be my husband, and I was no fool, I would be obeying him rather than the other way around. I was the one being married *off*. I was the payment for services rendered. He would be my Lord.

"You will wear this, Tristan," his smooth voice commanded in Markaytian which is a common enough language, one many provinces and kingdoms knew at least little of, but I was surprised to see the Elven Prince so proficient. "It is customary in my kingdom for you to have a mark of good faith placed upon you."

He opened his hand to reveal a ring. It's a beautiful piece of jewelry, even if I hate what it represents. A band of delicate twining circles on upside down, three-leafed-clovers, and a large blue stone set in the middle of the Elven crest. "May I?" he said.

Seeing no other viable option (I did contemplate running), I nodded. He took up my left hand and slid the ring onto the fourth finger. It fit perfectly. I didn't know what to do after that. I probably should've thanked him, but I couldn't. Instead, I stood there hating him for choosing me. There were plenty of men in Markaytia, couldn't we find him someone more suitable, with less important ambitions? I have the blood of a dragon and I'm not easily tamed. He has no idea what awaits him on the other side of the leash he placed upon me.

"You will not touch yourself—this is also a custom where I'm from—unless I permit it. I understand you are a virgin?"

I was already blushing by that point. "Y-yes."

How dare he ask such personal questions in front of my family? Unlike Lucca, I had decided to wait for someone special as Papa had, at least for my first time. I'd been on many dates and had a couple of short romances, but never found someone worthy of my virginity. Now I'd have to give away my coveted virginity to this domineering prick—beautiful, but a prick nonetheless.

"Good. You are to remain innocent until I deflower you. I will be the only one to enter you." His voice was no nonsense and to be obeyed. It was as if he already owned me—I hated that too. It was embarrassing, standing there, being talked to like that. We are not so blasé about sex in Markaytia. Not to mention, I was meant to be warlord, not a concubine.

"Do you understand, Tristan? I could make it easier for you. Perhaps a chastity device of some sort could be arranged."

He looked genuinely concerned about it as he conferred with his father for his opinion. I finally found my voice and interjected, quickly.

"I understand. Really, that won't be necessary. No touching myself without your permission, no sex with others. I'll do whatever you ask." *Just stop, bloody talking.* I needed him to be finished so I could leave and destroy something with my sword. I couldn't think of anything more ridiculous than his assumptions. Did he think me to have so little self-control? *I'm a Markaytian.*

His eyes were fierce as he regarded me. I didn't know a thing about him, but I got the impression that he would much rather take me with him in that moment than have to wait until our wedding day. Which begged the question, "When?" I looked to my uncle.

"Next spring. You will be married next spring," Uncle said.

I nodded. "May I be excused, Sire?" I ripped my hand from the Elven Prince's.

"Tristan *Arcade*," Papa began in his scolding voice, but I didn't care. Nothing seemed as embarrassing as Prince

Corrik discussing my deflowering like it was an ingredient in a cake recipe.

"Let him be, Eagar," Father said, to my surprise.

The king nodded his permission. "We will discuss the rest, Tristan. You need not be here for that."

Of course not, why would anyone need my opinion on the rest of my life?

I gave respectful bows to the Elven king and my soon-to-be husband, before I allowed my dragon's blood to rage and stormed out of the Great Hall.

Father was not pleased and spent several hours later that evening explaining to me why we do not storm out on Elven royalty. I was too angry to care about his lecture and made the mistake of telling him so. Since, according to Father, 'my brain had taken leave of its senses,' he decided to impress upon my backside the same lesson.

Painfully.

I was barely cooled the next day; both my blood and my bottom were still warm, when I arrived at the training fields. My father was there of course. I expected his cold demeanor, but I did not expect was the anxious look on his face.

"I'm to relieve you of that and your current duties. Go play." He reached to grab the sword out of my hand. *My* sword. The same one he'd given me on my seventh birthday.

"Father, I know I was unforgivable yesterday, I'm sorry for that. I'm going to marry him with good form, I promise. Please don't do this." We each had a hand on the hilt, the sword sat between us with the point of the blade aimed at the ground.

"*I* am not," he snapped. "It has been decreed by your intended. You are not to hold a sword, again. Since you are not to be named warlord, he saw no need for you to fight

11

any longer. You are dismissed from the royal guard and he would like you to be treated as the prince you will be."

"Princes fight all the time! Look at Lucca."

"For whatever reason, it was his wish. Your uncle agreed to it."

I knew what he was saying, though he would never admit to it: he hadn't agreed. That meant more to me than anything. Father had never shown me kindness. He was strict and uncompromising but knowing he would choose me over anyone else to be warlord, seemed to make up for everything. He made it clear on many occasions that he didn't have to choose me and once upon a time he almost didn't. I proved myself worthy and when he told me he decided to name me as his successor, it was easily the best day of my life.

The day he took my sword was the worst.

We looked our identical sets of eyes into each other's.

Mine are a sapphire blue, while Father's are such a dark shade of blue, they sometimes look black, but we've often been told that despite the differing color of our irises, it's that feature which defines me as the son of Arcade Kanes. We stared at each other for several hard moments, until I finally let go the sword and I walked off his training fields forever.

"If Tristan allows the Elven prince to live past their wedding night for taking his sword, I shall be surprised," I overheard Father say to Uncle one night as I snuck in late and passed the Great Hall.

Father and the king often discussed many things over a flagon of wine in the quiet of the dark night.

I smiled at that. My father was only taken to humor around Uncle and Papa. I felt better knowing there was the one thing between Father and I no one could touch. He knows I can fight and wanted to protect Markaytia and that me being declawed—well it was a bloody crime is what it was.

"Tristan, your face is going to freeze like that if you're not careful."

My scowl grows deeper. He can be such a cheeky brat sometimes, it's a wonder I'll miss him at all. Knowing he's irritating me, he pushes me further as he always does and flicks water in my face. "Who knows Tristan, maybe you'll like it?" he adds before he swims away to keep safe from my pending retaliation, but I don't retaliate.

"What do you think I'll like?" I yell after him.

"The sex of course!"

"*Lucca!*"

"Well, what kind of a person gets his husband to send for permission to masturbate?" Lucca pauses, a twinkle in his eyes. "A kinky kind of person, that's who."

Ugh. He may have a point. Uncle once told me: *the Elves are creatures; they are of a different breed than us Markaytians.*

His warning did not urge me to intrigue. I haven't made it a priority to study their culture, and that would include their views on erotica. I wanted to remain in denial while I could.

Lucca defiantly lies on his back, an impish grin on his face, as he floats above the water, acting like we have a thousand tomorrows together instead of just the one. He closes his eyes and hums a tune that reminds me of lighter days where having fun was all we need care about. His song calms the rage inside me before I fall back in the water and lay face up like Lucca. My long, dark hair floats around my face, my bare chest soaks up the sunrays. For now, I will take my cousin's lead, relax, and enjoy my last day in Markaytia.

Tomorrow, I will marry Prince Corrik Cyredanthem.

CHAPTER 2

*M*y nerves are shot.

Lucca's attempt to distract me doesn't work and agitates me further. "Come little Elven Concubine, let's get you dressed," he says, entering my room unannounced—like he owns the damn place—and rips my bed sheets away. I throw a pillow at him. He dodges it.

"I'm not going to be a concubine," I say, rolling over and stuffing my head underneath another pillow. *Maybe he'll go away if I ignore him long enough.*

"Don't be sour Tristan, this is already the worst day of my life."

The worst day of his life? Leave it to Lucca to think of himself.

"Don't call me concubine again, and I promise I'll do my best not to be sour at you *Luccalthizan.*"

He twists his mouth in distaste at the sound of his full name. I'm of the mind to tell him to leave, since I'm in no mood for his usual theatrics, but Lucca insisted that he be the one to prepare me for the ceremony today. I know his zeal for the task is only because I will be leaving forever, otherwise, he'd be content to let an attendant perform the mundane duty. The prince arrives from Mortouge this afternoon; we will marry at sunset and depart for Mortouge after breakfast tomorrow.

I make myself leave the warm blankets—they smell like home—I don't look back as I stand, my eye catches something new on the other side of my room.

"Is *that* what he expects me to wear?" I point to the ridiculous white pile of cloth hanging over my armoire, which looks like a giant rabbit costume you'd wear to the Spring Festival. *Utterly hideous.*

Lucca laughs. "It's not half-bad, Tristan."

"You don't have to dress like a great white ball of fur!"

"No. But I also—"

"—don't say it—"

"—don't look half as lovely as you."

We both know that wasn't what he intended on saying. Lucca never uses words like '*lovely.*' My mood takes a further plunge. Now I'm cheerless *and* vexed.

"Come on dear cousin. I see you shan't be teased this morning. Let's wash some of the sleep from your eyes and hope you improve your disposition before the sexy Elf Prince sees how grouchy you are before breakfast," he says, dragging me by the hand.

"That's still teasing," I mutter to myself, but follow him anyway.

The bathing hall is a chaotic mess, as usual, but more so on this morning. The royalty that resides in the palace, scramble to get ready for the ceremony, not paying any mind to Lucca and I—thank the Gods. We make our way over to one of the free baths.

Sam and Niña, our two female attendants, greet us and begin to disrobe me and my cousin. Prince Corrik wouldn't allow for another man to touch me so he arranged to have a female attendant assigned to me. *Controlling Bastard.*

Once, he let me go for an entire fortnight without allowing me release. It's a wonder I didn't murder anyone, though I do recall everyone steering clear of me for three days before the missive appeared that time. I thought of little more than tearing out the prince's violet eyes—the anger still a poor distraction against my aching cock.

I've learned that he—my cock, whom I've begun referring to in the third person—is a savage beast with a mind of his own, and once disturbed, is relentless until sated. Unfortunately for the two of us, I never know when relief will come.

The Elves are creatures of magic and he left an empty journal. He has a journal in Mortouge that is its twin, and when he writes a message in his copy, that's when a message appears in mine—*magic*. With it, a pen, also of magic which has given us the ability to write messages all this time. You'd think we'd jump at the opportunity to get to know each other, but we haven't—at least not me. I suppose he has written to me every evening. He'd make a sorry attempt to ask me questions and spark conversation in between all his commands for me. There were plenty by the way. His biggest concern was over whether I'd 'deflowered' myself or not. No, of course not. I made an oath didn't I? I don't know what Elves do, but Markaytians keep their oaths.

"Tristan," he said in one of his dictatorial messages, and I knew I was being scolded. "What have you been doing?" A simple enough question, with all sorts of implications; I read right through them.

"Nothing I shouldn't be," I responded, and hoped he could feel my anger through the damn book. He would sign off by writing the same thing in return every night: "Thank you, my Tristan. Sleep well."

It infuriated me. How dare he call me *his Tristan*? I cared little how true it was.

Lucca and I slip into the large bathing pool together. Either Corrik doesn't know I still bathe with my cousin or he doesn't care. We've bathed together since we were small boys—there is nothing sexual about it. Markaytians may be private over sex, but not over being nude. Niña takes extra care to wash and exfoliate my skin today; she applies softening ointments, and some oil to smooth out my long hair. While she turns to fetch a scrub brush, I notice a spot she's missed on her first pass over me—the head of my cock is leaking pre-come, enough to slick the head and send a jolt of pleasure through my groin.

Thankfully she turns back before I succumb to my cock's ability to hypnotize me like a python and use me as an instrument to get the sex he wants. She scrubs me with more force than usual, and my skin feels like it's burning. "I'll look better with my skin the color I came with, thank you very much."

"I'm so sorry, your Highness," she replies, but doesn't look sorry at all.

"We're not married yet, there's no need for such formalities," I say.

"Don't mind him," Lucca says from beside us. "He's just sore about having to lose his virginity tonight."

The three of them burst into laughter. If only they really knew what a deviant I've become; losing my virginity is the least of my worries. It's the only perk. Sex is a private thing amongst Markaytians as Lucca is well aware, even if that little cultural aspect has skipped his moral character. He knows better than to tease me about *that* in particular.

If he's not careful he'll be wearing a black eye to my wedding.

"How long's it been?" he pushes, his indecency without bounds. "I'll bet he wanted you good and randy for tonight, 'uh?"

I won't punch my cousin on my wedding day. "I'm not a broodmare."

"That's not an answer. Come on, it's just us. We won't tell anyone."

"Right. I'm going to be forthcoming with my private information so you can continue to make fun of me?"

"My guess is at least a week," he mock-whispers, as if his words are only for Sam.

"Lucca!"

"Maybe two. The last time the Prince made him go two weeks without mas—"

"Five. It's been five *Gods'* damned days," I say when he won't shut up.

He gives a self-satisfied smirk as he waits for Sam to finish rinsing his hair.

"That's *not* why I'm grouchy," I say.

"Sure, it's not."

"Okay, it's not the *only* reason I'm grouchy."

"I know why you're upset—you've every right to be—but it's all the more reason I should take your mind off things."

"By reminding me I have no control over my own penis?"

The two women giggle at that. I don't normally say such things, but Lucca's revealed enough that it doesn't matter at this point.

"All right. Maybe that wasn't the best thing to say, but it's kind of funny."

"Funny? How about I lock up your penis, and tell you not to use it except when I say? In fact, I know *just* what to leave you as a parting gift."

The look of horror on his face is worth having to endure this conversation.

"Okay. Point made."

"Good." Now I'm the one smirking.

Lucca behaves himself, for Lucca, the rest of the bath. Though I've gone longer without ejaculating, I'm especially on edge today. *What better way is there to relieve tension than with a long, intense orgasm?*

I say my goodbyes to Sam and Niña once I'm dressed, and Lucca and I head to breakfast.

Father is the only one in attendance. Not unusual, but I did expect more of the family to breakfast with us on this day. Arcade Kanes is a taciturn man so I don't expect a farewell speech, but I do hope—as foolish though it may be —for some kind words of approval. Perhaps an *'I'm proud of you, Tristan.'*

"Where have you lot been? And Tristan—why in the Gods' names are you dressed like that? The Prince will be here any minute. What if he wishes to see you? You can't see the Elven prince looking like you're ready to shoe a horse."

I sputter, not sure which question to answer first. I'm not *that* underdressed. I just didn't bother putting much into my outfit for breakfast seeing as I'm just going to take it off again. I don't say this to Father though. Wedding day or no, he'll discipline me if he sees fit.

"Sit down. Eat—*quickly*. There's no time for lollygag-ging. I would think you could act as an adult for one day. You'll never be anything but a child. *Irresponsible!*" He speaks only to me. He's never cared what Lucca acts like for the most part.

Lucca and I sit and begin piling food on our plates. My face burns the whole time, embarrassed that I've disgraced myself in the eyes of my father. I think about apologizing, but don't, knowing he prefers my silence. His eyes rake over me, and something makes him madder, but I can't figure out what. When I think enough time has passed for him to cool over our late appearance to breakfast, I take a chance and ask, "It's bad luck to see each other before the wedding, I thought...? He won't want to see me when he gets here, will he Father?"

"You'd better hope not looking like that."

I put my head back to my breakfast, not looking up again, until a messenger comes in to speak with Lucca. I get the impression he wants to speak with me too, but Father's tense demeanor has succeeded in wrapping tightly around me and the messenger stays keeps his distance. Lucca nods in my direction as the boy speaks into his ear.

I'm fast losing my appetite, but rather than draw attention to myself by pushing my plate away, I set to work finishing breakfast with a large glass of fresh milk. I think I'm home free, I'm about to ask to be excused, when Father stands with authority, his long chestnut hair sways with his movements, and he unsheathes his sword to point it at my face. He stands for what seems like a long time, his jaw tight, his upper lip curled. Cold eyes pierce me and his fingers are wrapped tightly around the hilt as he either finds the words he's looking for, or slits me belly to throat. At the moment, I might choose the slitting. Silence closes in on me and even Lucca knows not to utter a single joke. His eyes are glued to my father as are mine. Just when I decide it's going to be an execution, Father says the four words—*the only four words*—that could make this day worse.

"Do not disappoint me."

I don't get opportunity enough to form a response before he's walking away, his crisp boots echoing off the stone of the large dining hall, re-sheathing his sword as he goes. I sink low in my chair and run a hand through my hair.

"Don't listen to him Tristan. You know him well enough to know what he's like. He's nervous too. You are his only son and he has to give you away."

"Well, that's a fine way to say it."

I'm distraught as it is and now, I have a pit in my stomach. It appears that I can't live up to my father's standards—he has no faith in me—and now I'm expected to live up to those of an Elven prince? I know how this fiasco will end. I'll be sent home within two new moons.

"Your mother wants to see you," Lucca says.

"I'd better go now then. I haven't much time." I mean that in a few ways of course.

"Your mother will fix you up. When you return to your rooms, I'll be ready to prepare you. I've practiced," he says. His obvious pride elicits a weak smile out of me.

"Tristan, one more thing," he says, a cheeky grin spreads onto his face. "Your *Master* has arrived." He runs off before I can smack him for more teasing, but he needn't have worried—I'm too flustered by the news.

The prince is in the palace.

Lucca's risky little plan works—I'm no longer thinking about my father.

She sits in front of her dressing mirror, her attendant behind her holding the clasp of a stunning pearl necklace draped around her neck. Mother admires it in the mirror, deciding if it's the right one. Her raven hair, like mine, wraps around her body but whereas mine is bone straight, hers is arranged in bouncy curls that pop about as she tilts her head from side-to-side, trying to catch the pearls from all angles. Her shining grey eyes narrow as she shakes her head and purses her lips. "It's beautiful, but it's not right. Tristan will be accented with silver. I've got to have something silver to match," she says, to her attendant as her eyes lock onto the corner of the room, her lids suggest her focus is elsewhere. When Mother does that, I know she's off having a conversation with herself. She's nervous.

"You look beautiful no matter what Mother. Wear what you wish," I say.

"Tristan, my *dar*ling!" Her eyes light up like diamonds when she sees me. I wander into her open arms and squeeze her tightly. She pulls back and cups my face with her smooth hands. She searches my blue eyes for a moment and reads the turmoil in them with practiced precision. "What has your father said now?"

I pull away from her and turn to sift through the open jewelry box on her dressing mirror. I do not wish to speak about him, but Mother won't allow me to stew in peace. Never has. She nods to her attendant to leave us.

"Oh, Tristan. You know better than to invest in his behaviors. You know the sort of man he is—hard and rough to his core. I don't know how Eagar stands him."

My mother and father are not together. It's common practice in Markaytia for the warlord to choose a woman to

23

bear him a son to carry on his legacy. Father is in love with Eagar, my papa.

He and Eagar have been lovers since before I was born. Eagar fights alongside my father as his second in command; they've been in love since their first day on the field together. Love was instant for them and there is no one else for my father, but Eagar.

"Papa can stand him because he wouldn't dare treat Papa as he does me."

The word gentle could almost be used about the way my father treats the large, pretty man. I say pretty because while Eagar could slice a man in two without thought, his looks suggest he might have been a porcelain doll in a past life. He has narrow cheeks and fine bone structure, with long hair that went white far before the time it should have. Instead of making him look old, his white hair makes him look years younger than his actual age. He's got intense, emerald green eyes that always seem to be glossed over with tears because his heart pours out of them. He's used them to get me out of trouble with Father many times. I can't blame Father for loving Papa so. He's a hard man to not love with your whole soul. When I was born, he took time away from his regular duties and cared for me alongside Mother. He and Mother grew close. I went to Papa as often as I would Mother.

"Let's sick Eagar on him," she jokes.

I shake my head. "I'll be fine Mother. Father didn't help matters but the truth is, I have bigger worries than him. I'm worried about everyone I'll leave behind. What about you? What about Lucca?"

"You are a strong man, always wanting to take care of everyone," she says. "But as for me, you know I can take care of myself. Lucca on the other hand is an impish boy, but he will be fine. Not having you here will give him the opportunity to grow into a man and clean up his *own* messes."

Mother knows most of my secrets. She knows that half the time I was in trouble with Father, it was because of something Lucca had done. I could never stand to see him in trouble, and despite his protests, I always convinced Uncle and Father that I had been the irresponsible one, getting Lucca out of trouble as often as I could. Mother hated when I took the blame and allowed me to cry to her. Over time, she resented Lucca.

"All boys must grow up my Tristan," she says. "And though my heart is aching at the mere thought of having you gone, I know I must let my little birdie fly. I know this path is best for you. What you are doing for the kingdom is noble, and you will always be remembered in Markaytia." Tears stream down her cheeks. They're the words I wish *Father* would've said to me. For the last time ever she wipes my tears. "I know you'll make us proud, my son."

"**O**w! For the sake of the Gods Lucca. I thought you said you practiced?"

Lucca laughs as he continues braiding my hair. It's pure torture. *Why do people like this?*

"I did. That's why it hurts. I need to do it tight enough, you know, so it doesn't come apart when you and Prince Corrik are—ooo*ow*!"

I pinch him hard in the stomach and smile as I watch him nurse the sore spot.

"You won't be smiling long. I have to do that one over now," he says. Lucca must braid my hair in the intricate pattern, unique to the Elves for the Elven-style ceremony that will be performed tonight. I know how much he practiced and studied for this task—it's rare to see Lucca apply himself.

Finally, Lucca's finished. He spins me around in my chair so I can view his work in the mirror. Some of my dark hair has been braided into a Mohawk that runs down my skull. There is still some hair left to hang, and other parts are braided and twined with colored leather bands and jewels. Two braids sit over my right temple. At the ceremony, Prince Corrik will move them to the left. My new Elven crown will be placed over my head, and over my braids, which is an Elven tradition that will signify the marriage is complete. When I see how complicated the braiding patterns are, I'm grateful I have a cousin so devoted to me. I swish my hair from side-to-side and watch as they move and sparkle.

"You've done well, Lucca. Thank you."

"Of course, I have," he says, arrogant as ever. "Would you expect any less from me?"

"I'd watch what you say. I know more about you than anyone. I can think of several reasons why I might think you would shirk off learning how to braid my hair for the ceremony."

"Please," he scoffs. "I have just as much on you."

"You do. We're even when it comes to that. You have my promise that I won't share any of your naughty secrets with your future wife," I say without thinking. I won't be here. I'll most likely never know the person Lucca will marry.

"Wife you say...? How do you know I'll marry a woman?" I know he'll have picked up on my slip in talking about a future that will never be, and he veers the topic so we don't have to return to discussing what we already have many times over. *No need to dwell on it, Tristan. Keep moving forward.*

"Maybe you don't know as much about me as you think you do," he suggests, and for the first time I wonder if there *are* things I have missed about my cousin. "But to clarify, I will marry a man. I do enjoy being with a woman, yes, but you'll see, there's nothing like having a hard man underneath you." After saying a thing like that, he shoves something in my hand. I look down to see a strange looking mass of gleaming silver. It's heavy, and it resembles—

"A chastity belt, Tristan, a formal one. You are to wear it under your robes. It locks with this," he informs me holding up a key dangling from a chain looped around his fingers. I forgot about that. Wearing the chastity belt today will be a symbol of the chastity I have kept for him.

"I trust you can comport yourself if I leave you two alone?" His eyes flick to my crotch.

"Give me that," I say snatching the key from him.

He laughs. "All right then. I'll stand just outside the door. Call me back when you're done, and we'll proceed with the robes."

He slips out the door, and I'm alone.

Alone. Completely, alone.

Even with Lucca standing outside the door, I know his loyalties are to me. If I were to do anything I'm not supposed to do, he'd pretend like nothing happened. I know he's hoping I'll relieve my tension. Maybe I should? Why not? All this time I've behaved myself. It's my wedding day, shouldn't I get to do as I please, once, before I'm never allowed to again?

That's all it takes to convince me. Like a man gone mad with power, I pull my trousers and underthings down and my cock springs out hard and wanting. My dick relishes in

27

his freedom as the cool air hits him. *'Hello there Tristan,'* he says, *'I've been waiting for you to decide to play with me yourself.'*

Nasty, nasty, evil little blighter.

But he's too damn tempting—I ghost my hand over the head. I take a sharp, delicious inhale, and stroke my hand down his length. *'That's it,'* he coaxes, *'grab some of that cream over there while you're at it. It will feel so good.'*

Cream. That's a good idea. I almost thank my cock out loud for such cunning ingenuity. I grab the cream, rub it over the head and down the shaft in the same manner as before, only this time it feels much better. I get lost in the sensations as I fuck my hand and climb closer to orgasm— not far away after a five-day abstinence. I'm a hair's width from unraveling when Father's words ring through my head.

"Do not disappoint me."

That's one way to deflate an erection, even an erection well on its way to the promised land—think of your father. To my cock's dismay, I drop him like he's the wrong end of a branding iron and look myself over in the mirror. What have I almost done? *Almost proved my father right is what I've almost done.* I wipe the excess cream off my cock without problem. There's no flagging erection when I slip on the cold, silver chastity belt with ease, and lock it into place. I don't want to look at it but at the same time I must, morbidly fascinated with the thing and how it looks on me. The skin of my scrotum is pulled through a ring until my testicles are fully inserted. The shaft of my cock is pushed through a gap at the top of the ring. Then, my penis is inserted into the tube, which is so like the shape of my cock, if I didn't know better, I'd think someone had cast my cock in soap. The tube locks to the base and voila: no more erections today for Tristan, but there's a hole at the tip of the tube—I can still urinate. Thankfully, it's comfortable even if it feels a bit weird.

Satisfied that's done, I call Lucca in. He gives me a *'what took so long'* look but says nothing. Instead, he takes the key to the silver chastity belt from me.

"I get to be the one who gives this to the prince," he says, waggling his eyebrows. "Any words for your betrothed I should pass on?"

"Just hurry up, and help me dress," I say.

The first garment is a white, sleeveless, gown. It drapes over my body covering me from head-to-toe. The second piece is a long jacket. It's made of fine, white silk and has a V-shaped neckline embroidered with silver designs. The long sleeves bell wide and flare at my wrists. The jacket joins the other robe in the middle, at the base of my navel, then spreads wide, revealing the first silky garment underneath. The shoulders have silver etchings in the shape of fire—the only part of this get up I like. A larger sliver pattern encrusted with Elven diamonds adorns the jacket all the way down. The first layer of silk cloth flares out from the bottom of the jacket and covers my legs to the ankles. I'm basically wearing a dress with a long jacket over top. *Ugh.*

If that's not enough, Lucca helps me secure a white cape made from rabbit's fur around my neck.

"I'm going to die from the heat of this thing," I complain.

"Oh Tristan," Lucca cries. "You look stunning. More of a Prince than I."

"I look like a woman in a white dress."

"You're not, Tristan, you're the best man I know. You would've made a great warlord, and Prince Corrik is lucky to have you," he says, his lips quiver as he says what we've skirted all morning.

"Lucca, please, don't cry. If you do, I won't be able to go through with this." He's breaking my heart. Despite my request, tears stream down his cheeks.

"But this will be the last time you will be just mine, Tristan. After now, you will be his."

I can't say anything. He's right. Tears escape my eyes too as I realize that these are the last moments I'll spend with my cousin, my best friend, my brother. We embrace in a long hug as our best times flash before my eyes. I'll miss him the most out of anything of my old life. I smooth the top of Lucca's golden hair and kiss his crown one last time.

CHAPTER 3

I peer out of the tent that conceals me from the crowd.

I'll be the one walking *toward* Prince Corrik, which in Markaytia denotes the submissive person in the relationship, the person who is married *off*. It's not gender related as it is in other societies that either favor patriarchy or matriarchy.

I should've expected this. He's already proven to be the authority figure in our relationship. I lived all these years under Father's thumb, and now I'll have a new master.

I look out to the sea of people who sit in white chairs that are spread on either side of an isle leading up to a large, circular dais. I spot Lucca craning his head around, trying to see me. When our eyes meet, he waves to me like a lunatic. I smile at him until another set of eyes find me: Prince Corrik's. They glow an ultra-violet purple and look into me, searching for something. I can't look away. *Is there anything inside that ice fortress of a man?*

Lucca waves and jumps in his seat, making it easy to hear him above the crowd. He clearly thinks I've lost sight of him. *Why else would I have looked away?* Prince Corrik notices Lucca's display and frowns. The Gods only know what the Elven Prince is thinking, but I doubt Lucca's antics bode well for him. Or me.

If he could control himself this once.

"Tristan!" Papa's voice behind me rings loud in my ears as I duck behind the tent flap, where I belong in the first place. I don't miss the chastening glint—Papa has always been the hybrid of stern Father and Mother hen. "It is bad luck for the prince to see you—come away from there and let me have a good look at you."

"I don't believe in such superstitions, Papa." I don't quite snap it, but he knows something's up. His comments are too reminiscent of mine at breakfast to my father—the ones I got my head bit off over.

"Regardless, come here now, little man." Papa spins me around once I'm in reach of him. "So, Lucca can do the things he puts his mind to. Will wonders never cease?" He wraps me in his barrel arms. "What's got you in a huff? Was it what your father said to you at breakfast?"

"How do you know about that? And how come you weren't there?"

"Your father and I talk about everything, especially that which concerns you. I wasn't there because your father wanted to eat with you alone—*someone failed to tell Lucca.*"

"Yeah, to tell me off. And I don't know why he'd want to talk about me, seeing as I'm such a *disappointment.*"

"He didn't mean it like that."

"Then what *did* he mean?" I pull away. "Wait. What did he want to talk with me about?"

"I am sworn to secrecy on both counts."

"Of course, you are." I can't hide my sarcasm, and I

instantly regret talking like that to Papa. "I'm sorry, I didn't mean it."

"You meant it all right, but I can't say I blame you. I will tell you this: your father does love you, more than you know, and more than he'll ever say." Papa's said that before and I want to believe him, but I'm greedy and still want to hear it from the source.

"Let's put an end to this, shall we?" That's his polite way of saying, *enough, Tristan.* I know the tone well from my youth. This is not the first disagreement he's had the pleasure of ending between Father and me.

"Yes, Papa."

"Good. Now tell me, are you ready?"

"I'll never be ready."

"Well, I for one am proud of you. Some day in the future, you will have saved a countless number of people by this union. Everyone will be grateful to you," he assures me.

"I don't need them to be grateful to me Papa. Keeping our people alive and safe is enough for me."

"Alive is good." He pulls me forward again and kisses the crown of my head like he did when I was younger, and the world is right again.

"Coddling him to the end I see," Father says, his hard voice bites through our moment.

"Hello darling." Papa ignores his jibe.

Father pulls Papa away from me and turns him so he can look into his green eyes. He stares into them in a way that would make me quake, but Papa only smiles. It's an exchange I'm used to seeing. I've never had the meaning explained to me, but it does mean something. When Father is satisfied, he let's go with a smack to his bottom. "I'll deal with you later."

"Of course, Arcade," Papa says, putting his head down.

"You," he says, turning his black eyes on me. "It's time to go."

I nod. I don't want to test my voice under his fierce scrutiny. Father's long, chestnut hair, feathers over his strong shoulders. He's wearing his obsidian battle armor as usual. I can't remember many occasions where I've seen him without it. Today he's added the additional burgundy cloak over top, and the extra pieces of gleaming armor over his shoulders.

"Come then son, your destiny awaits."

———

The foreign Elvish music plays as my fathers escort me down the aisle. My heart speeds up as my limbs take me to *him*. I avoid looking at *him* and focus on the faces in the crowd. My family and court sit on one side, their forlorn faces resolved with admiration for my sacrifice. The prince's family sit on the other side, all of them beaming with happiness. I'm stunned. It's never occurred to me that they might be joyful over our union. I continue down the aisle and when I pass her, the beautiful Elven queen smiles at me. Her eyes are genuine, and she looks like she's restraining herself. She's a hugger, isn't she? Sitting beside her is the grand Elven king. He's an older looking version of, Prince Corrik. Streaks of silver hair flow through his otherwise blond locks and he wears them with pride. His presence is massive, leaking off him, oozing command. It's no doubt why he is king of the Mortougian Elves. He looks strong too, like he could spear a man easily, but wise enough to know when to use words to do the piercing.

The Elven king gives me an approving smile as I

approach the dais where Prince Corrik waits for me. Father releases my arm and makes to walk away, while Papa can't help himself, reaching up to fix a braid that probably doesn't really need fixing. Father has to take his arm and guide him away from me. I step up to the dais alone with my head bowed until the last moment. I finally allow myself to look up. The prince stands in front of me, tall and imposing. He's draped in cloaks of silver and blue. Unlike mine, his cloak does not join in the middle, instead, his entire chest and navel are exposed, revealing his well-toned chest and abdominal muscles.

His top cloak is adorned with sharp, silver and gold shoulder armor. Strips of fabric hang from them, enhancing his magnificence, and the hilt of a large, wide-bladed sword rises from his back. It's a gorgeous weapon and I imagine the finest Elven blacksmiths have crafted it. *I would love to get my hands on a sword like that and perhaps if I'm clever enough, one day I will.*

His hair isn't the way I remember. It's blond enough to look like it's been spun from gold, with violet highlights to match his eyes. It's mostly loose with half of it pulled off his face and the front cut short into bangs that are long over his forehead, resting on a slant toward his right ear. His *ears*— they were covered by his hair when I first saw him, but now they're free, unencumbered by the golden mien, poking out far above his temple and then turn in a graceful swoop back downward.

A stunning crown shaped like a winged creature sits around his head. As I come closer to him, I see that the winged creature is not a winged creature at all, but some sort of insignia. His ears are adorned with the same design that looks like it's been tattooed on in ultra-violet light, swooping up over each ear, and down his cheekbones. I smile, but Prince Corrik is expressionless. His lips are in a hard line and I catch his feral violet eyes before they dart down to my left hand to look at *his* ring on my finger.

An Elf that resembles both Prince Corrik and his father stands before us, ready to perform our ceremony. "Hello Tristan. I am Corrik's Uncle Fera. It is good to finally meet you. Allow me to be the first to welcome you to our family." Fera smiles at me, and I'm grateful to see someone else smiling on the dais with me. "Let us begin by getting you two to join hands," he instructs.

Our hands join for the first time since he put his ring on my finger; they are warm, smooth, and too soft for a warrior's hands, but I know better. Prince Corrik is a great warrior. He smoothens his thumb over my knuckles and deliberately over my ring finger, feeling for his ring—*his marking*.

"You are all here to bear witness to the union between Tristan and Corrik, and I am pleased to induct him into our family, and our Elvish way of life. You have been granted permission, and you will become an Elf." Fera directs his gaze at me with a serious grin. "From this point forward, you are no longer Junior Warlord, Tristan Arcade Kanes. You will be Prince Kathir Tahsen Cyredanthem," he pronounces in his strong Elvish accent. I want to tear my hands away from the Prince's. Anger builds in my gut and I try to calm down. I look to Father. He appears too calm as he nods for me to return my attention to Corrik and carry on. He knew. Father knew I would have to change my name.

And he kept it from me.

My name means everything to me. I expected that I would no longer be a Kanes, that I would likely take Corrik's last name, but to change my full name to an Elvish one, and keep nothing of my Markaytian name? I suppose the prince wants my body *and* my entire identity with it.

I can't help but wonder what an Elvish name like that means? Maybe it's the name befitting a pet in Mortouge. How am I to know? I don't know a word of Elvish. I can't even pronounce the name I've been given, and I've already forgot what it was.

Father glares at me, afraid I might say or do something about it in front of everyone. He warns me with his eyes not to act in usual, Tristan style. *'Just keep your mouth shut,'* they say. I will, but I can't hide how I feel—I'm like Papa that way.

Contrary to his prickly aura, the prince is *gentle* when he picks up the tight braids on my right and moves them to rest on the left of me. I feel precious when he places a crown, the twin to his, around my head and fixes it to make sure it sits just so—which can't be right. He's a cold heartless bastard. He lifts my chin with his forefinger and thumb until my eyes *should* look at him, but I can't face those cold purple rocks. I keep my head where he's moved it and look anywhere else. I hear the Elven monster promise to always honor and protect me—*please*, as if I need protection. This would be a good time to remind him, and everyone present that I'm the son of a warlord, but my thoughts are cut short as I'm asked to repeat after Fera and promise to honor and obey.

Obey. I never thought it would be me on this end of the wedding bargain, but here I am. This time my angry eyes blaze on my face, my lips curl as I snarl agreement—*this ceremony is just a formality anyway, do I really have to say all of this?*

Papa knows I'm upset. Father restrains Papa from storming the dais. That's what calms me down. I know Papa will risk trouble with Father to come up here. I can't let him do that. I spread a fake smile on, take a breath, and say the words. I also catch a glint of sunlight off the prince's neck and realize the sun's light is catching on a chain, which holds a key, *the* key to my virginity.

"You may kiss him Corrik, he is your life mate now."

He may kiss me? We don't kiss each other?

That only spins me for a minute as I realize, no matter how it's been phrased, I have to kiss him and in front of all these people. I've never held hands with anyone but Lucca in front of people, and now I'm to kiss someone? I would rather face an angry, two-headed dragon with only my sword than to have to endure this embarrassment. My breathing isn't right, but I don't notice that I'm at the edge of hyperventilation until I hear the sleek, hard voice.

"I won't bite."

I feel a hand against my cheek, it grounds me, his words cause a tiny smile to give way as I study the white floor of the dais—he's made a joke. *Unless Elves really do bite.* I focus on the warmth in his hand. It surprises me. The man looks like he could freeze lava, yet there's something warm underneath the brambles. With his other hand, he interlocks his ring with mine: they're a perfect fit. Each move brings us closer to the moment, my mind strains to grab onto something else that must happen so that the kiss doesn't happen, yet—but there's nothing else, and it's going to happen.

"Focus on me, sweet Prince. *Please.* Look at me." The tenderness in his voice is careful, and it doesn't escape me—he's begging. Does it bother him that I can't look him in the eyes?

C'mon, Tristan. You've conquered greater mountains than this one.

"There's nothing to be afraid of," he says, and that's what finally does it.

Afraid? I'll show him afraid. No one insinuates Tristan Kanes is a coward. I am a dragon.

I turn wild eyes on him and strike, meeting his lips like swords meet in battle. He's surprised, but only for a tiny second—I've caught him off guard—but once he's figured out what's going on, he dominates our kiss, grabs me around the waist, and pulls me into him. I can't back down now, and have him coo at me again so I get closer, pressing against his bare chest, fighting for dominance. That's when his tongue slides into my mouth like a dare— he's onto me. If he thinks he's going to win this battle, that I'll just roll over and *obey* him, then he's married the wrong Kanes. I may be leashed to him through duty, but what he'll find is that leash is attached to a dragon warrior.

I slide my tongue inside his mouth and tangle it with his sinewy Elven one. He tastes like man; I like it. My cock perks up from inside its cage, jolting me back to where I should be: at the ceremony. I pull away and push at his chest in one move and finally look into his eyes after avoiding them this entire time. I'm taken off guard—he's smiling. I was beginning to think he was incapable. It's a small smile, but enough to reach the creases of his eyes. Wonderment is sparkling in the cold violet depths, and somehow, he remains frosty in his mirth. "You are my responsibility now," he vows.

My mouth quirks at the corners into a sour expression— *I can take care of myself. I'm no one's responsibility.* If he's noticed I'm displeased, he doesn't say and lifts my hand up with his to the sky as we turn to face the cheering crowd.

"I am pleased to present to you, Prince Corrik and

Prince Kathir Cyredanthem of Mortouge," Fera says above the noise.

I look around, Mother stares at me with proud eyes, Papa is crying into Father's shoulder, the Markaytian king sits beside Lucca with a beaming smile directed at me. Lucca. He's laughing—*at me*. He knows my state of mind even if the prince does not. My anger makes me brazen, and I look to my right to check on what the Elven prince has got up to in the time I've spent staring out at the crowd. He's looking at the crowd as well, waving with his other hand as he holds steadfast to mine in the air. He must feel my eyes on him—he spins his head to look at me. He doesn't smile with his lips, but the skin around his eyes is relaxed just enough to suggest he *might* be happy.

This Elf is harder to decipher than Father.

"You are a good kisser," he says and winks.

I blush like mad and look anywhere but at him. *Why would he say something like that?* I change my mind about him—he's as insufferable as Lucca. When will it be learned that I'm not comfortable with things like kissing and sex?

His thumb and forefinger grip my chin tilting it up toward his face, so I have no choice but to look at him. His lips move in slow this time and chastely press onto mine. They're soft and warm; I like how they taste. When we part, I think I should say something but I'm too embarrassed and —*damn it*—I'm aroused. Thankfully neither of us has to say anything. It's time for us to walk back down the aisle for the first time as a married couple.

I try to find Lucca—who's ... *gone? Why would he sneak away now?*

I don't know, but there's one thing I'm certain of. Wherever he's gone, it means trouble.

Trouble for me.

CHAPTER 4

J'm handcuffed to a large war Elf—an Elvish wedding tradition. The married couple must spend their reception attached to one another literally. *I feel ridiculous.* We are seated at the head of an elaborate table in the Dining Hall. Being linked together has done little to spur conversation and even if I wanted to, I wouldn't get a word in with the prince. People have been accosting us all evening under the pretense of congratulating us, but I think they just want a look at the massive wonder. *I'm willing to give him away if they want him.* It's difficult having to move as a unit with someone I don't know. Lucca and I could manage this with ease. We often moved as one thought, knowing each other well enough to forecast what the other would do next.

But the prince and I are hopeless.

We've had a few awkward instances where I've tripped forward, forgetting I'm attached to a moving land mass, and again when he'd forget, yanking me in whatever direction he meant to go. I'm not used to tripping. I'm fucking agile. It's embarrassing as much as it's frustrating so I've succumbed to watching his lead, and allowing my arm and body to go along with whatever he deigns to do. I wish he'd let go my hand at least. He hasn't released it since the ceremony. He has no compunction dragging my hand where he likes, but I'm remiss to do the same. I can't seem to work up the bravery to ask for a turn with our hands. I try to slice through my bison steak one-handed—*impossible*. I push my plate aside. I could pick it up and chomp through it, but Papa would have a fit—he's taught me better manners than that. I'll eat tomorrow. The Elven prince looks down at me, his features twist in concern. "Are you not hungry, Tahsen?"

I think he just said part of my new name. *Why would he call me by my middle name over my first name, whatever it is?* "No, sir. I'm hungry, just having a little trouble," I say and glance to our linked hands, my cheeks heat. He chuckles like I'm an adorable puppy. I'm not adorable! I'm fierce, super fierce. I hide my scowl and eye my plate again.

"*You* may call me Corrik," he says.

"But you're Elven royalty, I couldn't do that."

"We are also married now, you realize?"

"Yes, I realize," I say, my face heating. I don't know why us being married should embarrass me, but I blush every time it's mentioned.

"Then why aren't you doing it?" he asks arching his brow.

I don't know, maybe because you're terrifying?

"You may also ask for your hand back." He makes a show of releasing my hand. "But I want you to return it when you're done."

A little thrill goes through me as he says that and I feel silly—it's just a hand, but he wants to hold it. I accept his offer and use my hand, his dragging through the motions with mine as I cut my food.

"What do you think you're doing?"

"Cutting up my meat." Can't he see I'm trying to be efficient? I thought if I cut the whole thing into pieces, I could avoid this nonsense of asking for my hand every time I need it. *Doesn't he hate this as much as I do?*

"Do you always slice it up like that? Into small child-size pieces?"

"No," I say. "But that way we can both eat in peace. I won't have to keep asking for my hand and therefore asking you to give yours up. It will be easier that way."

"And do you think a marriage is easy? That we can find shortcuts when our problems don't suit us?"

"No." I see where he's going with this. I'll bet this lousy handcuff tradition is an exercise to illustrate to the newlywed couple how one must give and take in a marriage —blah, blah, blah. I don't need a lecture or this game to understand *that*. Besides, for the prince, er, for Corrik and I, it's different. We're not in love. This game is pointless for us.

"I know marriage requires effort."

"It's more than just effort."

His eyes look through me, trying to read my other thoughts but I guard them and force a pleasant smile. "Of course, Prince Corrik."

"Just, Corrik."

"Corrik." I can't say his name without shyness—like I'm doing something I shouldn't.

By Gods, really Tristan?

He opens his hand, the one cuffed to mine, as a silent order to return it to him. I'm reluctant, but I place my hand in his. What good is it having a hand I can't use anyway? I can barely say his name, I won't ask for my hand again. I'm surprised when I don't have to. He continues to take my hand at will when he needs his, but he's careful to make sure to give me my hand when he can see I need it. I might call that sweet, but he isn't the sweet sort, not really. Sweet would be giving me my sword back.

During dessert, I hear a 'psst' at my feet. I look to Corrik —busy with a guest—lift the tablecloth and poke my head under the table. Lucca's there, on all fours. Of all the ridiculous nonsense. His smile schemes, eyes twinkling with the words he can't wait to say. "Lucca! What in the name of the Gods are you doing?" I whisper yell.

He dangles a key at me with a giddy grin on his face, the key to the blasted handcuffs. *So that's where he disappeared to.* I should be mad at him, but all I can think is how I want that key. I consider the possibility for a moment.

"I can't do it Tristan."

It feels good to hear my name again. "I can't live without you. Come, we'll run away together." He's serious, and absolutely mad.

"Don't be ridiculous, Lucca. Go put that key back where you found it." I shudder to think how he got that key away from Fera. "And go sit with your father where you'll stay out of trouble." In truth nothing keeps Lucca out of trouble, but it will keep me out of trouble. I can't accept his offer and he knows better. That's not the way a warrior behaves; a warrior accepts his duty no matter how much he doesn't like it.

"I mean it Lucca. Go before—"

I don't get to finish my sentence; the prince only needs one hand to drag Lucca by his foot over to his side of the table. *How will I get him out of this one?*

"What do we have here?" Prince Corrik regards him coolly, and with a tinge of amusement as Lucca struggles to stand on his feet. His eyes narrow and zone in on Lucca's hand and the key, which he snatches away from him.

"Prince Corrik, I can explain," I say.

"Heasi!" he yells.

I don't know what the word means, but it's sharp, and I imagine 'shut the hell up' is a pretty decent guess. I think of Papa in this moment, he never argued with Father once I found trouble with him; he'd become quiet, and submissive.

I do my best to mimic Papa. Lucca looks to me for some inclination of what to do, but I've got nothing. I don't know the prince well enough to predict what to say to him.

"Do not look at him, look at me." I've never seen Lucca respond so quickly to an order, not even when it came from his father. "While I may be understanding, dear Prince Lucca, my father may not be. He might see your little 'prank' as a breach of this contract. This is serious, I don't think you realize."

Lucca swallows. "I'm sorry Prince Corrik. Please forgive me. I'm going to miss my cousin. We will miss each other," he adds, to give the prince something to think about. Corrik doesn't look to care about Lucca's jibe; his lack of empathy is etched clear on his beautiful, stony face.

"Do you think you can get this key back around my uncle's neck without him noticing?"

I smile, I know he can. Lucca does too. "Does a dragon breathe fire?" He crosses his arms over his chest, his ego still intact.

"Go then. Before he realizes it's gone."

Lucca winks at me, and as always, leaves me with his mess to clean up. He's lucky I'm chained to an Elven prince or I'd clean his clock.

"He meant no harm," I say.

"You should not be defending him, *especially* to me."

He slams our joined hands on the table and I freeze. I feel obligated to defend my cousin, but Corrik's betrayed by my allegiance to Lucca over him. He's my husband, my allegiance should be with him now.

With tremendous effort, Prince Corrik's beautiful Elven face softens, and with his free hand, he turns my face toward him.

"Tahsen," he says. "I did not like that, yiah!" Using the hand joined to mine, he runs his fingers through his silky golden hair. It's an off-hand gesture and I can tell he's frustrated.

I have to fix this.

Since my hand is stuck going wherever his goes, it's in his hair too. I take over control of our hands for the first time tonight of my own volition and grab his. I've gotten used to holding his hand; it's familiar now. Our joined hands move as one thought back down to the table and the gesture calms him some.

I haven't been able to look at him with the enduring stare I do now. He really is perfect, and had we the opportunity, I think I might have liked to date him. Maybe in an alternate universe, one where we'd get to know each other before we wed.

Maybe 'alternate universe us' knows how to deal with this situation.

I start when he reaches his hand up to my face and rubs his thumb over my bottom lip. I think he might kiss me again. My heart picks up its pace; I get ready to kiss him. I'm relieved when he pulls his hand back, picks up his wine goblet, and nods toward mine. I grasp my goblet with my free hand.

"Las, nah! Lucca will put the key back. All is well."

I notice more Elvish slipping into his sentences. I'm

probably going to have to learn that Gods forsaken language. We clink our glasses together, and I am thankful for the wine to calm my nerves. He resumes his austere composure after that and it's easy to figure out his toast to clear the air has cost him in some way. We don't say another word to each other, nor does he look my way—yet I know he's cognizant of me. He doesn't offer my hand back to me anymore, securing his grip on it; I'm certain I won't get it back at this point even if I ask.

The music and dancing begin, and the prince and I are expected to start the evening off. Without a word, he pushes out from the table, and with a hard tug to my hand I'm up too. All eyes are on us; my breathing quickens. I don't know why this is nerve-racking. I've performed in front of people before; Lucca and I are complete hams. I suppose it's got something to do with what I am now. I am not Tristan the great son of our admirable Markaytian warlord, but cowed Elven husband and concubine. I don't want to be judged like that. I'd run for it if I weren't chained to a massive war Elf. We are in the center of the floor now, and the prince pulls me around to face him in a wild swoop. I gaze into his stony eyes—predatory eyes. By the Gods, is he still angry over the whole Lucca thing? I swallow. Quite possibly, but the look in his eyes isn't about Lucca, not exactly. Lucca's actions stirred whatever emotion is charging through him, but he's not thinking of Lucca.

He wasn't kidding when he told Lucca his actions may not be seen as a prank—but he wasn't talking about his father, he was talking about his own feelings. Lucca challenged his hold on me and won, that's what angered him more than anything else. He fights to control the rage within him like he's been doing since he discovered Lucca under the table, but it's not going well. We take frame, and the prince automatically assumes the dominant position; the hard lines of his unyielding body only know how to dance lead.

The orchestra begins soft, but our dance is a rigid, dour thing. I decide to get through this horrid moment by submitting to the Prince's hard turns and abrupt footwork. He still manages grace, but I fumble unable to keep up with his changes. I catch sight of Father, he looks disappointed, yet when doesn't he? I remember his words at breakfast, it's like they were a prophecy for now. If the prince would just slow down a half step, *I am* a good dancer. I'm considered as agile as Father; fumbling is not something I'm used to.

"I'm sorry," I say.

Nothing.

"Corrik, I didn't mean to choose him over you—I'm just used to defending him."

He spins me, it's fast enough to centrifuge the food I've just eaten, but my words have effect.

"Then it's good you shall be apart if you can't control this habit—it's a bad habit. How do you expect your cousin to grow if he's not left to suffer the consequences of his actions?"

I... I haven't thought about it quite like that.

"I'm not sorry, you know. I'll never be sorry for taking you away from here—you belong with me Tristan. You're mine." His directness is startling. I don't like his words, but I appreciate his honesty. I still hate him for it.

Wait. *Tristan.* He used my Markaytian name.

He's trying to calm himself. His fingers dig into my shoulder a little harder; it hurts. I need to do something before he loses the careful control he's constructed around his anger.

"Corrik, you have me." He spins me away then back to him dipping me severely, my nose is inches away from his.

'*You're damn right I do,*' he says without words. That didn't go how I thought it would. I need to think of something better. We continue to dance. He continues his graceful, yet rigid float across the dance floor, while I'm dragged along like a rag doll. During another death spin, I catch sight of Papa, he looks concerned—he knows I'm a formidable dancer, and that something's wrong. He and Father look good together. Much as Arcade Kanes is a cold-hearted bastard, he loves Papa. Their relationship is a flawless fairytale. When I was a little boy, I often asked Papa to tell me the story of their wedding—I may be a fierce, sword-fighting Markaytian, but I'm also a bit of a romantic.

Wait a minute—*their wedding*—I know what to do. I know how to demonstrate to the prince, *to Corrik*, that I'm willing to be his. My alliance will be with him from now on.

The song ends, and thankfully so does this Godsforsaken dance. If we have children, I certainly won't be recounting for them our first dance as a married couple—as any couple at all. I stop him from dragging me back to our seats by the stupid handcuffs chaining us together—the only time they've come in handy all night.

We've had plenty of Elvish traditions tonight, time for a Markaytian one.

"Corrik."

Slow and deliberate, I get down on my knees in the same way Papa did on his wedding and recite the same words he did. "I honor you. I trust you. I am yours." I try to give him the eyes Papa described giving to Father, it's harder than I thought it would be—my parents were in love, it was easy for Papa to look at Father like he was his whole world because he was: *he is*.

Corrik is the man taking my whole world.

I realize my eyes are closed when I have to open them. When I do, I see that the large war Elf has the most amazing expression on his face. I've surprised him. This isn't quite like Papa's story. After he pledged himself to Father, he buried his face into Father's thigh. Papa's a large man, but Father is larger and stronger, and was able to pick him up. Papa wrapped his legs around Father's waist, and according to Papa, they kissed the kiss of a thousand kisses. I've never had any clue as to what that means, but Papa always says that part with such a wistful gleam, I never questioned him. Some things are better left to wonder.

In my story, I have an Elven prince shocked to hell, looming above me. This is stupid. I shouldn't have done it. *You're a foolish man, Tristan Kanes!*

I want him to know I'm serious about this, about us. I'll work hard at our marriage because as much as this union was decided without my say so, it is now up to me to maintain the union honorably. He can never doubt my loyalties— *Markaytia's loyalties.*

"Tristan," he says my Markaytian name, his free hand slides through my braided hair to my cheek. "This is a gift I hold in high regard."

The crowd is quiet until Corrik gets down to his knees in front of me, gasps and whispers fill the silence. He's so large, he still looms over me and I have to turn my face up to see his. I can't believe he's on his knees before me—it seems wrong—this isn't a man who kneels, yet here he is kneeling before me: his concubine. One hand still on my cheek, he pulls my face to his, and our lips meet—it's like lightning all over again. I don't know if it's the kiss of a thousand kisses like Papa's story, but I know I'll remember it till I die.

The crowd claps and cheers when we part. Corrik

smiles as much as Corrik smiles, and I'm glad I've managed to thaw the ice mountain a little. I look over to my fathers, they are *both* smiling—my father seldom smiles—and it's not just any smile, it's one that beams with pride. He nods minutely; no one sees it, but I have. Corrik stands us up, and we both give a bow to our onlookers.

"Please join us for more dancing," he says.

The music starts again, but we return to our seats, thank the Gods. I don't think I'd like to dance after that performance. "That meant a lot to me, Tristan," Corrik says rubbing our joined hands with his thumb. He bends in for another chaste kiss. "I like kissing you."

I pull back. "I like kissing you too." *And Gods, do I.* "But Corrik, there are so many people—it's inappropriate."

"Oh yes, I forgot about your Markaytian sensibilities."
He's mocking me.

"There's nothing wrong with wanting intimacies kept private." I don't know where my sudden boldness comes from. I probably shouldn't speak to the prince like that.

"What makes you think you will have any say over what 'intimacies,' as you call them, will be in private, or not? I think I've demonstrated that I hold the key to those practices."

He's teasing me, pulling on the chain around his neck, revealing the key to the chastity belt I wear.

"Because you seem like a decent man. Am I wrong?"

"Indeed, you are. I am in no way decent when it comes to *intimacies*." His eyes sparkle on the word and his mouth smirks. He means it, he's proud of it even *and he's still* making fun of me. It would appear that he has more confidence talking of these matters than I do.

Markaytians are open with our bodies, but private about

what we do with them, unless your name is Lucca Kanes of course. He is the exception, not the rule.

I think the prince is flirting with me—I'm not sure. He's hard to read. "Then I'm left with no choice, but to bow to your mercy my Liege," I say hoping it will further our playful banter, but I don't think I should've said such a thing. His breathing gets heavier, and he's restrained again, his hand tightens around mine.

Thankfully the Elven king and queen interrupt us. "That was beautiful, Kathir," she says.

Ka-what? Oh yeah. My name—*my Elvish name.*

"Yes, my dear it was," the king agrees with her. They both smile radiant smiles and I wonder how such a rough character like Corrik could come from these two—I would think their son would emit the same sunshine.

"Thank you," I say. Corrik is still in the grip of whatever madness possesses him, his hand tightens further still; it hurts. If he squeezes anymore, he'll break something. The king and queen seem to understand what Corrik is going through and what he needs. "Ahhhhh, yes my son, after such a powerful display of devotion on both your parts you will need—"

Corrik shakes his head at his father, the king stops speaking, getting his meaning; I do too. There is something Corrik doesn't want said in front of me. I look to the queen, though I don't know why, it's not as if she'll tell me their secrets.

"It's time for the two of you to go upstairs," she says. They depart, and I'm left alone with an Elf that's gone stone silent and the vibe he's sending says he wants to sink his teeth into me.

Finally, he speaks. "They're right, we must go. *Now.*"

He doesn't drag me this time, my human speed too slow

for him. Instead, he heaves me over his shoulder—without any effort—and carries me out of our wedding reception like I'm nothing more than a sack of potatoes.

———

"Corrik! You let me down now! This is undignified!" I've screamed at him and pounded on his back the whole way up to our rooms to no avail. He won't speak, nor will he pay any heed to what I'm saying. He doesn't need to ask me where to go, it seems he already knows where our rooms are.

"Put me down this instant you lout!"

Okay, so I've gotten a littler braver on the way up here. I couldn't get away from him so I fought back in the only way I could: by shouting obscenities at him. Inside our rooms he puts me down and shuts the door while I let loose.

"Just what did you think you were doing carrying me throughout the palace like that? Of all the embarrassing—"

He waits with his free arm crossed over his chest until I stop my rants, which I do, but only because the way he's focused on me is unnerving. *What's he going to do?* When he still doesn't speak, I divest myself of the ridiculous rabbit fur cape and throw it on the floor. I'm still not over being carried through the palace, *my home*, slung over his shoulder. I could be forgiving, but I'm not in the mood.

"Have you nothing to say for yourself? No? Then I'm going to bed—you can consummate the marriage yourself."

I turn away knowing full well I can do nothing chained to him, but it's the gesture that counts. I make my best attempt at dragging him with me, but it's like trying to drag a large block of granite and I go nowhere. Yet with just a tiny flick of his wrist, I find myself pressed against the large

Elf's chest. He nuzzles his mouth into my neck and I shiver and freeze as his soft lips press themselves down my neck leaving a wet trail. It feels good, and for a brief moment I forget I'm mad at him.

But then I remember. "Corrik, *stop*."

He does and considers me angrily. I'm in this now so I put on my brave face and solider on.

"Corrik, explain."

"I should think it obvious."

It is obvious. He carted me off to fuck me, fine, that's what we're supposed to do, but I thought there would be a little more romancing. "Is that how this happens in Elvish Tradition? Cart your husband off and have your way with him?"

"Yes," he says. It's clear he just wants to lick my skin again.

"Well, you're in Markaytia now. We don't do things like that."

In truth, I don't know what it is Markaytians are meant to do on their wedding nights. I mean, I know they, well, they make love, but I'm not familiar with the details. I'm making things up as I go along because I don't want my first time to be with an angry Elf.

My words have effect. He smirks. "And just how do we do things *here* my little Markaytian?"

"With the truth. Something happened downstairs, Corrik. Even your parents noticed. It caused you to act like a barbarian. I want an explanation. I want to know who I'm letting have me."

"I'm afraid I'll have to disappoint you—you're not getting an explanation and you will let me have you anyway," he says certain of himself. He scoops me up, I kick wildly, but it does nothing to deter the Elf from his goal. He sets me down on the bed, hard, his angry eyes indomitable.

"Fine, take me if you must. But I do not consent to this."

I'm lying on the bed now, staring up at his beautiful form and I dare to cross my arms. *Will he still go through with this, even though I've said no?*

"I shall never force you into sex with me, Tristan."

So, I finally have one power.

"If you don't answer my question, then I suppose we will both be unhappy men."

"You don't mean that," he says. "You take your duty seriously and you know you must do this whether you want to or not."

My one power begins to crumble at the edges, but I won't give in yet.

"Well maybe you're wrong. Maybe I think my kingdom has abandoned me in giving me over to *you,* and I no longer feel I owe them anything."

To that the prince does something I do not expect; he bursts with booming, laughter. It's beautiful despite its lack of mirth. "That's the most ridiculous thing I've ever heard. You practically ooze patriotism. Markaytia could gut you and leave you for dead, yet you'd use your last bit of saliva to spit on anyone walking by who dared breathe a bad word against Markaytia."

Damn him. How does he already know me so well?

It's childish, but I roll away from him as much as I can with the handcuffs keeping us together. I don't want to look at him; I hate him and his mocking. Silence reigns for a time before a hand cards through my braids. It feels good and soothes me despite being attached to someone I loathe. I can't believe I was beginning to think he would be an all-right companion, prickly as he is. We were having a spot of fun downstairs—I thought I could *like* him.

"I can't tell you," he whispers, his voice soft now. "Can I promise to tell you some other time?"

What am I supposed to say? He's made it clear I can't say no—or I can but he won't tell me anyway so what good is his asking? I turn back to face him and his expression twists with concern.

"Oh, Tahsen." He uses his thumb to wipe away the stupid tears of frustration I've been ignoring. *Why does he look to care anyway?* "Maybe we *should* just go to sleep," he says.

I can't believe what he's just suggested. That's what gets him to forgo sex? Tears? No way. I'm not a child—it's just been a long, trying day. I will lose my virginity tonight damn it. He's right and I take my duty seriously—I will consummate this marriage for Markaytia. "Don't be ridiculous, we will finish the requirements for the marriage," I say in a business fashion and look him over keenly. "Whatever possessed you before, it's gone from you now."

"How do you know that?" he says.

"I'm not sure. Something about you has changed."

We are quiet again for some time, his hand is still in my hair like he needs to touch me. I look at his sword to distract myself, he's still wearing it and I wonder if he's noticed how many times I've admired his stunning weapon throughout the night. Its hilt is gorgeous with its simple design and the grip is wrapped in some type of leather with a gleaming pommel sticking out the end. The cross-guard runs perpendicular to the large, wide blade, which is inlaid with more of the same Elven designs, matching the upside-down clover on our crowns. I miss my sword all the more.

"Do you find my sword pleasing? Would you like me to

wear it while I bed you, my fire-breathing Markaytian?" he teases.

Huh. Fire-breathing? I do have the blood of a dragon coursing through me. I crack a half-smile at his compliment; he's trying to patch things up between us.

This argument is ending with a bittersweet resolution, but I'm proud at how I've handled myself.

It's time to move on. We must consummate the marriage. The moment is getting closer to where I must lose my virginity. That thought begins to dominate over all others and my breath picks up the pace. His free hand begins to smooth over my chest, undoing buttons and pushing aside layers of material—I hardly notice until I feel his hand, warm against my bare skin. I gasp, but my plea-sure is short-lived.

"What is this? Why was I not told of this marking?"

His hand traces over the large black, dragon tattoo on the left side of my body. The head is nestled into my neck with its mouth over my collarbone and the open wings flared over my left deltoid. Its body snakes down my left chest muscle and over the nipple—that part had hurt second most when the artist inked it into my flesh. The worst of it, was its tail that whips down over my ribcage and ends halfway down my abdomen. All warlords in Markaytia are marked with such a tattoo at their coming-of-age ceremony. It just so happened that Mr. Control-Freak decided to rip me out of that life, not long after I was named and marked. I wasn't very well going to peel my skin off—once a tattoo is on it's on for good.

"This will have to go."

"I'm not ripping my skin off, Corrik."

"Rip your skin off? By Ylor, no. I can remove it another way."

"Elves have ways to remove a tattoo?"

"Yes, and not to worry, it's completely painless."

I know I can do it because he won't expect it. I jump up grabbing his sword with a mighty heave (it's a lot heavier than I expect), as I force him to flip around, or be stabbed. I won't kill him, but I am going to make myself heard on this point. "You will do no such thing, Corrik Cyredanthem. This tattoo is *mine*. If you remove it, there will be trouble between us." I aim the sword at his throat, my hands shaking with its weight. I doubt I'd be able to do more with it than this. It's too heavy for me to wield.

Corrik is stunned.

"Promise me." I know I don't have much power over him. This is no more than a reckless show. He can grab the sword and have me pinned on the bed in an instant; this may even anger him to the point he will abolish the marriage and the treaty. I don't think sometimes, I just act, but it's too late now and I must follow through.

"For now, but you don't understand."

"That's not good enough."

There's something in his eyes. He looks scared, not scared because I'm going to hurt him, only scared because I'm holding the sword in the first place—he's frozen with fear and I realize I do have control, at least in this one moment.

"Fine. I promise. Now put that sword down, before you hurt yourself."

Hurt myself? He's just seen my tattoo, the one I earned for a reason. I may have been born with the requirement: the blood of a dragon flows through me as it does my father, but my father would have a new son, before he would hand the title over to someone unworthy. I don't flash his sword around carelessly, but with purpose; there's no way I could hurt myself. The very thought is absurd. It is heavy, much heavier than the swords I'm used to; I wouldn't last with this sword in battle, but my anger is ample fuel for this.

But he's promised me and that's enough so I slide his sword home to the baldric on his back. When I'm unarmed and am facing him again, I can feel the violence peeling off him as he breathes hard.

"That was a mistake."

"You are trying to tame a *dragon* Corrik, you best take care or you might get scorched." He's the one making the mistake.

He grabs me roughly and flips me on my back; I let him. His mouth attacks mine and he tugs hard at the nipple under my tattoo, intending to place his own mark there. He rubs, tweaks and squeezes it between his fingers. I arch my pelvis toward him.

Lucca always told me sex was the best after an argument with someone. I didn't understand it then and couldn't even fathom how that would work, but now, in this moment, I understand completely. I'm still fired up inside, the aftermath of my anger courses through me as it looks for a physical outlet: my husband.

Corrik is an infuriating, dominating ass and I hate him, but he's a sublime creature. His beauty is otherworldly—I've never seen anything like him and I'm certain I never will again. He's hard and supple and dreamy.

Since when does sex require love? I have a supreme specimen before me; it's enough to please my cock. His tongue prompts my lips open and I let him inside, allowing his tongue to seek mine, tangling with it. He doesn't bother with anymore of the buttons on my wedding attire. The thing I'm wearing is a gown after all, and he simply pushes it up to reveal the gleaming silver chastity belt.

I forgot about that. I know he's expecting to see it, I'm embarrassed anyway. My cheeks heat and I can't kiss him anymore. I pull away to watch with morbid fascination. He lifts the chain with the key over his head and dangles it before me. "You've remained chaste just for me," he says. I lost count over how many times he asked me that in the strange book he left me. I don't know what good it does to continue to state the obvious or is he mocking me? I'm not sure. I haven't grasped an understanding of the Elf yet. "More than that you've taken pleasure only when I've allowed it."

Is this a speech? The kind like when a new building is opened, and a ribbon is cut?

"You've been good, haven't you Kathir?" It's my Elvish name again. It has a harder edge to it than the other one he's been referring to me by. I have a bad feeling this isn't something good.

And then I remember.

Moments before I put on the chastity belt, I had some fun. I'm sure my wide eyes are what give me away.

"Tell me what you've done. Tell me how you've disobeyed me."

The best shiver goes through me, not arousal exactly, maybe something better. "Nothing. Well not *nothing*, but not something either—I only touched him!"

He becomes murderous. *"Him?"*

It takes me a moment to reason out why he's so angry about my referring to my penis as a 'him.' He thinks I've touched an actual him. "My penis! I touched him—it! I touched my penis." I've gotten used to referring to my penis in the third person, now I've given Corrik the wrong impression. "What I'm trying to say is, I touched my own penis—not another man's—without your permission."

I can see it's taking him a moment to process what I've said, his eye narrow and his pretty face twists as he finally comprehends. "You refer to your cock as a 'him?'"

"Yes." I have something new to be embarrassed about. No one was supposed to know that.

His laughter this time is a gorgeous, deep, tone, the smile it brings to his face making him so beautiful it's hard to look at him. But I am looking at him as I realize that for all his negative qualities, I do like something about him and it's laugh. In fact, I'm in *love* with it. I want him to keep laughing. "I used to talk to him when you'd let me pleasure myself," I blurt out the first thing I think of. He laughs harder; I continue.

"Mostly, I'd apologize to him—on your behalf—for making him miserable for so long."

His laugh continues, and his eyes—the dark violet ones —have happiness flooding out of them. I didn't think something so dark could look so bright. It's like magic happening.

"He talks to me too."

Corrik loses it—he's laughing so hard there are tears he has to wipe away—and I can't stop myself, I've lost it too. I'm entranced by his gorgeous laughter. Something that beautiful has to count for something. The Gods wouldn't bless someone horrible with a gift like that, would they?

"He complains half the time, and the other half, he just cries, w*hy do you never want to play with me, Tristan? Why do you ignore me when I ache? I'm magnificent*—oh yeah did I mention? He's quite the arrogant bastard." I go on like that until Corrik is gasping for air. I've managed to thaw the Ice Prince some more. I stare in wonder at him as he catches his breath.

"So, you touched *him* when you shouldn't have?" He

still smiles and plays along with my game, but I know it's a serious question. "Tell me about that."

I'm quick to defend myself. "Just the once, and it was *his* fault. *He* convinced me I should do it—I wanted to obey you, but he's incorrigible."

"What did your penis say to you then, that was so convincing?"

"Well, it wasn't so much what he said but the way he looked at me."

"He gives you *looks,* too?"

I nod. "I'm sorry, Corrik. I have been good—I only touched him the once, today—and he may have got me to stroke him a bit, but I stopped before it got out of hand."

"I'll bet he didn't like that very much."

I don't answer. The moment has died off, and I remember why I stopped; I didn't want to disappoint my father, it had nothing to do with the prince. It's probably best he doesn't know that. Especially since it would probably sound strange me telling him my father popped into my head mid-wank. Besides, the topic of my father is a heavy one. I don't want to go there amidst our already strange pre-coital conversation.

It's anti-climactic when he pokes the key into the lock and frees the comedic wonder. My penis doesn't care that he's been laughed at, he's got too much confidence and energy; he's ready to party. Corrik tosses the chastity belt along with the key on the floor.

"I can see why you had such a hard time. He does look like the kind to win a debate." He looks to my penis. "I'm sorry Mr. Kanes, I shall spend a great deal of time making things up to you."

"You will not nickname my penis Mr. Kanes," I say.

"Why not? He's mine now. I'll call him whatever I like."

I would say something clever back, I really would, but Corrik swallows my cock and I may never speak again. His mouth is warm and wet and slick. As quick as he's sucked me down, he spits me out, kissing the head and then bringing his lips to mine immediately so I can taste the flavor of my own cock.

"This *must* be the part where I get to ravage you? Markaytian tradition can't be so very different from Elvish?" he says with softness, fast regaining its edge. The way he looks at me—I could pretend that he loves me. Love may not be necessary for sex, but it does make it *more*.

"Aren't you upset I've disobeyed you?"

"I probably will be tomorrow," he says, like it's an inevitable thing he has no control over. "But right now, I just want to make you mine."

"Then make me yours, Corrik."

CHAPTER 5

*A*ll I can see are two glowing purple eyes.

The light of the candles is gone, scant moonlight squeezes through gaps in the clouds that have covered the night sky and into our bedroom's skylight. Corrik's happy laughter has vanished from existence: he's in a trance —I've never experienced anything like it and I must assume it has something to do with being an Elf. He reminds me of a person in the heat of battle. I'm afraid. I can't move and I won't speak—it's not wise to interrupt someone in such a state—anything could provoke an attack.

He takes inventory of my body and decides I've been clothed long enough. He unsheathes the great sword from his back and slices my gown in the right places, tears it from my body, discards it, and throws it to the floor along with the silver chastity belt.

I'm naked for the first time in front of Corrik—I hope I appease him. I won't be warlord, but I can still win victories for Markaytia and him admiring me would be such a victory.

"You are beautiful, Kathir, and all mine. No one shall

touch you or look upon you because you belong to me." He sheds his clothes, and when he's naked too, he tosses his sword with the rest of it—*it's just us now.*

His body is magnificent; it's what raw power looks like. Solid muscles contract and squeeze the flesh that fights to hold them in, reminding me of full water skins bursting at the seams.

"And I am all yours to look at," he says and takes my hand, the one attached to his, bringing it down to rest on the velvet skin of his cock. "And this is yours to touch."

His cock.

Mine is large, but his is *much* larger. It's long and thick with a head that mushrooms over his girth. His skin is white porcelain, but his cock is more of a cream, with full veins embossed on the shaft like twin lightning bolts.

It's bloody magnificent.

When I remember it will be going inside me, I start to panic—that *thing* is likely to split me in two.

I'm distracted when I feel something wet being slicked over my cock. It's Corrik's hand with something similar to the lotion I used earlier. My cock likes what's being done to him. I moan.

"That's *nice*, Corrik."

"Relax."

Do I look nervous? Because I'm not—I'm not at all nervous about being impaled.

He leans over me, placing his lips by my ear. "I'll go gentle for our first time, even though I want to fuck you senseless." *Does the Prince desire me that much?* I press into his hand, I love his hand, I could spend days with my cock holed up inside of it. It's a deep dark cave of wet wonders. *In and out, in and out ...* I'm building up, building, climbing—

"*Corrik, nooo,*" I cry when he takes his hand away. I'm so close, but I guess that's the point. He's in charge. He's in control. I *get* it.

Unless.

I put my free hand on my dick, and in short order, my hand is removed and slammed over my head.

"Do not touch *him* again, not till I say."

It's a threat, a promise, and hey did he just? Yep, he referred to my cock as a '*him.*'

He doesn't wait for a response, his lips crash to mine and we're kissing—no, he's trying to kiss me while I try to suck his face off. *Do all Elves taste this good?* His pelvis rocks into mine, our cocks touch and get to know one another; I tilt up so my cock can continue to find his. Something raw and powerful takes over, we aren't strangers anymore, we're lovers. He breathes in as he kisses me, taking my air with him as I exhale, and pull his breath back into me when I inhale. We dance like that, trading air back and forth with urgency, until he stops suddenly and reaches over to the table by the bed for something. I continue to attack him—an animal has taken over my body, Tristan is gone. All I know is I have to taste him: lick, suck, and nibble his skin. I breathe in hard so I can have his scent, my free hand claws down his back. He moves down out of my reach and kneels at my entrance. I lift my head to look at him as I pant like I've run the distance of two cities. By Gods, this is it, the part where he impales me with his monstrous appendage. *Be brave, Tristan. You've faced far more terrifying situations; you can do this.*

Nope, doesn't help. I'm terrified.

"Accck. *Corrik.*"

Without warning, he coats everything with slick lubricant: my cock, my balls, and most specially my hole. The liquid isn't cold, but it shocks me. He doesn't apologize and uses the lubricant to glide his hand up and down my cock some more, before settling one finger at my entrance. With more care than I thought him capable of, he slides his finger in to his first knuckle a few times, before he twists it in deeper. He knows what he's doing. Once he's able to work the whole finger into me, my fear of his large, Elf-cock, begins to ease, relaxing my entrance, making sure it's open enough to accept his cock. Besides, I like what he's doing now.

"You may grab your cock now, Tristan. I want to grab it, but I can't."

It seems the handcuffs thwart even him. No matter, I'll gladly grab my own cock. It's slick with lubricant as I slide my hand up and down in time with his finger. He adds another. By this time, I'm drunk with lust and press down on both his fingers.

"Add another," I beg. "Please?"

He's more than happy to oblige.

I've taken to sex quite fabulously; I want more, I crave something I can't name. I moan, writhe and sigh on his fingers—I've lost count of how many are in there—I pump my cock and climb toward climax a second time. Once again, he pulls everything away. *Evil bastard*. His cold, purple eyes look down at me, filled with an emotion I can't name. I'm going to pretend that it's love. I don't care if I'm called a sap for it; I want love present here, now, as he takes me.

"Don't feel so bereft my darling. Don't you want to see what my cock feels like in there?"

Yes, yes I do.

If multiple fingers feel like that, I'm all in, I want that

mighty cock to fill me—want him to pound into me, make me scream.

"Take your hand away from your cock; only I will touch you now."

I obey and move my hand to the side of my body.

"Legs up, spread them wide—open for me, Tahsen."

He uses the softer of my Elvish names and it feeds my fantasy that he's in love with me, that I'm not a concubine, but his true husband—someone he treasures.

I bend my legs toward my ears spreading as far open as I can and expose my hole. He presses his thumb into the pucker and teases it some more. "Corrik. Please," I beg harder.

The corners of his lips tug slightly—Corrik's version of a smile.

Unless he's laughing.

He dumps lubricant onto his member with one hand and I'm left to suffer, watching as he pumps his cock, coating it. Finally, after what feels like a thousand years, he lines the head of his cock up with my hole but doesn't push in just yet. Instead, he reaches down to grab my free hand and slams it over my head like before. I'm vulnerable, but I'm too high on this sex mountain to care. With him over top of me, I can clearly see his intentions. He leaks possession seeking to dominate me. I shiver with terrified excitement.

His voice, normally a hard, decisive tone, has changed to an otherworldly hiss. "That wedding was just words, but this is different. Once I claim you, you will be my mate for life. We will be bonded by flesh, and by magic."

His words should scare me more, but they don't. I like what he says. I don't want to want him, but I do.

"Go on then, make me yours."

He emits a growl only a creature could and when he

does, his teeth flash, sharp as razors; the moonlight glints off them.

With a mighty thrust he slams into me and I hear thunder in my head or did thunder actually happen? I'm not sure. All I know is that Corrik's cock is deep inside me. It's larger than all the fingers he had up me, and it's not nice at first. *It hurts.* Corrik either doesn't notice or doesn't care; he continues his thrusts. I wince as he slams into me, and for the smallest of seconds, I'm concerned he really is going to split me in half.

But I remember how much I wanted this, I remember how long I've waited and how much I deserve this. My sexual prowess has been locked away for too long and I won't be denied the enjoyment of this moment for anything—even big, arrogant war Elves whose parents spoil him with whatever trinkets or humans he decides he needs. I let my body relax and bear down so my entrance opens for him once again. The pain is gone in that instant—I'm able to enjoy the benefits of having a mate with a large cock.

Corrik is overtaken by something he's not in control of at the moment, but I'm not afraid—the worst that can happen is pain, the best, intense pleasure. That's all I feel right now, pleasure—pleasure deep and intense. Our souls sew together as we become one as we become mates by flesh and by magic. Whatever that means.

The thunder is back. It clashes noisy inside my head as Corrik pounds the life out of me and I climb closer to climax. Up, up, up and, *I can't.* I want to come so bad it hurts, but I can't. I don't know what's wrong until I hear Corrik's voice rich with haughty, mirth. "What's the matter my Tristan? Is there something you need?"

Asshole. He knows what I need.

"I need to come," I say and even though I'm hot all over, I blush another level deeper.

"Ask nicely and I may consider it. *You* don't need to come to satisfy the ritual."

That's news to me. In Markaytia, both participants need to come to consider the marriage legitimate. Once again Elvish customs differ and Elvish customs rule. The way he pounds into me now, there's no way I can back down—I'll say whatever he wants me to, beg even.

"Please, Corrik. Please let me come." I'm desperate and scared he'll say no.

He stills his cock and I writhe around it with a whimper as he pets my cheek with his free hand, his other still holding mine steadfast over my head, bound to his by the handcuffs. "You're so pretty, especially when you beg—*stop moving.*"

His lips stretch over his teeth, so I can see every one of them. "You should not have provoked me, now look what you've done. Our wedding night was supposed to be perfect, I was going to be so soft, so gentle." He slams into me again, and it does hurt, but it also feels so, so good. I moan and beg and swear to him I'll do anything if he'll just say I can come.

"You will—you will do everything I ask," he tells me.

Fuck, yes, whatever. Just say the Gods damned words!

"Come hard, sweet baby boy."

And I do—harder than I ever have before. He comes too, filling me up with his Elven seed. I hear the thunder again, and I know it's done. I'm his mate now.

He's also mine.

It's a sudden feeling that grips me, courses through me. It must be the Elven magic. I feel like he's my possession as much as I am his. He might hold the leash and all the authority between us, but he's mine too, and I'll make sure he knows it.

He collapses on top of me. He's panting; I'm panting, and I wish he'd get off me. The weight of him grounds me and keeps me in the present so I can't fly away in my mind. We stay like that for some time until my silent wish is answered. He rolls off of me taking his cock with him. We both lie on our backs and stare at the ceiling. I feel a comfort between us like we've known each other a hundred years, yet I don't remember a day. My feelings of hatred aren't gone, they're full force, except now I feel I can tell him.

"I hate you."

I expect the creature from before to return, but he doesn't. Instead, I hear Corrik's soft voice, the one he used earlier, drift regretfully over to me.

"I know." His cuffed hand finds my cuffed hand and he squeezes and rubs his thumb over my wedding ring. We lay like that for the Gods only know how long. Come is leaking from my ass, come is splattered all over my stomach. I should feel dirty, but I don't. I'm not going to bother to ask him to get up with me to clean. I'm going to close my eyes, fall asleep and worry about it in the morning. It's come, not toxic waste.

He doesn't agree that we should fall asleep like this. He stirs beside me, then he's tracing over my body with a warm, wet cloth, using all the care in the world.

"Corrik, where on Earth?" First there's handy lubricant and now warm towels? How convenient.

Corrik waggles his eyebrows trying too hard to be impish when he's clearly still pensive.

"Someone thought we'd need these. Most likely someone from my side of the family," he says.

Of course—bloody, kinky, Elves.

He takes care as he cleans me, but there's no more quarter smiles from my Elven prince—he's still thinking about whatever it is he's been thinking about since the end of our mating. When he's finished cleaning us both, he returns to his position beside me and resumes his silence. Now I'm going to find it impossible to sleep. I wish he would've left me alone. That way I could continue thinking about what a domineering ass he is, but now I'm confused. *He cares enough to take care of me—if I didn't matter to him, he would've just left me, right?*

He rolls over on his side to face me so he's over top of me, while I stare at the ceiling. His fingers trace the small bruises on my hips where his fingers gripped me tight.

Their existence seems to calm him—he visibly relaxes. "Close your eyes, Tristan," he orders.

I don't want to, but I also don't want to provoke him again for his sake. He seems more affected by it than I am. He continues to trace the marks on my hips, and he knows that though my eyes are closed, I'm not asleep. His voice sings in my ear, a haunting Elvish lullaby. I can't understand a lick of it, but the melody is calming. Calming enough for me to drift off to sleep.

CHAPTER 6

*L*ike a guard dog, I jump up out of bed the moment I hear the latch from the bedroom door click open and just as quickly as I jump up, I'm pulled back down. I'm still handcuffed to a large Elf and somehow through the night I've ended up spooned against him. I blush hotly as I think of the night before. It wasn't all petals and honey, but it was still bloody fantastic. I wince as the light of the early dawn shines through the window and into my eyes. Corrik jumps when I pull on him. The person assaulting our door enters; it's Uncle Fera—*what is he doing here?*

"Well, well nephew. What a prize you've acquired. Will I get to borrow him? Sometime in the near future perhaps?"

Still sleepy, it takes me a moment to process his words and realize I'm indecent. *Have these Elves never heard of privacy?* I'm not skittish about being naked in front of people, but being naked in this intimate a fashion with my partner is of a different nature. Corrik pulls me into him and growls at his uncle as he hastily covers me with a blanket.

73

"He's not going to be shared. Remove the cuffs and be gone," he says.

Fera smiles, unaffected by his nephew's grunting. As Fera moves closer, I draw back into Corrik on instinct—an interesting contradiction—but his words are worrisome. *Is that what Elves do? Pass their mates around?* For once I'm glad of Corrik's inherent possessiveness.

"Look Corrik, all of those worries for nothing. It seems he doesn't want to be free of you just yet."

As I scuttle back against Corrik, the irony is not lost upon me. I'm depending on Corrik—the man I've resented for a year—to protect me from dangers unknown: his uncle. This is ridiculous. I'm son of the Markaytian warlord, not some frightened little bunny. I stare at Uncle Fera with a dare in my eyes. *Try to have a turn with me and your cock will find its way to the bottom of the ocean.* He laughs at me. I know I'm no threat to him, and it's clear he thinks I'm cute. Yuck. At least he finally pulls the chain holding the key over his neck and unlocks the cuffs.

"You have a lovely cock," he compliments as casually as one would comment on the weather in Markaytia. I expect Corrik to come to my aid again, but instead he smiles as much as Corrik smiles, in agreement, like I'm a prize-winning hog. I'll skewer the both of them—just wait till I get my hands on a sword because I will despite Corrik's restrictions. Fera pauses, a mixture of shock and happiness blooms on his face.

"I see you've already marked him—very good."

Is that a thing?

Corrik changes the subject. "When should we be ready, Uncle? I'm anxious to get home." To get *me* home he means —I can read between the lines. And I can also see he's working hard to hide something from me. He's terrible at it.

I don't think he's let anyone else in on what he intends to keep from me. His parents and now his uncle almost give him away.

"We shall enjoy breakfast with our Kathir's family and then we'll depart. Is that soon enough for you, Nephew?"

Corrik nods and his uncle leaves. Alone and uncuffed from one another, I'm finally able to push myself away from the great war Elf.

"Where do you think you're going?" He pushes up casually onto an elbow. I try to decipher his mood; it doesn't look good. Is he still upset over the way things went last night? Why brood over it? It's not like much can be done about it, unless he's a time travelling Elf? I doubt it.

"Going to get ready for breakfast."

"Get back here. You'll go nowhere until I say."

Bossy Bastard.

I narrow my eyes and make my displeasure known but obey and return to sit on the bed. "Yes, my Liege?" I'm flippant.

In a heartbeat, he flips me on my back and pins me with his knees on either side of my body, my arms between my body and his knees.

I've provoked him again.

"You cannot do that with me," he hisses. "My anger is something altogether different from anything you've ever known—you don't know what you call to battle young dragon warrior."

'We know this much; they are creatures,' my uncle told me once. *Is that what Corrik is trying to get me to understand?*

"Okay Corrik. I'm sorry," I say as bravely as I can, but I'm shaking. He climbs off me and faces away.

"I will hurt you. I'll like it and I'll admire the marks I'll leave on your skin." He restrains himself, barely able to maintain control on the wildness inside him.

"Please," he says. "At least attempt not to anger me."

"Yes, Corrik," I say, but it doesn't seem to be enough.

We sit in silence; he's having a hard time. "Come kneel before me." That's not so hard. I do it quickly. He remains seated on the edge of the bed, and I kneel slowly between his knees; my face is level with his huge cock.

"If you continue to disobey me, this won't work."

I take a sharp inhale, *is he breaking us off?* I thought that couldn't be done once we were bonded by flesh and magic? I can't allow this marriage to end—I'll be Markaytia's biggest disgrace.

"Corrik, please don't get rid of me, I'm sorry. What do I need to do? I'll make it up to you, I promise. I'll do anything."

His eyes widen. "Get rid of you? I'll never get rid of you —you're mine now." He grabs me roughly by the scruff of my still braided hair. "Do you understand the true meaning of that?"

I shake my head because I don't, but I'm learning. I'm just glad he's not returning me.

"I'm trying not to punish you on our first days as a married couple Tristan, but you are making it difficult."

I come up with an idea. "I could have my father punish me."

That angers him more, his hand twists hard into my long hair. "You are my responsibility now. I will punish you if I see fit to punish you, no one else."

"Of course, Corrik. I only meant that if you didn't want to—"

"Of course, I *want* to. I've wanted to since last night and the mess with your cousin. It got worse when you told me you touched yourself without my permission and when you continued to provoke me—by Ylor! You pulled my own sword on me, Tristan. I'm merely working to hold back for your sake. Do you wish to ride home with a sore arse?"

I shake my head. I don't mention that it's already sore—sore from his cock.

"Then this must stop."

"Don't drive yourself mad over it. You're going to have to punish me at some point, we might as well get it over with."

Father had to punish me often. Lucca and I tended to do the things that got me into trouble with him. Father promised me he would stop punishing me the minute I stopped acting like a child, but apparently, I never did. Even when I grew to be a man, I could only go so long before the chaos inside me took over.

"I'll decide if you're to be punished or not," he says pinning me with his eyes. I look at my knees. Then he cards his hands through my hair. He nudges my chin up and then signals for me to stand. He pulls me in between his knees, nuzzling into the marks he left on me.

"These will be enough."

I bring my hand to ghost over the marks. "Does marking me mean something, Corrik?"

He nods. "Yes. It means everything. I need to see my marks on you; they soothe me. I'll mark you again, Tristan. I will mark you many times over. I won't be sorry for what I do—it's part of my nature—Elves are different than humans. It's best if you try to behave," he says, his lips quirk into a quarter smile. "Now you know what I did not wish to tell you," he raises his brow. "How did you get me to do that?"

"I wasn't trying to. Why wouldn't you want me to know that, Corrik? If anything, it helps us."

"That's what Mother said."

"You should listen to your mother," I lecture.

His eyes smile even if his lips do not. He's pleased.

"Corrik? Are you going to punish me now?" I hate having punishments hanging over my head.

"No. I *should* spank your naughty bottom, but I won't this time

"Spank me?" I shrill outraged. "That's a child's punishment—I'm a man now." I expect that from my father but not my husband.

"Nevertheless, that is what you can expect from me if you choose to disobey me again." He's serious. I remember something else he hasn't mentioned. Now that it seems I'm in the clear, maybe I shouldn't ask—he might change his mind about punishing me—but I want to understand him.

"Corrik, last night, after we consummated our marriage, I told you I hated you."

"I remember." His voice is hard.

"It bothers you."

"It does."

"Why didn't you mention it in your list of my transgressions?"

"That's how you feel—much as I don't like it—I'll never punish you for how you feel."

"You don't like that I hate you?"

"Are you always this obtuse? Or is it just around me? I suspected you to be intelligent."

"Corrik!"

"Of course, I don't want you to hate me."

He doesn't? I was certain I meant nothing to him and that he didn't care what I felt. *Don't get carried away, Tristan, someone saying they don't want you to hate them isn't exactly a declaration of love.*

78

"Come my husband." When he moves, the morning sun hits his forehead in a spot that was covered by his crown yesterday. I didn't notice in between all the sex: A translucent tattoo is beneath his feathered gold bangs, semblant to the pattern of the insignia on his crown and the ones on his ears. It's stunning, and I can't help but reach out and touch it.

"What is this?" I ask.

"That is the royal Elven crest," he states with pride. "I was born with it, but you will have one too someday."

"I will? How is that possible?"

"So many questions. You will have the crest when you finish your transition to becoming an Elf, and you will get one because you are my husband."

His pride over this radiates through him—he can't wait for me to become an Elf. "Nawh. Go clean up. We must leave soon."

He sends me through the doors to our private bathing chamber with a hard slap to my right ass cheek. When I'm out of his sight, I have to rub the sting out. I'm more than glad he chose not to punish me after that, his hand *hurt*. I'll be working hard not to attract his ire in future.

Now to see if I can remove all these ridiculous braids on my own.

The outfit's not terrible.

Elven design, hand crafted, and clearly made for travel. It's beautiful and I like it. I don't like that Corrik chose it for me. It makes me feel like a doll. Corrik should know how I '*feel*' about playing this dress up game. He said I could share with him my feelings; he's going to regret saying so.

There's also a small pack and a sleek pair of knee-high travel boots. I dress and look for Corrik. His clothes are gone, including his grand sword. He didn't mention I should wait for him so I decide to take this opportunity to do something that came to mind as I bathed. Using a quiet, unused route, I transverse the hallways back to my old bedroom. I see no one on the way of course. Lucca and I became adept at using these old halls, ones no one uses anymore. There are newer more efficient routes in use nowadays. We did lots of sneaking around in our youth.

Nothing in my bedroom has been moved; it looks as if I still live here and only spent the night in my other room down in Father and Papa's barracks.

But I don't live here now.

Nostalgia sweeps over me as I take in all of the items I'm not allowed to bring with me: the large, embroidered Kanes Family Crest on the wall, my medals and trophies I've won over the years for sword fighting and archery, and of course the trunk with my old battle tunics I had once used at practice. I open the trunk and pick one up, bring it close to my face and inhale the scent anchored within. It still reeks of blood and sweat, and I sigh—*home*. It's not been a full hour since Corrik has practically begged me to behave; yet without guilt or remorse, I stuff the tunic into my small pack and look around for what else I should bring. I add my dagger, the one with the Markaytian crest embossed in gold over the hilt, and something Papa gave me when I became a man: the ring his father gave to him. A brilliant white gold band studded with emeralds like the eyes of all the men in his family. Inside is an inscription: '*Submit to the Heart.*' I wish I could take the whole room, but it's all I can fit in my pack without raising suspicion. For a brief moment, my conscious flickers, but would Corrik really be that angry over a few personal items?

If he is, do I care?

He said he's never getting rid of me and he seems to mean it. I should have no worries as to ruining any treaties Markaytia has made with Mortouge. Right? Fuck it. I'm bringing them.

I stroll over to the dining hall guessing I'm supposed to meet Corrik there since he left me no instructions. By the look of distress on Corrik's face as I spot him searching for me in the hallway, I think maybe I was supposed to wait for him. I shake my head; we need to work on our communication despite his taciturn ways. He has the look I'm beginning to recognize—the one that says I'm in trouble.

"Where were you?" he says.

I don't need to think about my answer, Lucca and I are the masters of evasion. "Lavatory."

"For thirty minutes?"

"My stomach is upset," I say knowing that could mean many things. Maybe I'm nervous about leaving my home, maybe I'm worried over the man I've married—the things he told me would frighten men less brave than I to their core—maybe I'm disappointed in our sexual escapades from the night before. Though for the record, I'm not. *At all.*

I'll let him wonder.

I don't expect his eyes to soften with concern. "Upset? How is it now?"

"I've had worse. I'll be all right. I think I just need to eat something."

The lie works better than I planned and serves as a distraction. I bask in my victory as he leads me into the dining hall and to my seat.

Everyone is present. Well almost everyone—not my father. It's just as well; it looks like my little detour has made us late and everyone's begun eating without us. I'd rather not have Father know I'm still arriving late to breakfast as a married man. But while it takes the sting out of his absence, I would *almost* prefer his disappointed glare to his not coming at all.

"Good morning little man," Papa says.

"Papa," I hiss.

"Sorry, Tristan. You are a married man now—I shouldn't be calling you that."

He's hurt. I don't like to see him hurt. "It's all right, Papa."

He smiles. "No matter how big you get, you will always be my little boy. Why don't you plate up then? I can't have my son starve his last morning in Markaytia." He struggles to say the last bit; tears shine in his emerald eyes. He turns away and wipes at them. "I'm sorry, Tristan. Arcade told me I shouldn't come, he almost forbid it, but I need to tell you something."

"So, how was *it*?" Lucca interrupts, waggling his brows.

I whack my cousin and I look over to Corrik to see what he thinks of Lucca asking such a personal question about our wedding night, but Corrik isn't even there. He's gone over to talk with his parents, and I notice his mother and father keep looking at me out of the corners of their eyes as they talk with their son in what appears to be a serious conversation. It's like they fear I'm going to bolt or burn up the treaty at any moment.

"Has the prince got you that googly-eyed you can't stop looking at him? It must have been good—why I bet you wish you were still alone with him in your bedroom, so you could—"

"—*Lucca.*" I look to Papa beside us, Papa's blushing like I expect him to be.

"It's all right son. Chat with your cousin, but come talk with me before you leave," he says.

"Didn't you enjoy your night?" Lucca says without remorse. I forgive him because he's Lucca. His question has a complicated answer, but I know Lucca only cares about the sex part of the night so I answer him about that even if I'd rather not.

"The Prince is an excellent lover."

"The Prince is an excellent lover," he mocks. "You sound like you're reciting the alphabet. C'mon. Don't I deserve more details than that? I've always been forthcoming with my sexual escapades."

"Maybe more than you should have been."

"Fine, so you won't give me details, but you really did enjoy, yes Tristan? I need to know my cousin is well taken care of."

I wonder what he thinks he could do if I wasn't '*taken care of,*' but instead I think back to the moments the prince's engorged cock slammed into my most private place and the sensations of ecstasy drumming through me. My cheeks feel warm. "It was everything I hoped it would be."

He smiles wide. "Good. That man may be a prickly bastard, but at least he's good in the sack."

"Ah, our dear sweet Lucca," Corrik says returning to his seat. Damn it. Did he hear what Lucca just said about him? Probably. I remember my vow and don't defend him—my cousin is on his own this time.

Lucca shudders before he turns around to force a fake smile at Corrik. "Good morning, Prince Corrik."

"Thank you for living up to your end of our bargain."

"My sincerest apologies, Prince Corrik. Thank you for

not reporting me to your father. It was a foolish, childish action."

Lucca is a talented actor. He's not sorry at all, he's never been sorry for anything in his life, but he's managed to convince his father of his 'remorse' many times.

"Very foolish," Corrik agrees.

Lucca takes that as his cue to return to his seat, but he lifts his glass from across the table at me, most certainly toasting to my lost virginity.

I decide to keep silent and eat as per my papa's suggestion and I remember he came here to tell me something. I'm curious as to what so I decide to take my plate over to that side of the table and eat with him. I don't get far.

"Where are you going, Kathir?"

"Nowhere," I mutter as I take my seat again.

"Good. I'd rather you didn't sit with your cousin—he gets you into trouble."

I want to say that I get myself into trouble, but that doesn't seem like the best defense so I keep my mouth shut and eat. I don't bother explaining that I intended on sitting with Papa and Mother. He most likely wouldn't care.

Breakfast is often an informal affair, more like a party. The king prefers this way. He enjoys watching everyone move around and have a good time. Father disapproves of the king's disorderly meals, but he usually attends.

Once I finish eating, I dare to ask Corrik permission to speak with my uncle. It doesn't look like he wants to let me go. "How is your stomach feeling?"

"I'm all right now—the food helped."

"Very, well. Don't be long."

Does he really care that much, how I feel? I approach my uncle at the head of the table.

"Ahhh, Tristan my boy! Your aunt was looking forward to this day. She would have been proud of you, as am I."

My aunt, and Lucca's mother, died shortly after I was betrothed to the Elven Prince; she died in childbirth. Lucca's baby sister was a surprise.

The pregnancy with Lucca was hard on the queen and they decided not to have any more children after him because the king was terrified of what might happen to his Georgina. When she became pregnant with Anna, the king begged her to terminate the pregnancy, but the queen refused. The pregnancy was worse than with Lucca and the queen could not handle the birth. Anna, was not strong either. She died only days after the queen.

Many things happened this past year, that being just one of the terrible things.

"I'm sorry, Uncle Amarail. We miss her."

"That we do, son. That we do. But today is a day of celebration! You are like my own Tristan, every bit a son to me as Lucca and I am so happy to have seen you wed into a good family. I hope you will have the joy of children one day—they bring such happiness to a heart, especially when you witness their success."

Does the king consider my marriage to Corrik such a success for me? I know it is for the kingdom, but for me as well? I don't want to ruin his good mood, especially when strong emotions could resurface. "Thank you, Uncle Amarail, for everything. You are a good Uncle. I will miss you."

We embrace and he pats me on the back. When we part, Papa is there. "Tristan, could we have that conversation now?"

Papa pulls me aside; he looks nervous.

"Papa? Is everything all right?"

85

"Yes, fine. Everything is fine, but there's something I should have talked with you about long ago. Tristan we are similar, you and I."

He's redundant, trying to say something big, but I haven't the slightest clue where he's going. "Papa, of course we are alike—you raised me."

"Yes, and well that's not what I mean, but well it is what I mean, but damn it Arcade!"

"I'm not Arcade, I'm Tristan."

"Yes, I know who you are. I'm cursing your father."

"You're not making much sense, Papa."

"I know," he says with a heavy sigh. "Tristan, do you remember much about your father and I growing up?"

"Of course, I do."

"We have a *special* relationship," he begins.

"I know that."

"You do?"

"Yes. Everyone knows. It's clear how much you two love each other. Everyone always says how you're meant to be together—it's because you're special."

"No, I mean, yes, but that's not what I'm referring to." He can't seem to find the words.

"Papa just come out and say it. It must be important if you begged Father to allow you to come up to breakfast just to speak to me."

He pauses. "I never said that—how did you know I begged your father?"

"You said he almost forbid it. I know what that means."

"So, you did notice," he says half to himself. I'm confused. "Tristan, what husband has to ask his husband for permission? It isn't—"

Papa goes silent as he looks with scared eyes behind me.

I turn to look into the black eyes of Arcade Kanes. He ignores me and grabs Papa by the arm.

"You're a mess Eagar. This is why I didn't want you to come."

"Just because you have no wish to see me off, does not mean Papa would be so heartless." All my anger at him, built since yesterday, comes out in one sentence. He turns those angry depths on me and raises his hand to strike, but he stops. Instead of slapping me for talking back to him, he roughly grabs my chin and turns my cheek toward Papa. "The prince will sort him out. He's fine. Let him figure out the rest for himself—that's an order."

Let me figure out what for myself?

I start to seethe; my breath becomes rapid. I don't care about the scene it will cause, I'm going to let Father have it once and for all—*I've lost all opportunity to win his praise anyway.*

Before I can say one word, Lucca grabs me by the arm. "Not now, Tristan."

It takes me off guard, cooling my rage, and I see Papa's eyes pleading with me to listen to Lucca and let it go.

"But Papa—you wanted to tell me something. It seemed important. You can't just let him tell you what to do."

But Papa always let Father tell him what to do.

Father's stone stare is unforgiving, my words offending him in a way I don't expect—on behalf of Papa. Father pulls Papa to him as tears fall from his eyes. I have no idea what just happened. Lucca begins dragging me away. "Lucca, no." I try to pull away from Lucca and toward Papa. "Papa!"

"It's okay Tristan," Papa says.

Father pulls him away and out the doors to the dining hall. Lucca drags me over to his side of the table. He sits me down and shoves juice in my hand. "Drink that. Everything is fine."

I drink, but only because I can't speak. *What was that?* I'm not sure, but I think I hurt Papa again. Only this time it's worse. My heart is broken. Out of everyone, I love Papa most—even against Lucca. I didn't even get to tell him that, instead I wounded him.

"Las, Kathir." Corrik's cold voice breaks into my brooding. It takes me a moment before I realize he's talking to me.

"Nawh," he growls before he storms out of the room.

Apparently, I'm to follow him. "All right, already," I mutter glaring in his direction as he walks away. I look to Lucca apologetically.

"I think you should go Tristan," he says with a smile. "I don't think he likes me very much."

"Well, you've certainly made an impression, as always."

"By Ylor! Kathir, come!" He pokes his head back in to yell at me.

I cringe. I'm not doing a good job of obeying him. I stand up and run after the prince as he stalks ahead of me until we are outside where the Elven guard is preparing us for departure. Ignoring me, Corrik adjusts the saddle on a white horse as he adjusts the hair on the top of her snout.

"This will be your horse, Waii. You will take care of her as we ride home," he says then with his Elven strength, Corrik lifts me onto my horse like an adult would boost a child, and I can't help but pout like one too. Nothing is going my way this morning.

"Stay here and *away* from your cousin," he warns.

It's like I've been put in a 'time-out,' but I don't reply, and just obey. I've made enough of a scene for one day.

I watch from atop of Waii as the rest of the Elven royalty join us. I scan the crowd for Papa and relax when I see him with Mother—my mother looks at me forlorn then turns into Papa's side where he shelters her. Papa waves at me, but I can see he's keeping tears at bay. He's trying to relay that everything is all right, but I don't believe him. I look around for Father, but he's gone. I don't suppose he'll want to stay to see me off after that catastrophe.

I consider getting off my horse to go apologize to Papa, but then I remember my new master, who most likely has eyes in the back of his head. I've angered him again somehow; I'd better not provoke the creature within him anymore. Uncle looks to me with a smile, his arm wraps around Lucca, who for once, isn't smiling.

When the royal Elven entourage is settled, they thrust forward and tap their horses waving goodbye to all the attending Markaytians. Corrik joins us, and signals with a grunt for me to follow. I give a last wave to everyone as I turn my back on home.

N one of it seems real until we pass through the gates of the palace and into the Markaytian village. I've passed through these gates many times, but never with the knowledge that this will be the last time. My heart clenches with regret at having to leave my family. I do not hold the title of warlord, but it makes me no less a warrior than I am. A warrior accepts his duty to his people, and my duty is to be a husband to the Elven prince. I don my battle face as I would my armor, and bid my horse to put one foot in front of the other, steadfast into my new life.

Some distance from the palace walls, I hear shouting from behind me. I recognize the voice at once. It's Papa.

Regardless of the repercussions from the prince, I turn my horse. He's shouting something at me. But I need to get closer to so I can hear it.

Corrik sees what I'm doing and turns his horse, following me.

From here, several things happen at once. Corrik grabs my horse's lead and drags me away, Uncle latches onto Papa and holds him to prevent him stepping any further from the palace walls. Desperate, Papa shouts louder, and equally desperate, I tug harder against the strength of the Elf holding my horse back so I might close enough to hear what Papa's saying.

I still can't hear, I need to get closer so I jump off my horse. Corrik follows suit. I'm ahead of him; however, and I'm close enough to Papa I can finally make out the words he shouts over and over as the great war Elf engulfs me and drags me back to my horse.

"I'm sorry Tristan! It's my fault!" He sobs. "I'm sorry, Tristan, it's *all* my fault!"

"What? What's your fault?" I yell back, but he can't hear me. I'm too far away.

The last thing I see is Papa being dragged by Uncle and several guards inside the gates. Tears stream down my face as Corrik drags me kicking and screaming and the entire Elven entourage has stopped to stare at me. I expect Corrik to yell at me, and right now I hope he does. I hope he's angry. I hope he hurts me.

But he does none of those things.

He's gentle when he wipes my messy tears with his thumb.

"Come D'orhai." His voice is soft and coaxes me into a numb calm. I don't care who's watching, I grab onto him—he's all I have now, even if it's just in the capacity of master.

He lifts me onto his horse so I'm facing him when he mounts the large black stallion, and I curl into his body, slip my arms into his robes and around his torso. My skin touches his skin and I cry.

I don't want to look at her anymore, at Markaytia as I perform my last duty to her. Leaving. I'm happy to have Corrik's scent surround me as we ride away.

CHAPTER 7

"*A*re you still there, my husband?"

Corrik abandoned his usual taciturn ways and has been trying to get me to talk for the past hour, but he needs to get the hint; I want to wallow in my own self-pity. Thus far, he's blathered on about his home—sorry *our* home —in Mortouge but I don't care if they have talking trees, I want to figure out what Papa's last words to me mean.

I push away from him. "I can go back to my horse now."

"Nonsense. You're a mess." It reminds me of what Father says often to Papa.

"I insist."

Two cold, violet eyes glare down at me and suggest I tread carefully. I'm in no mood to heed them so I glare back with the same challenge; he wanted to marry a dragon? He's got one.

"My apologies, I forgot. The world evolves around *your* desires," I say. His fists tighten as do the lines of his face; I'm provoking him again. *Good.* "And for the record, my name is Tristan. *Tris*-tan! You cannot take someone's name from them." I'm not sure why I say that. He hasn't called me by the other name much since last night, but it's just another thing on the list I resent him for.

He growls at that and I've lost all the leniency I'm going to get from him. "Sassem Ylor, Kiya!"

He whips the reigns, furious, and moves us beside his mother who is riding alone with guards while the Elven king rides ahead with Fera and his General.

"Take him. Take him *now* before I hurt him."

He thrusts me onto the back of her horse and rides ahead to join his father and uncle. I wait for the queen to scold me, but instead her soft laughter rises from in front of me; her omniscience is apparent with the way she conducts herself—she's a wise maternal being. My mother has a playful way of softening the edge of her tongue when she speaks, but for the queen it's in her blue eyes; I recall them from the wedding. I wish I could see them now.

"That is my son," she says, the echo of her laugh still hangs in the air.

I can tell she's not one to state the obvious so I assume she's referring to his character. I remain quiet as we cantor on behind the men of the royal family. I'm just grateful I'm not being told off.

"I shan't tell you he's a kind man, but he is a good man. Nevertheless, he is harsh, and he'll never feel sorry for it."

Yet he was soft with me earlier. *D'orhai. Sounded like an endearment.* I'm surprised I remember the Elvish word he used when he picked me up off the ground in shambles. It was sweet and I'd say it was kind.

"Despite his undesirable qualities, we all love him— adore him even. You will see. There's something no one can name that makes everyone love him."

Is she trying to insinuate that I'll fall in love with him? No chance of that happening—I don't even like him. "Yes, your highness."

She laughs when I use her title. "Kathir, please call me Mother or at least Purinettira. We are much closer than 'your highness' now. I want you to know I can relate with how you must be feeling right now. I know how it is with arranged marriages—the one between the king and I was as such. I hated Vilsarion a long time—sometimes love must grow. I know one day you will love my Corrik."

The tone of her voice suggests she's smiling—if only Corrik would smile half as much as his mother does—but how can she smile and know I loathe her son? How can she ask me to call her Mother?

"You know nothing of our ways, my dear, but you will soon see you were born to be an Elf. As you know, we allow few outsiders to frequent our lands, but you are special. Only someone special—like you—would have my blessing to marry my Corrik."

I'm special, am I?

Why do they keep telling me I'm born to be an Elf? Shouldn't I have been born an Elf in the first place if that's truly my destiny? No matter what they say, I'm a dragon, not an Elf.

"Thank you, Mother," I say.

She's given me many high compliments, I want to return them in kind so I start with honoring her the title, Mother, as she's asked. It feels strange to call another that. I've two fathers, and only one mother, but I think I can make room for a second Mother.

When she figures out I'm not in the mood to talk, we ride in silence and I watch the terrain change. I know this area—we are still within the borders of Markaytia—but we've traveled far from the palace, which is in the heart of Dragon's Rock. We are well beyond the village and farther than Lucca and I would dare travel on our own, though we often did with my father and his guard. Father never went anywhere without at least ten men and he expected the same of me.

We keep to the road South. Mortouge is to the North, but this road is much easier to travel than it is through the thick forests behind the North wall—*a journey much easier made with just two.*

The Elven entourage is several hundred men and women thick—supple, strong looking warriors—maybe during the time I'm not needed as his sex toy, I could convince Corrik to forgo his silly notion that I shouldn't have a sword and be permitted to fight alongside them. It wouldn't be as warlord, but it would be a satisfactory second prize. Fighting alongside the Elves would be honorable. It's said that no human has the strength to fight with the elite band of Elven warriors, but according to the queen I'm special—once I become an Elf it might become a possibility.

By the time the sun sets low in the sky, we've made it to the borders of a town called Umbria, a Southern town where it's decided we'll stay for the night.

Corrik rides back to me and the queen. "How is my delinquent doing?"

"Corrik," she chides. "Leave the boy alone."

Corrik says nothing in response, nor do his features give away what he's thinking as he rakes his eyes up and down, analyzing me. Once he's decided whatever it is he's decided, he dismounts and gestures for me to do the same. I follow behind him, but I notice that most of the other members of our party head off in different directions as they enter Umbria. Only about fifty men and women remain with us as we all travel on foot to wherever Corrik is leading us.

"Where are they going?" I ask.

"This town doesn't have an Inn large enough to provide for all of us; we shall have to stay in different Inns."

I notice Corrik's parents head off with a different set of guards, and Fera heads off with a couple of the male guards wrapped around him.

"Only fifty guard with us Corrik?"

He raises an eyebrow and smirks. "What's the matter? Scared my little Markaytian? Never fear, I shall protect you."

"I'm not scared, I just wondered. My father used to travel with far more men, even to Umbria." I came here once with Father; we always kept a full army with us, the men who couldn't fit in the Inn slept outside of it so they would be close by. He would never split them up.

"Your father is a human, we are Elves," he replies, implying that humans are the inferior species. *If he thinks humans are inferior, why marry one?*

His horse is given to the stableman—I've no idea where Waii has got to—and we head inside. I blush when he grabs my hand. I've not stayed at this Inn before. It's quiet yet full of patrons who drink beer and eat pub stew.

The barkeep is younger than I expect. I thought I would see a round old man, balding with a white beard, but instead it's a tall man with short, dark hair and tanned skin. He's clean-cut and greets Corrik full of sunshine—I immediately don't like him.

"Hey! Corrik, you're back!" He sets down the glass he's cleaning to shake hands with my husband.

"That's *Prince* Corrik, actually," I snap. Why is he familiar with my husband? Oh, I get it. They must have stayed here the night before the wedding and this 'man' must have been his last-night-before-he-was-married-sex. I can see it in his eyes; he looks Corrik over now, feasting on him, sexing him up in his thoughts.

"Sorry. This is my husband, *Tris*-tan," Corrik annunci-ates like I did earlier instead of telling him my Elvish name.

"Pleased to meet you," he says. "I'm Alvin."

Right. Sure, he's pleased to meet me. Our handshake is curt and uncomfortable.

"Everything's set for you. We reserved the Inn for tonight, as you requested. We are honored to have the Elven royalty among us again so soon," he says with his perfect smile.

"Thank you, Alvin," Corrik says, his lips tug minutely, which I know is his form of smiling. *How dare he smile at this miscreant!* I'm an inch away from slicing his lips off with the paring knife I spy beside the limes, when Corrik pulls on my hand and leads me up the stairs. Guards are stationed outside our room and we go inside; I'm thrust toward the bed.

"Nothing happened between Alvin and I—not like you think it did."

"Whatever do you mean?"

"You know what I'm referring to, you were glaring hard enough to light him on fire."

"Well, the man was practically slobbering all over you."

"So, what if he was? You *hate* me remember?" This time his lip ends are tugging harder; it's almost a half-smile and I can't help but gloat that his smile for me is bigger than his smile for the barkeep—*so there stupid Alvin.*

"Or perhaps that's changed?" His eyes look hopeful.

Have my feelings changed? No. I don't know why I feel this surge of jealousy except that if I'm stuck with Corrik, he should be stuck with me. "If anything, I hate you more than before—you flirted with him back. I'll thank you kindly to remember you're a married man now. Have you Elves no respect for such a contract in addition to having no decency?"

His face brightens like it did the night before and he lets loose the laugh I love. It makes it hard to stay mad at him, but I solider on with a glare worse than the one I gave Alvin.

Corrik moves closer to tower over me, still laughing and nestles his hand into my long, dark hair to grab the nape of my neck. I have no idea how any of the things I've just said could make him this happy, but they have. He presses a soft kiss to my lips and pulls away looking at me as if I'm dear to him—for a moment I pretend I am. It's much better than the truth.

He rubs circles on my cheek with his thumb and then he pulls away. "Get ready for bed." *That's it? Get ready for bed?* He hasn't apologized for what happened downstairs, and we haven't even begun to talk about earlier today when he dumped me on his mother's horse and ignored me. Well, if that's how he wants to be, fine, but this little concubine is closed for the night.

He hands me a bag, inside are more versions of what I'm already wearing. It's got some items for washing up, like soap and shampoos, and there is even a kit for shaving. It's a well-stocked bag only missing one item.

"Corrik, there aren't any night clothes in here."

"Don't worry D'orhai—you won't need any night clothes," he tells me with fire in his eyes.

"Arrrgghhh!" I yell and throw the bag at him, which he

dodges. This time he only smiles, without the laughter, and it's just as beautiful. It freezes me for a minute, until I remember how frustrating he is, and continue to the small bathing room. There is no room for a full bath, but it is a nice ensuite, which has partial plumbing—at least there is a toilet—but no sink. Instead, there is a basin with fresh water and towels, a mirror hangs above them. It will do.

Corrik stays away from me while I wash up. I remove my shirt, tuck it into the hem of my travel trousers, and use the towels and soap provided by the Inn to give myself a light wash. The ride wasn't hard today, and I was a mere passenger, but I got sweaty and dirty, nonetheless.

Out in the bedroom, I see Corrik remove his shirt and pants; I take a sharp inhale and watch as the curve of his bicep meets the bulge of the head of his shoulder, the muscles of his oblique wall stand out like they've been embossed over his ribcage. His round ass juts out from his large thigh with the gold locks of his hair falling to outline the whole picture, making him look like an angel—except I know better. Corrik is an angel fallen.

My cock likes the look of Corrik's naked form, and I'm forced to remind *him*, my penis, that we're not on tonight, we're too angry. Except my pants continue to get uncomfortable, and I have to take them off. I focus on my task and jump a mile when I look up to see Corrik in all his naked glory, leaning against the door frame with his arms folded over one another. He smirks arrogantly, his large cock hard, his eyes zone in on my also hardened member. How long has he been watching me?

"Come," he orders then moves away from the door.

"I'll bloody well take my time. I don't care how sexy you are," I mutter, hoping he can't hear me. I'm finished anyway, so I hang the towel, and return to the bedroom.

He's lying on the bed, his hands pillowed behind his head.

"Don't you need to wash up?" I'm suddenly nervous. I know what he wants, and I've already decided not to give it to him, but the task might prove more than I'm up for at the moment. He did say he'd never force me, but I'm starting to believe he might never have to. He shakes his head.

"Elves don't sweat?"

"You know we do. You saw evidence of that last night," he says. "But, not to worry, I won't smell—not yet—I'll wash in the morning."

"Do you have built in air fresheners or something?"

"Or something," he says. "Now come."

I join him on the bed but remain as far away from him as I can. "Well, night then," I say and roll over, away from him. The candle on his nightstand is still lit. It's obvious he wants to have a conversation; I'm making it obvious I don't. He doesn't say goodnight in return, so I know our silent argument isn't over.

"Why do you dislike your Elvish name?"

I stop pretending I'm going to sleep. That question fires me up and I turn on him, so I face him when I respond. "How would you like it if I told you that from now on you will have a Markaytian name?"

He frowns. "What would my Markaytian name be?"

I try to think of something horrible. "Octavious."

"Why Octavious?"

"Because it's stuck up and priggish, just like you."

His face splits into that beautiful smile of his I love, and he laughs at me again.

"I don't see why that's funny; I've just insulted you."

"I don't feel insulted, not when you're so damned adorable when you try to get mad like that." The laughter lights up his eyes now, turning them from cold, purple depths to bright violet beams.

Adorable? *I'll kill him with my bare hands.*

I pounce and prepare to punch him in the face, drawing my fist back. I release it with all my might, but he captures each wrist as I punch. My hair flies everywhere as I struggle to get him to release them. When I give up, realizing I can't escape his iron grip, I settle on glaring down at him. He smiles at me like I'm a wonderment sent by the Gods and his eyes focus on the large black tattoo of the Markaytian dragon embossed on my skin.

"It's seems we've aptly named each other. I *can* be stuck up and priggish at times, even my mother says so, I don't mind admitting that. And *you*—you are a dragon warrior— you have a fiery spirit."

"Dragon warrior? Is that what Ka—is that what my Elvish name means?"

"Yes. The first time I saw you, I decided you looked as though you could fight a dragon. I know your name, Tristan, means *great warrior*, and that Kanes is the family of the Dragon—I know you have dragon thrumming through your blood," he says.

I'm not sure what to say. He's put a lot of thought and research into my new Elvish name.

"It's embarrassing. I can barely say Ka—it."

"It's, Kaw-th-ear. Ka is like the sound of the crow, but with a gentler caress, and 'thir' is like 'ear' with the 'th' of a thistle, Kaw-th-ear, *Kathir*"

"*Kathir*," I try, saying my first Elvish word aloud. I still don't say it quite right. "And what about the other?"

"Tahsen. The first sound is 'T' like the first sound in 'Tom' in your language, but it is put together with ahh, to make T-ahhhh."

"T-ahhh. Tah," I repeat after him.

"Good. The second syllable sen, is like sun in your language."

"Tahsen," I try. "And what does that one mean?"

For a moment it feels like he doesn't want to answer, and for the first time I think the Elven prince might blush. He takes a breath. "It means, my heart."

CHAPTER 8

"My heart?" I squint at him.

He releases one of my hands and moves my long hair aside. "Yes."

"But I thought—"

"—I am well aware of what you thought, but it isn't true, well, not *all* true. I do intend on taking you for my enjoyment as often as I like."

His words make me shiver and my already hardened cock begins to ache. Damn him for being attractive and sexy in every way. In moments he's sitting up beneath me, and his mouth is on my neck, hungry and possessive as he teases the skin with his teeth. A moan escapes my lips.

My vow not to have sex with him long forgotten, I join my lips with his and open them to make way for his tongue. His hands wrap around my body and pull me to him. I press my cock along the curve of his belly, and his hands find my ass squeezing my cheeks hard. I moan again, but this time into his mouth. He sucks me into a kiss, and I can't breathe until he releases my mouth. I pant as I look into glowing purple eyes. With one sharp tug, he flips me on my back and the glowing, ultra-violet eyes pin me in place. "Alvin is nothing to me, and you are everything. Never doubt that."

I swallow, and nod as I fist the cotton sheets, and he attacks my mouth again. Wet pre-come leaks from my weeping cock and I want him to just fuck me already—but I won't say it, y*et*.

His mouth moves down my body; he licks and sucks his way to the crease of my inner thigh, right next to my poor cock who begs for attention. He gets none. Corrik's mouth nips the sensitive skin next to my cock and I thrust my hips at him hoping he'll take me inside. Instead, he pops his mouth off my thigh and breathes on the poor bastard till I finally beg. "Corrik, damn it."

"Problem D'orhai?"

"You know there is. *Please.*"

He uses his tongue to coat my entrance with saliva and my cock hurts more—it's not what I had in mind; it's making things worse. He circles a finger around the smooth, wet, ring of muscle there, and teases the opening before sliding his wet finger inside. When he does, he hits the spot inside of me that makes me whimper with more pleasure and soon there is a second finger added. I don't hear myself request the third, but it's there and before long he's hitting that lovely spot inside of me, reducing me to a quivering bundle of nerves.

"Corrik, please. I need you inside me."

"How can I refuse you when you beg so prettily?"

My knees end up by my ears, my legs splayed obscenely open, and he drives his large cock into me, angling just so to hit that nice spot inside me, over and over. I'm groaning and almost screaming his name, but I don't think anything I'm saying is intelligible; I'm too overcome with torturous pleasure as he makes my body climb to the peak of climax without allowing me to go over. It's driving me insane in the best way. He's claiming me all over again and I love every frustrating second.

"Come for me beautiful boy," he says as he drives his cock over the magic spot inside me. I come hard and so does Corrik, releasing his seed into me. He rolls off me and I'm left to pant labored breaths and gain my bearings. My hand has fallen on his stomach, he's not breathing as hard as I am, but I feel sweat glisten there—I remember what he said earlier about sweat.

"How about now?" he asks.

"What?"

"Do you hate me now?"

That isn't fair him asking me a question like that after intense, wild, passionate sex. "I hate you a little less."

"No matter. Seeing as pounding my cock into you seems to be the key to you hating me a little less each time, I'll have you in love with me by the time we reach Mortouge."

"Love you? That's a bit much to expect considering."

"I'm the Elven prince—men would kill to be with me; you should feel lucky I chose you."

"You arrogant, self-centered, prick. You think I could love you after you've taken me from my home. If you wanted me to love you, why not court me?"

"Because I wanted to make sure you were mine. I take what I want, I don't beg or ask," he growls not sorry for any of it. "Besides, there's nothing wrong with arranged marriages—Mother and Father had one."

I know that already. Arranged marriages are less common than they used to be in Markaytia but are still the norm in most other places. Father and Papa fell in love and married with ample consent from Grandfather before he passed—I foolishly thought the same would happen for me. "And if my uncle had refused your offer?"

"I would have taken you anyway."

"I see so if polite and civilized, doesn't work, you barge in and take what you want."

"I won't lie to you Tristan—trust is too important amongst Elves—I'm sorry if it makes you continue to hate me, but at least you can depend on me to tell you the truth if nothing else."

I change the subject. "Why do you keep calling me by my Markaytian name? I thought I'm an Elf now?"

"It upsets you."

"That doesn't seem to stop you from doing what you want, Corrik."

"Yes true, but *I* don't want to be angry with *you* and when you are upset, you anger me."

I'm quiet for a while as the night washes over me and the exhaustion from the sex seeps into me, my eyes slowly close.

"Oh no you don't, D'orhai. I'm not finished with you yet," is the last thing I hear before Corrik is on me again and takes me as many times as he desires before he allows me some sleep.

I wake up exhausted and sore.

I was awoken too many times during the night by a sex-crazed Elf with a cock I can't seem to say no to.

"I forget you're only human," he says as he watches me rub sleep from my eyes and gingerly move from our bed to wash up. It's barely past dawn and we must be on our way.

"I'm fine." I want him to stop thinking I'm weak.

We make it downstairs to a full pub-style breakfast of eggs, sausage, stewed tomatoes, fresh bread and ale. Alvin is serving our crowd of course, but an older man who looks like him with the same dark hair peppered with grey and two women; one younger one older assist him.

I don't know Corrik near well enough yet, but since last night I see differences in the way he is with Alvin and me. To Alvin, he offers the same polite smirk he did last night, with me there is a warm comfort that doesn't exist between the two of them. It's not enough to appease me—I only feel a little less like I want to slit Alvin's throat—and I wonder where this strange jealousy comes from? It's not like I should care, but I do. Maybe him being my husband creates an innate sense of possessiveness?

"Desist your glaring at once," Corrik scolds me.

"Fine," I snap in no mood to argue. I'm sitting on my sore ass and I'm grouchy because I'm tired. I plaster on a fake smile. I almost get through breakfast, but that Alvin bastard decides to touch *my* Corrik. Without thinking about it, I grab his wrist and twist it behind his back. The plates he's holding crash to the ground, loud, drawing unwanted attention my way. None of the Elven eyes staring on deter me from my mission of putting this guy in his place.

"Do not touch my husband again," I hiss in his ear.

It's as far as I get before Corrik grabs me by both my arms and pulls me off Alvin, tossing me backward. I'm only just able to get my footing when he scolds and demands. "That's no way to treat our hosts. Apologize."

"Never."

Father and Papa would be appalled at my behavior and I'd never have spoken to Father that way. I'd have apologized immediately.

Alvin looks at me with a sneer on his face. "I thought Elves had better restraint over their spouses, Corrik?"

Asshole. This man knows more about Elves than he ought to.

"Yes, an oversight on my part, which I plan to rectify this instant. Come." He grabs me roughly and drags me through a silent pub. The rest of the guard has returned to eating, but I know they are aware of their new prince being dragged up the stairs like a misbehaved five-year-old. We return to our room from last night. The bed is still disheveled, but our things have been removed and packed with our horses. Corrik throws me against the wall, my back hits it hard and he slams the door shut.

I seethe with anger at him, at Alvin, at the situation I find myself in. *What will he do to me?* I may be a formidable fighter, but I know I'm no match for an Elf, especially not Corrik.

"I've been lenient with you. I should've punished you from the start, on our wedding night. Now, you dare disobey me in front of others? I cannot let this go; my leniency was a mistake."

"He had his hands on you. What would you have done if it were the other way 'round?"

"I would have killed that man."

"Then you are a hypocrite if you punish me for the same thing."

"I am not punishing you for that—I felt it prudent you apologize, and you chose to disobey me—*that* is why you will be punished."

"Would you have apologized?"

"I wouldn't have needed to. You are not me and I am not you—our statuses are different, you know this. I decide when particular actions are appropriate and when they're not. Certain things are expected of you, and different things are expected of me."

"How am I supposed to live up to those expectations if you won't tell me what they are?"

"I'm about to," he says. The stone in his stance has not wavered once he's set on punishing me, and nothing I say will deter him—I still think he's a bloody hypocrite. Why should a set of rules exist for me, and not for him? He grabs my hand and yanks me forward to the bed and sits down with me standing at his side. "Corrik—what are you doing?"

"Pull your trousers down, *now*."

My cheeks heat as I realize what he intends to do. "You can't spank me like a child. I won't let you."

"I'll spank you however I see fit—you're mine. Besides, who's here to stop me?" His eyes are pure challenge, and he has a point—no one could stop him, and no one would dare try. *Damn Elves would probably agree I deserve it.*

"Me. I say you can't—you said you would never touch me unless I gave you permission, I don't give you permission. I don't deserve it—not like before."

"That was in reference to sex, and I will keep my promise in that regard. The same does not apply for punishment—that doesn't make any sense—who *desires* punishment? How often does the person being punished agree they should be punished? Did you agree with every law and consequence in Markaytia?"

"Well, no."

"Yet you agreed to live there and thus obey all laws set by Markaytian rule. Now you have agreed to become an Elf, thus you will obey our laws or suffer the consequences. People *need* punishment; they seldom want it. I am your husband, so I will decide when, where and what your punishments will be. You will accept them whether you want them or not. You will eventually come to trust my judgment in this matter, but for now, you're just not going to like me very much."

Fuck. I really can't stop him—he's going to go through with this, and he's right: I did agree to follow Elvish law when I married Corrik, hell, I vowed to *obey* him on our wedding day. There's only one thing left I can do—I'm not above begging. "Corrik, please. I'm sorry, I didn't know. I won't disobey you again—don't do this, it's undignified."

"Ah, your Markaytian sensibilities again," he says. "No matter. They will dissipate too in time. I dare say some already have. I guarantee that after this experience, you will have learned to listen when I give an order. Enough of this nonsense and do as I have instructed you. If I have to do it for you, it will be worse."

With as much pride as I have left, I pull down my trousers.

"You're an intelligent man. I think you've gathered enough from what I've said that I don't need to lecture you further —why must I spank you?"

"Because I disobeyed you," I say, my cheeks as flushed as they can be, hot tears of frustration leak from my eyes.

"Correct. I can afford to be more lenient when you disobey me in private, but in public you cannot be seen defying me."

I nod instead of arguing like I want to since that would be seen as more defiance. I'm thrust over his lap, and he slips his fingers under the waistband of my undergarments to take the last of my dignity, making my ass bare and ready for his hand. Corrik is strong—I already knew that—but it's impressed upon me again when his hand hits my ass. It *hurts*.

"Fuck. Corrik. Not so *bloody* hard!"

"I dare say it's imprudent to curse when one is being punished," he says as he continues.

Corrik uses a maddening pattern of three whacks to one side and three to the other, over and over and over. I work at holding still, thinking if I do this it somehow saves my dignity, but it gets harder to remain still as the spanking progresses. The burning is unpleasant, it stings and I want to be let up.

"Corrik, I'm sorry. *Please.*"

"I won't allow disobedience," he says continuing to spank me. "You will obey me."

It gets harder to remain still and without wanting to, I attempt to move out of target range. He tightens his grip, and all I can do it kick my legs. I'm not quick to tears, but they start falling, and I cry over my helplessness. There's nothing I can do. I'm getting this spanking for however long he decides I'm getting it.

It's a long time before he's decided I've had enough. He helps me stand up, returns my clothes to rights and then pulls me in between his knees so that I have look him in the eyes.

"You have two minutes to wash your face and return downstairs. You will apologize to everyone, specifically to our hosts, which includes Alvin. You will sit beside me and not utter another word for the rest of breakfast."

"Yes, Corrik."

When he's gone, I run to the little washing up room, and pull down my trousers and pants to see what it looks like after a spanking like that. My ass is pretty red, but it's not bruised like it feels. I rub it to try and remove some of the sting, but it still throbs—Corrik has proven himself at yet another talent. I'm still miffed about Alvin, but I don't plan on disobeying Corrik anytime soon.

Two minutes isn't near enough to wash myself up properly, and when I return downstairs, I'm sure everyone can see evidence on my face that I've just been disciplined.

I make my apologies to the crowd, our hosts, and Alvin —who smirks at me like the prick he is—and then take my place beside Corrik. I'm sure it's transparent how uncomfortable I am. I want to crawl under a rock; I'll be glad when we leave Umbria, never to return. I eat in silence, not in the mood to talk with anyone. Alvin comes 'round a lot. He fills Corrik's water, flirts with him, but at least he never touches him. Corrik does not respond to his advances using a kind of indifferent voice I hope he never uses with me.

"Are you all right?" Corrik asks on our way out to the stables. "Do you need to ride with me again?"

It'll be any wonder if I can ride at all. My ass still throbs. "I'll be okay, Corrik," I say, careful to keep my voice even.

Corrik nods to one of his men, and I'm given my horse.

"Hello, Waii," I greet her. She seems to remember me and gives a small whinny, scuffing her hooved foot—I didn't realize I made such an impression. I smile. Corrik watches the interaction between Waii and me.

"I wish I had your talent for making creatures fall in love with you," he says. "I'm trying to tame this dragon you see."

He's flirting, and I think about ignoring him, but decide that's probably not the best plan after just having been spanked. I don't have to be flirtatious, but there's nothing stopping him tossing me over a bale of hay in here if I'm rude. I can't hold back my retort. "It's easy. It's called kindness."

"There you are—my dragon warrior—I thought I lost you."

"You ordered me not to speak."

"For the duration of the meal. You may speak again," he teases.

"By your Liege."

"Oh, come now, will you pout about that punishment all day? It should be forgotten—that's how it works."

I'm not mad at him, not really. I actually feel *relaxed*— but he doesn't have to know that. "I wouldn't know how it works—apparently I'm to learn by experience," I say and mount my horse. It's more uncomfortable than the bench was at breakfast; I instantly hop off and look to Corrik as a form of complaint. I can see the regret in his eyes—that he didn't spank me harder—but he does take some pity on me.

"Let's walk together awhile. I didn't spank you *that* hard —you'll be fine to ride again in a few hours—we'll take a smaller guard so we can make better time when we want to catch up to the others."

I'm surprised he'd make such a concession. "Thanks."

"Just be sure to tell my mother about this—she seems to think of all her sons, I'm the only one incapable of kindness."

Corrik keeps his word, and we walk alone leading our horses with only ten or so of the guard. The stony Elf is quiet for hours and so am I—until I can't stand it anymore.

"They are very beautiful," I say looking toward the small guard we have with us.

"All Elves are."

Apparently, they are not humble. "Will I be that beautiful when I become an Elf?"

"You will be the most beautiful Elf there is. Since you are already beautiful, when you become an Elf, your features will be unmatched."

I'm not in the mood to hear his compliments. "Where will we go now?"

"We'll head South another day, then make our way northeast for another two. A ship waits for us in Port Tyreadin."

"A ship?"

"Yes. Have I finally found something that scares my great Markaytian dragon warrior?"

"No, I just haven't been *on* a ship."

"Scared."

"Not scared."

"Terrified."

"*Corrik.*" I try to push him, but it's like pushing a slab of stone. He laughs at my attempt.

I try harder, plowing my entire body into him sideways —he barely misses a step and grabs me by the hand whipping my body into his as he presses his lips to mine, hungry. I respond in kind, my tongue twines around his—for a moment—until I realize we have company and I pull away from him. Our horses have long stopped walking and so has our small guard of ten. They aren't looking at us, but I blush all the same.

Corrik shakes his head. "We must cure you of your Markaytian sensibilities, D'orhai. Things are very different in Mortouge."

He keeps saying that, but it's all the explanation I get before his tongue wraps around mine again. This time he squeezes the sore cheeks of my ass, and my cock lights up like a firecracker. I moan into his lips. He pulls away and leaves me gasping for breath.

"Come."

With the nod of his head as a signal to our guard, he pulls me with him to an alcove in the trees. I look up; all I can see are the tips of the pines as they reach toward the sky. It's dark in here, but there is sun peeking through the holes between the trees and I can't hear a sound. Not even the footsteps of the giant Elf that accosts me, slams me to the ground, and begins feasting on my neck. I'm panting, my cock is rock hard, the skin on my ass aches—I want him, but not enough to stop thinking about the guards that can probably hear us, even deep in the trees. They are Elves, and with that comes enhanced auditory, as well as superior optic capabilities.

"Corrik," I pant. "Please. Can't we do this later?"

"But I want you now." He continues down my body and rips my trousers open, my cock is happy to see him, Corrik notices.

"You see?" he says as he grips my cock at its base. "*He* wants to play with me. You're out voted."

He swallows my cock in one bite, and in the wet cavern of his mouth, my cock finds such delight he stops all flow of blood to my brain, and I don't think of the other Elves any longer. I didn't realize the powers my prick possessed till now. For a man who never smiles, his lips are awfully smug around my cock—still don't care—as he sucks. Two fingers slide into his mouth next to my cock then they move to circle my hole. The mixture of sensations—my sore ass, the tingles he sends around my hole with his wet fingers —*unreal*.

I buck my hips further into his mouth until I'm sure I'll feel throat, but I don't so I keep fucking his mouth. I think I'm going to come, but I think wrong. As if he senses my impending orgasm, he pops his mouth off my cock and kneels up pulling his cock out of his pants.

"Suck."

The order sends a jolt of pleasure to my cock, who is lonely and cold without Corrik's mouth and I scramble to obey. I don't have as easy a time as he did. I'm not practiced

—scratch that—I've never done this before, but how hard can it be?

Really fucking hard.

Corrik's cock is huge. If I thought it was big as it pounded into me on our wedding night, I didn't know what the word big meant.

I do my best and try to fake like I'm a natural, swallowing his cock down like he did mine. I gag like the amateur I am. I pull back to regain my breath and my pride, and resume a little less eagerly.

"By Ylor!"

Corrik doesn't seem to care about my lack of experience. He shoves his cock further into my mouth, it hits the back of my throat and I gag again. His fingers grip my hair as he continues to fuck my mouth. I try to relax my throat wanting to be better at this, but there's no hope, he's too big. My gagging doesn't seem to bother him, and it doesn't bother me I realize. I'm still able to breathe, and I like it. I like the feeling of him over me, his large hand in my hair and in control—my cock aches. I want more like this, but I don't know what the 'more' is exactly.

Corrik does. "Off," he says, but he physically removes me from his cock with his hand still in my hair.

"Turn around. Put your hands on the ground."

I do. *Yes, sir.*

His hands rip my pants the rest of the way off. They trace over my sore ass; I wince, it still hurts. "I like this, Kathir. I like this very much—seeing your ass red, knowing it's because I made it this way. Your bottom is going to be this red a lot."

I groan at that. It may feel good during sex to have a sore ass, but it did not feel good during the receiving—nothing about it—and it doesn't feel good the rest of the time either.

I hear the pop of a cap. *Does Corrik keep lubricant on his person at all times?*

Yep. Yep he does. He slicks the cool liquid up and down my crack as he dips a finger into my hole, which he's loosened some.

"When you're an Elf, we won't need lube, Tristan," he whispers then works two fingers in, then three, until I'm open enough. He positions his cock at my entrance and once again his large member is pounding deep into me.

"By Gods. Corrik—Ow!" I say as he smacks my ass. He responds by doing it again. Oh yeah, that's right, he *likes* my ass red by his doing. My cock likes it too, combined with his cock being in my ass—fucking traitor—I'm out voted again so I give in and enjoy. I moan and arch into each thrust and slap, my fingers dig into the dirt until I see stars. I spurt hot come at the ground beneath me; he moans too as he releases his come into me.

We both fall to the ground panting. He's out of breath too—*for once*. He spoons me and pulls the hair from my face, planting a kiss on my cheek.

"Why do you hate me?"

I don't expect that question—not after sex like that. "I don't want to talk about it."

"Then it can't be important."

"It is."

"Then I order you to tell me."

"Is that how it's always going to be? I don't want to do something so you order me to do it?"

"I always get my way D'orhai," he says.

I push away from him; he grips me tighter.

"Not always," I say even if it's been true so far. "I'm going to win this time."

"Win?"

"Yes, win."

"Win what? I wasn't aware we were at war—I assumed that we were on the same side."

"No. We *are* at war—I was meant to follow my father and become warlord. You've taken that from me, and now I'm an Elven concubine, a bed slave, a nobody. I hate you for it." There, he wanted to know why I hate him, he knows now. He wins again.

"*Beloved* nobody," he teases. He doesn't deny the rest. *Stupid Elf.*

"This is why I didn't want to tell you—you don't care anyway."

"I'm sorry I took the future you thought you would have."

"Not sorry enough."

"No, but only because I know we belong together."

I try again, to pry free from his hold, but can't. "Corrik, shouldn't we head back?"

"We will, but we're not done talking."

"What more is there?"

"You need someone like me," he declares. "You just don't know it yet. You are better off with me than without me."

Arrogant bastard. "How can you know that?"

"Elves can *see*. We have visions."

"I don't believe in hocus pocus, Corrik."

"Wait until you get to Mortouge, D'orhai. You will wonder why you didn't. And Tristan? You aren't nobody, to me."

I want to ask more questions, but one of the men from our guard barrels into the forest.

"Prince Corrik, come quickly, your sword is needed."

CHAPTER 9

"*O*nce upon a time, in the beautiful kingdom of Markaytia, there lived a young warlord. He would get up every morning at sunrise to practice, not stopping until the last ray of sunlight would disappear from the sky. There were times he would travel with his father and his father's men. Together they would protect Markaytia and the provinces surrounding Markaytia. Now, the young warlord does nothing but sit on his arse while others do the fighting—*like a maiden in distress.*"

Using two rocks, I make like one rock is telling a story to another rock. "Why isn't he a warlord anymore?" I make the purple rock say to the green rock. "Because his husband is an overprotective, unreasonable, lout," I respond to the purple rock, with the green.

"You wouldn't say that if you knew of the dangers we face," the stone-faced warrior left to 'protect' me says.

"We're not yet outside the province of Dhrystone, I know the dangers of these lands."

"And do you also know the dangers that follow us young *Warlord?*"

I glare at him in return but say no more. He shouldn't be calling me that. *No. I didn't realize dangers followed them, or us I suppose. What sorts of dangers follow Elves?* Silence passes between him and I, until I can't stand it. "What's your name?"

His face breaks into a wry smile. "Diekin."

"At least that one's easy to say—Diekin," I repeat to test it out.

"Very good. Now be a good little boy and go back to playing with your figurines."

I deepen my glare. He may look at me as a faux prince, but I was Markaytian royalty once and I still think it brazen for him to speak to me like that. Besides, even if I am a concubine, I'm a *royal* concubine.

"Just who do you think—" It dawns on me mid-sentence, he's been speaking fluent Markaytian all this time and that becomes more important. "How did you come by my home tongue?"

"Elves are proficient in many languages."

"I know that, but why are you so fluent?"

His eyes smile thinking of something he's not going to tell me. "I have known Markaytian a long time, but Corrik made all in the royal court master it when he knew he was to marry you."

"Royal court? Who are you?"

"I thought you would never ask—I'm Corrik's brother-in-law. I am married to his twin sister."

"Brother-in-law? Corrik has a twin?"

"Yes, only she's prettier."

I doubt there's anything prettier than Corrik. "How many siblings does Corrik have?"

"Five hundred and seventy-four."

"Five hundred seventy-four!"

"The king and queen have lived a long time—the king comes upon his five thousandth birthday this year. Didn't Corrik tell you?"

"We haven't had much time for talking," I mumble feeling foolish. I don't know anything about my husband, or his insanely large family. We've spent most of our time fucking or fighting.

Diekin waggles his eyes like Lucca used to. "I understand, young Warlord. Ditira wouldn't let me leave our bedchamber for a full moon cycle after our wedding."

I ignore his inappropriate comments in favor of learning more. I wish I'd thought to ask Corrik some of these things. "How old are Corrik and his twin?" I'm not going to attempt her name yet.

"Two hundred—that's when Elven women reach child-bearing age—but men don't reach manhood until three hundred, so you and Corrik must wait a bit longer to have a child."

His words make my heart race. "Can Elven men have babies?"

He laughs hysterically—I don't know what's so funny. They're the ones living till they're older than rocks, my question isn't that crazy. "Not to worry, young Warlord. No. Elven men cannot have babies—the only race I know of who can are the Dyela and those men are half sea creature."

That both relieves and intrigues me—half-sea-men that can bear children? He must notice my wide eyes. "If Corrik lets me, I'll take you to meet them sometime. They're a pleasant people, but no promises—I doubt Corrik will let you out of his sight for a long time. I wouldn't either if you were mine, you are very attractive."

I blush. *Isn't he married?*

"You are easy to tease, Kathir."

"I'm just not comfortable with sex."

"You will be."

"Why does everybody keep saying that?"

"We are all sexual beings, Kathir. Elves just choose to explore their sexuality openly."

"My uncle said you are creatures," I say and swallow a little, nervous, but not nervous like I am with Corrik. I already feel comfortable with Diekin. "Is this true?"

He thinks for a moment before answering. "In a way, I suppose. I guess that is how others would see us—like we have a creature that lives within us and is responsible for our urges."

He looks up like he can hear something coming through the opening in the trees. Nothing is there for a moment then Corrik appears, sword still in hand. He sheathes it as he approaches—I don't miss that it's coated in blood.

"We were followed."

"How could they follow us this far without our knowledge?"

"I don't know," Corrik says. "But they won't be following us back."

"We need to go. Tristan, you're riding with me."

I think about complaining, but when I see how dark my great Elf's eyes are, I follow behind him without a word.

We ride at a pace I'd never have been able to keep on my own, my poor, tender ass aches and I hold steadfast to Corrik afraid I'll fall off. We've been riding at least six hours, like the wind's chasing us and might swallow us whole if we slow. We've veered up to the North in relation to Markaytia, and are headed into a region I've learned of in my studies but have never been to. Father never took me North. I'm excited to see what lies beyond this point.

Diekin's been one of the men in our guard all this time, and he follows us closer now. The mood of our entourage is subdued, a stark contrast to the joy that beamed from them earlier. I still don't know the details of what happened, Corrik threw me on his horse without a word.

One of the guards ahead of us signals for us to stop and it's decided we're to set up camp for the night. Corrik drags me to where his mother sits with his uncle, Diekin is two steps behind.

"Stay with him, Diekin, while we check the area and then we can make fires for cooking."

"I have a babysitter now? This is insulting, Corrik." I cross my arms over my chest, trying to look menacing.

Corrik turns his body toward me, heated energy pours off him. He's in no mood to have this argument, but I can't take the secrecy any longer. I'm used to being one of the first told when anything suspect happens.

Corrik grabs my arm. "Excuse us," he says, and drags me a short distance away.

"Why are you being difficult?"

"Because no one will tell me what's going on."

"It's not your concern—you're well taken care of."

"I don't want to be taken care of; I can take care of myself—I can help Corrik. *Please.*"

"You can't help us with this. Now I suggest you behave unless you need help?"

Why is he talking to me like I'm a child? "No. I don't need help," I snap.

The great Elf pulls me in by my waist and kisses my

lips. "Good, I want to get this done so I can take you to our tent and ravish you. Behave yourself."

I roll my eyes. The man must badly want to finish securing the area if he's ignoring the attitude I'm giving him. When he pulls out of the kiss, he searches my face for something, I give him a pleading look. "Corrik, I want to help. If I can't be warlord, maybe I could work alongside these men and women. I would be—

"No."

"But, Corrik—"

"—no."

"Why?"

"This is not going to be a conversation. I have said no, this matter is closed."

I fume silently as he lays down his orders with no explanation and yeah I'm pouting—*actually* pouting—but Corrik tends to bring it out in me. I think about what Lucca would want to do to the Elven Prince for being domineering. *He'd retaliate by going anyway*. I should, but this is just a scouting mission, I'll save a grand rebellion like that for something important.

"Go wait with my mother and not another word about this, Kathir."

I turn to go.

"I believe, yes Corrik, are the words you are looking for."

"Yes, Corrik," I say with no generosity and storm away.

I feel childish.

And not because Corrik's mother and brother-in-law are babysitting me. I shouldn't have acted the way I did. Papa told me many times that if I wanted something, pouting wouldn't get me there.

I throw a rock at the fire we've been given permission to build. Word came an hour ago that our location was secured, but that message came without Corrik.

"He'll be back soon. Corrik has a temper to rival the Gods—he's angry that anyone would dare follow us, he'll want to blow it off before he comes back to you," Diekin tells me as I watch the light from the flames jump on his face, with the warm crackle popping in the background.

Really? He hasn't seemed to have a problem displaying his temper in front of me. "Tell me about his other brothers and sisters, how does that work? Do they all live at the palace?"

He laughs. "Oh, dear brother, you *are* curious, but that is good. First, Mortouge is large—far larger than Markaytia. There are *seven* smaller kingdoms within the province; the members of the royal family are spread out between the kingdoms. It would take me eons to explain it all to you—you'd never remember it anyway, but you'll have plenty of time to learn once we're there." He pauses. "Corrik and Ditira are the youngest born to the family Cyredanthem so they remain in King's Keep with a few of their other siblings, but most notable is Alrik—he is first born, and you will get to meet him."

He leans down making to whisper in my ear but speaking loud enough for the queen to hear. "Corrik and Alrik do not get along. He thinks Corrik is spoiled."

"Diekin," she chides. "He's not even here to defend himself."

"I'm here and I heard that—you would not misbehave like this for my sister," Corrik says. He looks less angry than he did before, I don't think he's truly upset with Diekin.

"Corrik you're here," I say and realize I'm relieved to see him.

"I believe I just said that," he says, his lips twitch in each corner.

I look over at Diekin who is smiling wide, alongside the queen.

"Go you two. We'll send dinner in—the tents should be ready," the queen says.

"Tents?"

"Come," Corrik says. "I will show you."

The tents are larger inside than they look on the outside, they *are* magnificent; *but is all this really necessary for one night?* Corrik leads me into a sectioned off 'room,' where there's a bed set on the ground— a cozy looking mattress drown in blankets and pillows. There are tapestries strewn up on all four walls of the tent and a grand Pegasus Sigil for the house of Cyredanthem.

"I hope some time with my mother has you in a better mood. I could not find my patience while I rode and am likely worse than when I left; I won't be able to hold my temper."

"Corrik I—"

"Quiet."

How am I supposed to apologize when he won't let me speak?

My large Elf stares at me in silence, raking his eyes up and down, and a small shiver of terror runs through me—maybe I've been too hasty with my behavior, maybe I've angered him beyond his endurance? The air is thick with his restraint, his muscles are taut from preventing them reaching out to touch me, all the lines in his face are gone except the one between his brow, which frowns down at me. I don't know Corrik well, but I know him well enough to read that look; he's disappointed. I can't hide my shame; I look down to my boots. Corrik sighs. "Don't look like that—look at me, Tristan."

I do, but I can feel stupid tears in my eyes. I don't want to cry, but I can't handle this feeling inside me, and I don't know what to do with it. I wish he'd allow me to apologize.

"I know you are sorry. Is that a bit better?"

I nod, remembering not to speak.

"I need your obedience now more than I need your apology. You will understand some day, promise. Get ready for bed, our food will be here, then I will *need* you."

The night was spent with Corrik's cock down my throat. He was vicious as he rammed into my mouth, hot tears of shame and regret poured down my face. The whole time I wanted it. I wanted him to pound into me, to use me, to claim me. My cock was rock hard, and I was surprised at my own words after he came down my throat and I swallowed every drop like a man dying of thirst.

"Corrik, please—I think I need..."

"I know what you need D'orhai," he said as he brushed the hair from my face and used his thumb to wipe away the last of his come on my lips. He put me over his lap again, like he had earlier that morning and spanked me until I felt at peace. I didn't enjoy being spanked, for several reasons, but I knew I needed it. While he spanked me, many thoughts drifted through my mind. Mostly, I thought of Papa and how well he always behaved for Father. *Did Father spank him?* I'm not sure, but it would make a lot of things make a lot of sense. For example, the way Father would tell him, "I'll take care of you later."

I didn't conclude anything about that, but I did resolve to behave myself—his hand bloody well hurts! Besides, his look of disappointment is getting to me. It's almost as heavy as Father's.

And, I don't hate the Prince. Not anymore. Something's happened between us that oddly, I think has to do with spanking. I don't know what, but something.

Afterward, he wrapped me in his arms and sang his soft Elvish lullaby and I drifted to sleep feeling wrought with emotional exhaustion, but also like I'd come out the other side, more whole than before.

This morning, I get to ride on my own. A smile creeps onto my face as I gaze at Corrik when he turns to look at me. He does not smile in return, of course (honestly, the man needs to learn to smile more) but his eyes light up the smallest amount with delight. He faces front again and I watch the lines of his body, mesmerized as they move in rhythm with his horse.

"Stop making googly eyes at your husband and talk with me little brother," Diekin says, coming from behind to ride beside me.

"I am not making 'goggly' eyes."

"You are." He smiles satisfied.

I scowl at him. "What do you want Diekin?"

We trot at a moderate pace today. I think the Elves are worried I can't keep up; we travel much slower than I ever did with my father, but I don't mention it. I know they are trying to pay me a kindness; I don't want to belittle their gesture.

"I want to get to know you. Tell me something about you."

"That's quite vague. Where shall I start? With my birth perhaps?"

He laughs. He's far more animated than Corrik, and easier to like. "Tell me something fun. You look like the type to get into a lot of trouble."

"And incriminate myself?" I glance to Corrik's back. He may be a ways in front of me, but I know how well Elves can hear. *My arse is sore enough, thank you.*

"Corrik's not likely to be upset by something you did in the past. Come on. Let's have it."

"All right, but then stop pestering me. Agreed?"

"Agreed," he says with a goofy grin on his angular face. Diekin is quite attractive.

"When I was six, my cousin and I stole pies from the chef, and ran off to eat them with the pigs in the palace farm. When my papa found us, we were covered head to toe in mud—we looked like mini-mud people," I say and smile at the memory.

He lets out a loud chuckle. "See? I can always spy a brat. You and I will have great fun together."

I don't know what he means by that, but I don't think I want to find out. I think his kind of 'fun' is like Lucca's kind of 'fun' and I want to stay out of trouble with my husband.

"Any more stories like that?"

I want to remind him he promised to stop pestering me, but I can't crush the hopeful look on his face. This man is charming like Lucca. Perhaps the resemblance to Lucca is what makes me continue or perhaps it's the feeling of having a companion again, either way, I regale him with several stories of my youth—*there are too many times Lucca and I were up to no good.*

When we stop to eat, Corrik leaves again to scout the area, this time Diekin goes with him. Since we are beside a stream, and the stream is in view of the guards that are left with us, I take Waii to have a drink. It's the first time in days I'm alone.

I brush my hand through my long locks of hair. I love my hair, but I've always associated it with being me, being *Tristan.* I find I don't feel much like him anymore. I don't know who I am after last night. Being with this Elf has awoken things in me.

"There you are. Have you eaten?" Corrik says.

"That was a quick scout."

"Diekin convinced me to come back."

Silence passes between us for the magnitude of those words. *Could Diekin know what I've been feeling since I woke this morning?* It's nice of him to send Corrik to me, but I'm not sure if Corrik's the thing I need either.

"Have you eaten?" he repeats.

"Not yet."

"Come."

He leads me by the hand, and I tug Waii to follow. I pass her off to one of the guards and Corrik takes me away from the group—still within sight, but in an area more private.

There's a pale blue blanket over the ground and a spread of food set up under a tree on a small hill. There may not be candles, but it's not any less romantic. I blush.

Corrik clears his throat uncomfortably. "It has come to my attention that a 'date' might be in order."

I try to decipher who would bring this to his attention and I narrow it down to Diekin and the queen. I hide my smile by looking down; he gently nudges my chin up and places a kiss on my lips. "Does that mean I've done well, Tristan?"

"Yes," I say. "Thank you."

"Well, let's eat then."

He serves me, attempting to act like a gentleman on a first date I presume. He's graceful yet rigid. I swear, Corrik's the only one I've ever known to pull both those off at once. I thank him when he gives me my plate.

"I heard you, when you were talking with Diekin and I found I was jealous," he says as he eats.

"Jealous?" I would laugh at him if I didn't know he's serious.

"I want to know those things about you, I want to know everything about you. I wish I'd thought to ask you questions, but I've never been particularly good at chatting."

"I've gathered. You prefer to order people about and be done with it," I say.

"Yes, but since being with you, I've come to see the error in doing *only* that."

"You've only been with me a few days, Corrik."

"Yes, and it took far less than that for me to know that I, *Sassem*! Why is this so difficult?"

It's my turn to soothe him. I rub his arm and take his free hand.

He tries again. "It took far less than that for me to know I would do anything to make you happy because that's what makes me happy. If I don't know you, how am I to do that?"

He seems exasperated by the prospect I might be

unhappy and I realize I haven't felt unhappy since our wedding night. Not really. I may have been confused, upset and angry *at times*, but there has been an undercurrent of contentment existing alongside all of that. No person can be a ray of sunshine at every moment; I get the impression that Corrik has this unrealistic expectation for me.

"Corrik, I will be unhappy sometimes, but it doesn't mean I'm not happy."

"You hate me," he says with all the bitterness in the world.

I shake my head. It's time to tell him my little secret. "I did hate you, *really* hated you. I no longer feel that way." I don't expand—Corrik is arrogant enough without me giving him reason to make him more so.

My words do anyway. He smiles, a straight line of pure arrogance. "I knew you couldn't hate me forever. No one does."

"That can hardly be true."

"But it is. People always hate me quite passionately at first, but they never hate me long, though I've never had someone hate me quite as passionately as you," he says. He has to be the best at everything, even being hated.

I whack him in the shoulder. "You conceited bastard."

He laughs. "No more. No less." He doesn't apologize for it and can't. He's right; we are who we are, no sense in apologizing over and over for it. Corrik's ability to remain true to who he his despite some of his character flaws gives him a mysterious attraction—I find I can say with truth that I like him.

In the spirit of being who *I* am, I pick up a handful of what looks to be trifle and smear it on his face. His eyes widen as he registers what I've done, but not long after he flips me on my back and towers over me. I submit easily. I know he's stronger—I won't win—so I lay still and look up to dark violet eyes full of mirth. "How dare you little husband, I could eat you and no one would care."

"I hope you will," I tell him in a voice I hope is seductive.

He leans in to nip at my neck and delicious shivers find their way to my cock as trifle is smeared along my skin. "I shall. I think I shall."

CHAPTER 10

"*A* wedding gift for you, D'orhai."

The wind blows through my hair as I eye the ship moored on the docks of Port Tyreadin from where I stand on the shore, and investigate the architecture. I notice the ship's hull has been carved from a type of wood I don't recognize. The wood is a deep aqua green making the ship look like it has been carved from marble. A majestic neck swoops up from the bow of the ship; a dragon's head arches high above the water with the sides made to look like the dragon's folded wings. It looks like a great warrior and stares down at us.

"Wedding gift?"

"Yes. Commissioned the moment I returned home after the second-best day of my life—the day of our betrothal."

It has been several weeks of travel since our little 'date' and because it went well, the prince has been forthcoming with his feelings to the point I've become uncomfortable in a new way; mostly because I don't feel the same. I've grown fond of my Elven prince, a bit territorial even (which I still claim is some kind of Elven Voodoo ignited via sex magic on our wedding night) but I don't feel as strongly about him as he claims he does for me. I know it hurts him every time I don't respond in kind, but I won't lie to him. In the many weeks of travel away from Markaytia, I've gotten to know him, and I dare say, life might not turn out so badly for Tristan Kanes—now to convince him that Tristan Kanes is always better with a sword. I've attempted many ways to discover the reason for his 'Tristan Weapons Ban,' but he refuses to discuss it with me. I've concluded it's either something important, or stupid.

Markaytia has; lakes, rivers, streams, and a gorgeous bay, but no direct access to open ocean. You would have to travel for days down the river of Rainayta to meet with the sea. Father never liked boats much so he seldom made such a journey; he's never taken me. "I've never been on a boat Corrik," I remind him. "But I do thank you. It's magnificent."

We board the ship with all our gear, horses, and the other Elves. The women of the guard are fierce and look intimidating. I haven't talked to one yet, but I want to.

Once we've made it aboard, we are greeted by more male and female Elves and to my surprise, people who are not Elves. They look human, quite like Markaytians, only just on this side of more than human, like they are beginning to slowly evolve into Elves. They're the most beautiful humans I've ever seen, enough to make me self-conscious. I'm considered attractive in Markaytia, but compared to these sublime humans, I'm an ogre. If Corrik has some kind of human fetish, I can't fathom why he'd choose me over one of these fine creatures.

Some of the people—both Elf and human—are dressed in attire that would suggest they are here to take care of the ship and us. There are, of course, more members of the Elven military.

I'm fascinated to see these humans. Corrik explained to me that many races of humans and other creatures were once permitted to make their home in Mortouge, until a great war that happened even before he was born, and his father would not allow anyone else to join his kingdom or the realm. The humans residing in Mortouge now, are the descendants of the humans from the time before the restriction.

"Come. I will show you around."

I enjoy Corrik's excitement as he teaches me. "The right side is starboard; the left is called portside. The front is referred to as the bow, and the back the stern. Those there," he says as he points to the largest of the sails, "are the main sails. They gather wind to pull us through the water."

The wood is carved with beautiful detail, pictures, and Elven inscriptions, which feel marvelous as I run my hand along the designs. Corrik watches my wonderment amused as he continues to explain everything and all things 'boat.'

The wind blows through my long dark hair and from what Corrik tells me, we'll have a good day sailing due to the lovely gale. He seems to love this ship; a lot more than I imagine I will.

"Do you sail often, Corrik?"

"Often as I can. I have many duties, but I would like to take you on voyage and show you places you've never seen— it could be our honeymoon since we won't get one now."

Corrik leaves things unsaid, like why we won't get a honeymoon immediately following our wedding as is the usual tradition. To be honest, I hadn't thought of a honeymoon because I hadn't realized the Prince's feelings for me and presumed he'd merely come to retrieve his betrothed;

that I was nothing more than a chess piece in a treaty-forged alliance. The prince has since made his feelings clear to me—I believe he does care for me a great deal; I've learned some of how to read Corrik's taciturn demeanor. I suppose a honeymoon would be expected now, *but why wait?*

I don't bother asking. I know it's something Corrik doesn't want to tell me, and I don't fancy arguing at the moment, not with him looking as he does now. I could watch Corrik forever. He's become the most fascinating thing in my world.

He stops in front of large double doors. "This will be our chambers."

He opens the doors to a set of rooms that are far too exquisite to be on a ship even of this magnitude. The anteroom is large, and beyond it, I can spy a four-poster bed in a room all its own. A fire is already burning and there is white wine chilling on a small table beside a plate of cheese and fruit.

"We head North, D'orhai. It will be cold, but the fire will keep you warm," he tells me, directing me to sit in front of the fire. He pours the wine. "I know you're not used to the cold."

Warmth rises in my chest when he calls me by that Elvish endearment and it's not just the fire—he's called me that since our first day together. I wonder what it means but don't ask, worried he'll make me try to pronounce it. Instead, I sip the wine, allowing the bouquet to hit my nose first before the dry liquid hits my tongue. It's lovely wine.

"I think we should talk, Tristan."

Hmmmm. I like the sound of that. Talking usually means fucking; I take another deep sip of my wine and put the glass down ready to be ravished.

"Not that kind of talk, though I do enjoy those 'talks' immensely," he adds. "A real talk."

"Am I in trouble?"

"Should you be?" he asks. I can't recall anything I might have done, but it's hard to tell with Corrik; he hasn't exactly gone over the rules insisting I *learn by experience*.

"No, Corrik."

"Then you have nothing to worry about. We will be in Mortouge in a few weeks, our culture is quite different and it's going to be a shock to you. I couldn't tell you before—the Elves find it better to remain somewhat elusive—but I can tell you now.

"I've told you some. We are open with our sexual urges —but there's more. We display ourselves in ways that will offend your Markaytian sensibilities. Nevertheless, you will be expected to adapt to our culture since you will become Elf."

"About that—how will I become Elf?" I'm more interested in that. I probably should be concerned about the Elves and their sexually deviant ways, but I'm not. I've enjoyed Corrik's sexual deviance.

"Again, I must disappoint you, Tristan. It's better you just see. You wouldn't believe me anyway." His lips tug into his quarter smile and I admire how beautiful he is.

"Fine, Mr. Cryptic." I take another sip of my wine. "Is that all you wanted to warn me about? Sex? I don't think I'm quite so sensitive over that topic anymore."

"Yes, I know. I've created a monster, but it goes beyond sex and it's more about how we Elves believe everyone is constructed; Elf, Markaytian, or otherwise."

"Constructed?"

"We all have urges. In Mortouge we honor them instead of hiding them. Though I will admit these tendencies are far more pronounced in Elves. We almost can't control them."

I take his last words for what they are: a warning. I've experienced firsthand when he's in the grip of these 'tendencies,' and I've only scratched the surface of this side of Corrik. "And how do you think I'm constructed?"

"You are submissive, D'horai," he says plain and simple.

It's the first time I hear the term, but I know what the word submit means. "I was a junior warlord Corrik, how can you think me submissive in any way? And let's not forget my dragon's blood."

"This is not an insult to your bravery, strength, or heritage. You are all of those things. I could only have a mate who is these things. Can you imagine any other with the likes of me?"

Did Corrik just make a joke? I'm not of the mind to laugh at it just now. "But I'm terrible at obeying orders," I say. I'm sure he knows I'm thinking of our long journey thus far. He's had to spank me more than the one time at the Inn.

"That's because you're also a brat," he says, smiling in a fond way. "Submissive doesn't always mean being good at obeying orders—it's the need for them at all. With that is the need for consequences."

"I've never desired to be punished," I say narrowing my eyes.

"I didn't say you desire it. I said you *need* it—there is a difference."

I'm sure there is. He seems to know what he's talking about, but I still don't quite understand.

"It's my job to keep this balance between you and me. As the *dominant* or the *top*, I provide the rules and the consequences—that's what will keep us both grounded.

This is how we Elves honor one another in our relationships."

"What do you get out of this deal? What does a dominant desire?"

"Control, possession, worship—we crave them. For me, there is one more thing—I want your pain, Tristan. I am also a sadist."

I shiver. A sadist? He really is going to hurt me. "What do you mean by my pain?"

He's already spanked me enough times—but that doesn't sound like what he means.

He smiles wider. "So many questions, Dragon Warrior —but as you remember, I believe in learning some things by experience; this will be one of those things."

"But Corrik—I should get to know if you will hurt me."

"You will. I want your pain, but I want you to give it to me—after you do then I will take it."

"That makes absolutely no sense."

"It will. For now, you have my word you will be unharmed—except a minor spanking when you're being exceptionally difficult."

Minor spanking? I'm not able to sit half the day. "Corrik, I'm sorry. I don't mean to be stubborn—*that* I get from my father. I wish I was more agreeable, like my papa."

"You're young D'orhai and have yet to grow into the man your papa is, you're more like him than you realize. Your stubborn streak will get you in trouble, but I will like that as much as I will be irritated by it."

Papa used to say that too—that my stubborn pride was what got me into predicaments with my father.

"Corrik, I need you to give me something."

"You want something? Name it and it shall be yours."

I want to laugh at his declaration, but since the thing

I'm going to ask is the thing I don't believe my Elf to possess, I don't make fun of him.

"Patience. Please be a bit more patient with me...? I don't know your ways but I'm willing to learn."

"They're not just our ways, Tristan. All creatures are this way, some will admit to them, some won't. That is the only difference between Mortouge and Markaytia in this regard: we don't hide our true nature—nothing good ever comes of it."

I nod unsure what I'm nodding about, but I don't get long to think, the great Elf descends on me and pulls me up to him. "Enough talk for now my little Markaytian. Let's christen this room."

His lips capture mine in a claiming kiss, but it doesn't escape my notice: he's failed to promise what I requested.

CHAPTER 11

*H*ours later, I stare out at the endless sea. I'm thinking. *Dominant. Top. Submissive. Brat.* I've barely begun to understand what those mean. I already know I obey Corrik—that goes without saying, it was part of our vows. I'm used to that kind of a relationship anyway, Papa always obeyed Father. But what of the other things I'm learning?

"Penny for your thoughts young Warlord?"

I turn to scowl at Diekin. "Do not call me that. I'm not Warlord." We have this same argument over and over.

"You are. It is in your blood whether Corrik wants to let it out or not."

"What's that supposed to mean?"

"Why do you think he sends me to babysit you when you can clearly take care of yourself?"

"I'm unfamiliar with every danger—you said so yourself."

"Yes, but that's not the point—no warrior can know all danger. I was merely pointing out that perhaps you require help with *some* dangers. I did not mean to imply you could not face danger, now, answer the question."

"How am I to know? That damn Elf won't tell me anything. *Learn by experience*," I mock.

Diekin laughs. "Infuriating, isn't it? Most Cyredanthems are that way. Fine. I will tell you since you insist on being difficult. He knows of the dragon in your blood, but has others surround you, to protect you so you won't have to use it. He does not want you to fight, Kathir."

"But why?"

"That I don't know. Why don't you ask him?" he says with a cocky smirk. He knows I'm still shy with Corrik. It's odd. I've become less shy with him in all matters sex, but something as harmless as talking still proves difficult.

"I *have*. Bloody bastard won't tell me a thing."

"Well, I'm neither here to babysit nor to tease you, brother, but the latter comes rather easily to me," he says, with a wink. "I wish to offer myself to you."

"Diekin. Does Corrik know? He'll kill you with his bare hands."

He laughs. "Not my body—though Ditira is not quite like Corrik in that regard, she is not opposed to sharing me."

I don't miss how he says that, like he is Ditira's property.

"I meant, my ear and my experience. I have something to offer you that is not sex, but I am happy to see sex is at the forefront of your mind these days," he teases. "No. What I have to offer you is to do with our nature. We are alike, you and I."

Those words are familiar and immediately I remember Papa on the last day I saw him.

'We are alike Tristan. You and I.'

"Diekin, do you mean you are a submissive?"

143

"Yes. I'm Ditira's submissive," he says with all the pride in the world. "I'm also a proud brat."

I don't care. The sky is spinning. My gut has dropped a thousand feet and is then plunged into ice water. Was that what Papa was trying to tell me? Was he submissive to Father?

Growing up, I understood Father's word as law; Papa acted in the same regard, but I thought it was because of Father's title, Warlord, and Papa's as his Second. Father was in charge on the field, I saw no difference with him being in charge in our home. It seemed right, normal even and so I never questioned it.

"Kathir, what's wrong?"

"Nothing, I need to be alone."

"Okay, but I mean it. There is much you are going to learn, and it will confuse you. I'll be better at helping you with particular aspects than Corrik will be because you and I are the same. Dominants—especially Corrik—can tend to be pig-headed, they do not possess patience; when you need me, I will be here."

"Yeah, I mean, I will Diekin—I've really got to go."

I leave poor Diekin confused and run to Corrik's and my chambers. I'm not watching where I'm going, and I end up running smack into the person I don't want to see right now. Corrik.

"Tristan?" His voice is filled with concern.

"What?" I snap.

The concern quickly becomes laced with anger. It doesn't take a lot to provoke him, and I have; yet right now I couldn't care a wit, I *want* to provoke him. When I glare instead of apologizing, he slams me against the dark wooden wall. "By Ylor! What's gotten into you?"

"Nothing. I want to be left alone."

His eyes rake over me and then scan back up to mine. "And you shall." The steel in his voice momentarily removes me from my confused anger as he drags me into our chambers. Once inside, he tosses me on the bed and for the first time I'm scared of the large war Elf—*will he hurt me now?* He mentioned he's a sadist. I don't know what that entails—*maybe I'm about to find out.*

He searches in one of his bags and returns with two thick leather straps. Dear Gods, is he going to use one in each hand?

"Turn on your stomach."

"Corrik I'm sorry—"

"Turn on your stomach."

I do as he's ordered. I can be brave. I've taken a strapping before, it's nothing like being sliced through with a sword, which I've endured as well.

I'm shocked and relieved when he takes my forearms and binds them together behind my back with one strap and uses the other to do the same with my ankles. Once he's finished, I roll to the side. "You ass! I thought you were going to beat me with those."

"The day is still young," he growls, looking like he does want to beat me within an inch. I can see the now familiar restraint in his body.

"I will leave you now. *To be alone,*" he says.

A moment ago, I wanted him gone, now that he's leaving, I want him to stay. "Corrik! You can't leave me like this. *Please.*"

"You asked for time alone and that's exactly what you'll get."

In no mood to be generous with me, he turns and stalks out, a slamming door all he leaves behind; while I fume on the bed tied like a hog ready for roasting.

Bloody straps are all I can think about.

I have another thought that ferments inside my brain; part of me wants him to beat me, to feel his strap on my bare skin, to feel my skin heat red and the endorphins circle around in my blood—*to cry until I'm physically exhausted.*

Since, I've been thinking about Papa and his final message to me and the inside of me is *chaos*.

I fight my bonds. I tug, wiggle, pull and hop around on my stomach and it's at least thirty minutes later that I realize they were secured by an Elf, a clever Elf who apparently knows something about tying a person up. Once I realize the decision to be still has been made for me, something else takes over and I relax. I sink into the bed and let the bonds hold me—like it's Corrik holding me—as I think.

I think about Father and Papa. All the times my father berated Papa and all the times Papa would say, "Yes Arcade. Of course, Arcade." *Was that part of how he submitted?* I also think about his words to me on the day after my wedding. *'It's my fault, Tristan. It's all my fault.'* Is he the reason I'm like this? Did he raise me to be this way without my knowledge? What is 'this way?'

Whatever it is, I don't like it. As much as Papa raised me, I was also raised by my father to be a strong warrior—I've got the blood of a dragon in me—if Corrik wants me to submit to him he can earn it.

The door opens and Corrik returns to see I'm not much better off than I had been.

"I demand you let me go, Corrik."

"I see you need more time alone." He pretends to be irritated, but he's not. He's in a much better mood than when he left. I wonder if it has something to do with me being tied up?

"Fine leave. Who needs you?"

I wiggle around on the bed like *I* intend to leave but of course I can't.

"Enough, Kathir. I'm going to release you and then we'll talk about what's bothering you."

I'll talk with him of nothing, but I'm silent so he'll unbuckle me. I sigh relief when he removes the strap from around my forearms; I didn't realize how sore my shoulders had got. I don't have time to rub them; however, before he turns me over his knee without releasing the strap around my ankles. In one motion, my travel pants are pooled around the strap at my feet and my underthings too; my bottom is at his mercy.

"This isn't talking, Corrik," I brat at him.

"You're a slow learner then my little Markaytian—this is how I talk." Without further pre-amble, he makes quick work heating the cheeks of my bottom with his hand. When it starts to sting, I wiggle and squirm to get out of target range but he's too strong and my ass is further assaulted. He doesn't say a word and I wonder how he can define this as talking? It doesn't take long for the tears to come because of the sting, but also the frustration of getting spanked without any choice in the matter.

My feelings turn to my real problem. I think of Papa, Father, what Diekin's said to me ... They're right. There's something different about me that's clear to Corrik and Diekin, that has been left undiscovered by me until now. It's a strange realization because I don't know what a submissive is, but I know it's part of me. I know I feel better when Corrik gives me what he seems to know I need even if I don't know I need it myself. I cry, releasing my anger and frustration; succumbing to the pain. I let the tears drown the chaos until I'm soothed.

Corrik seems to realize I've reached this point. He flips me up and makes short work of removing the rest of my clothes and the last strap around my ankles. He tosses me on the bed and undresses himself as I watch him and try to sneak a hand back to cool the fire on my cheeks.

"Do not touch your bottom—just feel the burn," he instructs.

I don't know if this is meant to be more punishment for mouthing him off or if there's a reason for it—either way I have no choice but to do as he says. I enjoy the view of his naked body and let the pain wash over me.

Corrik takes a bottle of lube from the nightstand drawer and flips me over to slick the crease of my hot cheeks. I inhale, sharply. "Ow! Corrik," I protest.

"No. Take it. *Feel.*"

I do. I let him press his finger into my sore cheeks, the ones that still burn, and then two fingers and then three, and when I'm prepared, he turns me on my back. "Up."

He switches places with me and sits on the bed. His cock is rock solid and the skin looks like it's going to burst open. "You're going to ride my cock, Tristan."

I look hesitantly at the thing that will impale my sore ass but approach him anyway—like I would an angry dragon. "This isn't about punishment, Tristan. I need to be inside you."

"But it will hurt."

"Yes. I want you to take my cock anyway."

My pain—he wants my pain. He gave me what I needed and now he's taking what he needs. "You said you would never force me into sex."

"If you truly do not want this, say stop and I'll let you

go, but I don't think you want me to stop—I think you want me to *make* you, am I right?"

His words stun me for a second because he's right—I do want him to make me. I nod a small nod.

"Come then, it would please me greatly."

I want to please him. There's nothing better. I climb over top of him on the bed and kneel to either side of him as he backs up against the headboard. His hands are gentle, but my cheeks still hurt when he pries them apart. When I slide down over his cock the burn is intense—but I like it. My cock is just as hard as his looks. We share a look that is intense and meaningful before I slam down hard and begin to ride him and am lulled by the sound of skin slapping on skin. I push my hands through his long gold hair as he pushes up and presses his cock all the way inside me. I'm on top, but he's in charge.

There's heat, we're sweating, and our bodies slip and slide against one another as he claims me from below. He sucks my left nipple hard, and I cry out at the pain, so much pain all at once. Pain in my ass cheeks, pain from my nipple, and then Corrik's hand grabs my cock, and all thinking is gone. It's slick with lubricant and I fuck his hand as I ride him. The sensations overcome me, and I beg him, "*Please… please…* May I come, Corrik?" I'm used to having his permission in things—it feels right I should ask him this.

"Come for me, sweet boy."

I do—all over his stomach—and at the same time he comes inside me. We end in a kiss.

Corrik takes the time to clean us both and then wraps me in his arms, spooning me from behind. "Can you talk now, D'orhai?"

I nod because somehow, I can. As if all of what I just

went through, including the spanking, released what I was holding onto. "I'm like him, Corrik. No one told me."

"I assume you refer to your papa?"

"Yes. How did you know?"

"I'm a dominant, D'orhai. We sense these things from miles away."

"Have you ever been wrong?"

"Not in all my years and being an Elf, I'm exceptionally good at knowing. We are taught to see and acknowledge these things from very small. But back to you—you feel better now, yes?"

"I do, but *why* Corrik? Why does *that* help me?"

"Does it have to make sense? Can't it be enough that it does?"

"I suppose it will have to be—at least for now—but I've never felt quite this way before, like I'm out of control inside."

"You did, but you've had your father to help you—you just didn't know he was doing it. He is an exceptional dominant and you need someone who is quite strict—at least at times. He helped you before you knew you were out of sorts. He was able to do that because he's known you since birth. We've only just begun to know each other—we're learning. In time I will come to anticipate your needs.

"What you feel in this regard will be more intense than it ever was, I will bring out your submissive nature as much as you'll bring out my dominant nature. I almost couldn't contain myself on our wedding night, my need to dominate you was strong—I wanted to hurt you, see my marks on your body; I didn't like anyone touching or being near you."

It's a big admission. I think on what he's said. I'm also beginning to understand why it would have been difficult for him to explain all of this without some kind of experience for me to draw from. Even now as I'm in it, it's hard, on our wedding night I would have been lost. "What will that be like Corrik? When you mark me—no wait—I already know what you'll say."

"Oh really? Have I become predictable already?"

"You'll say, *'learn by experience'* and I'll roll my eyes when you're not looking."

He laughs. "You should ask Diekin about it. I won't force you, but I highly suggest you do."

I nod, perhaps I will. "What?" I ask when I see he's still staring at me.

"I want to tell you that you were right to speak up to me about your tattoo," he says as he caresses it lovingly. "It is 'you' to me now, I can't imagine you without it."

I'm touched and don't know what to say in return—that means more to me than anything he's said or done so far. It's him accepting me for me, a warrior by skill and by blood. I smile, but then my stomach growls.

"I've never heard a stomach growl as often or as loudly as yours," he says, pulling me off the bed and handing me my clothes. "Come. We'd better get you something before your stomach eats itself."

CHAPTER 12

"*D*oes Corrik know you're out here all by yourself, young Warlord?" Diekin says, amusement leaking through his words. He won't stop calling me that and I've grown tired of arguing with him over it, so I let it go.

We've been at sea a full day and we are into another night. The sky is dark and the stars twinkling. I wonder what my family is doing on this night as I ride across the open ocean. I decided to take a walk while Corrik met with some of his guard, I see he's sent Diekin to check up on me.

"Obviously. You're here."

"Very good. You're catching on."

"Is he worried I'll fall off the side of the ship?"

"Perhaps. Or perhaps it's those dangers I spoke of lurking about."

"Okay, spill it Diekin. What's following us?"

"I cannot tell you," he says with mock sincerity. "Corrik will tan my pretty little hide."

"You'll deserve it—you shouldn't have teased me about it."

"All right, but only because I could use a good hiding—by the time I see my mate again it will have been sixteen weeks," he says and the large Elf smiles. "Not to mention, *you'll* owe me one."

"Fine—out with it."

"Other Elves; *Rogue* Elves."

"Rogue Elves?"

"Yes, Rogue Elves," he repeats as we walk further toward the bow. "Elves that were once of Mortouge but were banished long ago. Over time their numbers have grown—they have become a problem."

"Is that who was discovered following us several weeks back?"

"Yes, but it's a bigger problem than that—they shouldn't have been able to follow us, Kathir. We've got protective magic weaved around us; we should be invisible to these Elves. That we are not means either that our protection magic has failed, or they have found a magic source stronger than ours."

"So naturally, Corrik has become overprotective."

"Aren't you a sharp one?"

"*Diekin.*"

"Hey, I can make fun all I want—I'm going to be the one with the sore ass for telling you."

"You *want* to be spanked."

"No one ever *wants* to be spanked—not exactly anyway. We desire the resolution the spanking brings. To be spanked, well, I wish that part wasn't necessary—except for in fun." He waggles his eyebrows at me.

"Why is it necessary?"

"That's a tough one to explain and every time I try, words don't seem to be enough. It's a thing inside, the way I am wired. Ditira expects me to behave but understands that sometimes I need her help. Spanking seems to connect to that place inside of me and bring about instant calm."

"Corrik seems to think it's better experienced."

"It is hard to put words, I guess. For those of us who need it, we understand that we do. It always existed for us and in Mortouge we honor this part of us, this need, rather than analyze it too closely. Like how some people enjoy the sky without worrying about where its beauty comes from. If you insist, I put words to it..." He thinks a moment. "It is a few things. It is repentance you can qualify when you feel you've done something that needs forgiving, and it is freedom. Oddly, it feels easier to surrender and let go when there are boundaries versus where there are not."

The words alone relax me, and I can't deny that I relate.

"Everyone lives within boundaries of some kind—what if Markaytia had no rules?"

"There would be utter chaos," I say.

"Exactly. There must be rules—even for adults. People like you and I like prefer people like Corrik to make rules for us so we can relax into the freedom of following the rules. You must trust him to know your chaos and steer you from it."

"How can I trust him when I don't know him?"

"That will be the challenge—the journey you two will travel together. It is the same journey any couple travels together. There will be mistakes along the way; the two must find the path through. When it is you who makes the mistake, you will seek physical means to absolve the guilt of it—that is the way of a submissive. When a Dom or a Top makes a mistake, they make it up in different ways, but you can be certain they will *never* make that same mistake again."

"You sound as if you enjoy being submissive."

"I do. Every second. I love my mate; she is strong." He loves Corrik's sister, I don't love Corrik. "Submission is beautiful. It is a gift we give."

I remember what I did out on the dance floor on our wedding night—oh Gods. Corrik, the arrogant bastard, must have thought that I was only minutes away from falling in love with him. That must have been a grand, submissive-like gesture.

I remember another thing. "What about when there is no guilt? I'm sure you saw what happened in Umbria."

"Yes. I was there."

"Corrik spanked me for that." I blush. "I didn't allow him, and I didn't feel guilty."

"First, you are his so it is his right whether you want him to or not—it is what you agreed to when you married him."

Not that I had a choice in marrying him—that was decided for me by my uncle. But I get what he means.

"Part of submission is following the rules whether you agree or not. When you break those rules, you will be punished. There will be times you will realize your error at some point during the chastisement and other times you won't—either way you broke the rules, and you will be punished for breaking them."

"Right. Well, it sounds like the dominant gets all the fun."

He shakes his head. "Never. It is far more fun to be a sub or a brat," he says. "We get to goof off and have fun while they make all the rules and have to be responsible."

"Yeah and pay for that fun later."

"How did you feel after? Do you harbor resentment?"

"I complained a little but other than sore and embarrassed, I was fine. And, much as I hate to admit it, I felt *content.*" I tried to feel resentment, but it just wasn't there.

"Ah, you, see? You did benefit, even if you didn't consciously understand."

"This talk has been helpful, Diekin. I'll try to keep you out of trouble as long as I can."

He smirks. "What fun would that be? I am glad to help. As I said, it's hard to put words to something like this and even with the best words, it will only register with those who seek to understand. Those who don't, never will. You've experienced what I say so you know firsthand what I'm talking about."

That's a lot to think about, but since the conversation's going so well, I consider asking him what Corrik suggested, about marking. Diekin has spiked my curiosity.

"Diekin," I begin as I look up to him, but I don't get to finish, because something is here with us. Diekin is staring off to the night sky so he doesn't notice. I look to the bow of the ship where silent movement catches my eye. I tap Diekin and point. He can see better than me and probably would've caught the movement before me if he were looking down instead of up.

"Kathir—go back to your chambers!" he yells as an Elf jumps from the shadows.

Diekin takes a defensive stance in front of me and in an instant, the quick Elf is on him. They begin to circle each other, to look for openings and conserve energy. Despite the blackness of the night, I can see the fire in Diekin's eyes.

The other Elf, who I assume is a Rogue Elf, looks similar to Diekin, only he's lither, less bulky and his skin is a deeper, tan shade. He's fucking agile. When he finally takes a first slice, I can see the precision in his movements. It's only Diekin's own formidable skill that moves him out of the way with enough time.

I don't leave like Diekin ordered; he might need my help. I'm unarmed though; I need a weapon. The deck is suspiciously quiet, other than the clash of steel from the swords of the two fighting warriors. *Where is everyone?*

I hesitate to use the weapon I know I have on me. Concealed in the belt pack at my hip, is one of my secret items: my Dagger. I'll use it if I must, for now, I move to grab the broom I spied earlier. I can't help but survey rooms for weapons or weapon-like things. I've done this all my life but more often since Corrik forbid me my sword.

When I turn back, Diekin looks over to realize I'm still here and it gives the Rogue Elf the time he needs to break through Diekin's keen defenses. All of this happens in an instant of course—Diekin is already looking back at the Elf when the Elf pierces him, straight through his right lung.

Diekin gasps like he's drowning and falls to the ground. The Elf doesn't bother to waste another moment on him; he turns his attention to me and when he pounces, I realize how helpless I'm against the strength of an Elf. I'm trapped and no amount of struggling throws him off me. I'm not used to this; only my fathers could defeat me in any kind of fight, but this fight is going to be over before it starts, *unless.*

No choice now, I've got to use my dagger. If I can reach it, I might be able to inflict some damage; at least get him off me, maybe buy some time. I pretend to submit, and the Rogue Elf smiles as if to say, *'that was easy'* lifting his sword. Meanwhile, I'm moving my hand down my thigh, fingers like an inchworm, toward my small pack—the pack that has now become instrumental in saving my life. My hand hits the opening, I can feel the cold, leather handle—still, there are scant seconds of seconds left, I know it, I can feel it. He will strike before I get the chance.

Doesn't mean I won't die trying.

I don't particularly want to die now, but this is my preferred way to go, in battle, even if I've barely got the chance *to* battle this time. I've known my whole life that I want to go out in battle, not dying old in bed, but what I don't expect, my last thoughts are of Corrik—violet eyes that read me, strong shoulders that can hold me in place; the laugh I've fallen in love with. I even think about the firm hand that disciplines me.

I gain enough purchase on the handle to swipe the blade upward, but not enough to do the damage I need to. It is; however, enough. I feel the sword sink into me, but not where he would have liked it to. It pierces my shoulder—the pain explodes and my world narrows to it, my vision turns to shadows and all I can see is an outline as he pulls the sword viciously from me and readies to strike again. I hear the clatter as my dagger drops from my hand after being pierced; all I can do is try to struggle as I prepare for his sword to stab me again. This time it will be lethal. I'm about to die, but I won't die a coward. I keep my eyes focused on his and dare him to strike me again.

His sword never comes. The Elf falls to his knees, injured, not dead and Corrik is there behind him. I hear the sickening, suction of a sword being pulled out of flesh. The Elf falls onto my thighs. I can barely make Corrik out due to my pain-induced, shadowy vision, but I can feel the thunderous rage peeling off him. He shouts orders in Elvish and rushes to my side.

"*Tahsen.*"

"Diekin—!"

"He will be all right."

"But, I saw him die."

"He will be fine, D'orhai."

I make to rise, but he puts a hand to my chest and slides an arm under my legs and shoulders. I decide not to make an issue of him carrying me or report the list of injuries I've sustained in my short life that are worse than this one, nor do I demand to walk because my Elf has gone silent. That never means anything good with Corrik.

He carries me to our bed, and I don't want to get blood all over—he shushes me. "Sleep, D'orhai. Everything is taken care of. I will fix you." He says nothing about blood on the sheets; it's all I'm worried about. What a thing to worry about as I bleed to death.

I struggle a bit, trying to fight him. *How can I sleep at a time like this?* Seeing I'm in no state to obey his will, he forces his hand by gently stroking my hair and laces it with his Elven magic. I can feel it wash over me. My eyes get heavy and darkness falls.

"Tristan?" he says when he notices me waking. I don't know how long I've slept, but it feels like days.

"I'm okay, Corrik." I'm better than, I discover as I test the shoulder that should in the least feel some discomfort, but there's nothing to prove it was stabbed at all.

"I was worried." I've not yet seen fear in the great war Elf's eyes; I see it now.

"I'm not dead, I really am fine," I assure him again. "Is Diekin okay?" I saw him fatally stabbed, but Corrik promised me he was going to be fine.

"He is alive and well, but he is Elf, you are human. Both

of you were healed with Elven magic, but you will take longer to recover than he did."

I want to thank him for reminding me of my weaknesses, but now is not a good time to tease him.

"Diekin waits to kill the man responsible; we are going to question him, but I made him wait a few days. I wanted to make sure you were okay first. I knew I wouldn't have all my wits about me if not."

"I'm coming with you," I say and try to rise.

"I don't think so." He pushes me down. "*You* are going to rest. This is not a matter for you to deal with."

"I have dealt with matters like this before."

"No. You stay here, and I had better not catch you out of bed, Kathir." His face hardens, but this time I can detect the fear beneath his anger. None of it matters. I'm done being a doll. I felt alive for the first time this journey when that Elf jumped me; it forced my body to remember what it was like on the battlefield.

I push against his hand, knowing he will be gentle with me for the moment. "I'm coming with you, Corrik. Let that be an end to it," I say using Papa's words. I've heard him say that to my father and in those times, my father would quietly acquiesce anything Papa demanded. *Will it work on Corrik?*

Maybe in time; not today.

"By Ylor! I don't know what's got into you—must have hit your head when you fell—you know better than to talk to me like that." It's true. I know what my disobedience does to him. He stands, the room fills with his restraint and he positions his face inches from mine. "You will not leave this room," he hisses then makes to leave.

"If you do this without me, I shall never speak to you again—you have my word as a Markaytian on that," I say.

He knows my dragon blood has spoken and if he wants to fight with a dragon he can and he will lose.

He's mad—mad enough to light this ship on fire, inches away from violence. "Get dressed, I will return to retrieve you," he says between grit teeth and storms from the room almost tearing the door off its hinges as he exits.

After what seems like decades later, he returns. He's still angry with me. He thrusts something out at me; I recognize it immediately.

"Explain this."

"That's my dagger." I reach to take it from him, he yanks it from my reach.

"I can see that," he says gesturing to the Markaytian Crest on the handle. "What is your dagger doing aboard this ship?"

"I brought it with me," I say defiantly. He slaps me hard across the face and tears sting my eyes as the pain radiates from my cheek to my head.

"That will be quite enough impertinence out of you. Explain properly."

"I visited my room before we left," I admit. "I took a couple choice items I didn't think would mean anything to anyone."

"You did this in secret. You were told not to take anything. Where is the other item?"

I actually have two more and I don't want to give either to him, but my lie ensures I can keep one. Furious, I storm over to my pack and unzip it. I know he'll go crazy over the battle garment, but he might understand the ring so I fish that out. "Here," I say as I thrust the ring toward him.

He accepts it taking reconnaissance of the illegal item. "And there are no other items in that pouch? Are you sure? Do I have to check?"

Yes, I'm lying again, but why I ever thought I could get along with the cantankerous Elf is beyond me. I feel no remorse in it. "No," I say trying to look offended. After my threat earlier, I doubt he'll test me further than that.

"You'd better not be. If I find out otherwise you will be one sorry Markaytian."

Wanting to change the subject, I look to the ring in his hand. "May I keep it?"

"What is it?"

"My papa's family ring—see there's an inscription inside." I direct him where to look and he does, *"Submit to the heart,"* I read to him, "and the emeralds represent the Sterling family's eyes."

When he's satisfied with my explanation of the ring, he closes his fingers over it. "You will earn it back."

My jaw drops open. "But Corrik—"

"—feel lucky that I'm not throwing it off the side of the ship."

I am, but I don't think it's fair I should have to earn it back—*it's mine.*

He pockets the ring. At least the battle garment is still in my possession, which only leads me to the second less heartening realization: He's still aiming to trust me even though he shouldn't.

"And the dagger?"

"Will stay in my possession."

"May I *earn that back too?*" I can't hide my sarcasm.

"No weapons for you—you've no need—"

"—it saved my life."

"I saved your life."

I'm uncertain if I can argue with that. *Could he have still saved my life if the sword had pierced my heart? How reliable is Elven Magic?* I don't know.

"Come," he says holding out his hand for me and ending this horrid conversation.

"Where are we going?"

"Where do you think?"

My eyes light with mirth. We're going to question a Rogue Elf.

CHAPTER 13

*H*e is tied to two wooden slats that are nailed together in the shape of an 'X,' in the dungeon of the ship, which Corrik conveniently left out of his tour. The Elf is naked and marked with long, red welts over his pale body. The pain he is in does nothing to diminish his triumph—it's written below the surface of his bruises. I look for the place where Corrik's large sword should have come through to his front, but I can't see it and assume he, like Diekin and I, has been healed. He's thin but muscled and if he weren't chained to the wooden 'X,' I could picture him jumping wall to wall like a spider. I see now that his skin is a shimmering copper, like he's been out in the sun often. His cock is hard as nails and has a leather ring tied around the base. He moans and mumbles incoherently.

"You will sit here and not say a word while we question him," Corrik says.

I've learned well enough that arguing with him in private is one matter, in public another. All I can do is give him plaintive eyes which he ignores, and sit on the chair in the corner. At least I still have a clear view of the proceedings.

Diekin is here with us, along with the Elven king and a dozen guards. The man is chained up well, *why so many guards?* The queen moves over to stand beside me. *Of course, the weak human is seated while the strong Elves stand.* Diekin looks to Corrik, who nods and then walks within the eye line of the Rogue Elf. Diekin says something to him in Elvish. *I'm not going to understand a thing.*

"He asked his identity," the queen whispers to me. Corrik looks back with a smug smile and I cross my arms and lean back in my chair.

"Hmmm," the queen says when the Elf answers back.

"What is it?"

"Well, he was very rude."

"I'm sure I can handle it," I say.

"I think in Markaytian the equivalent is 'fuck you'."

Did the Queen just say fuck you?

As the interrogation progresses, we learn he is the Rogue Elf, Heilren, sent to kill me. He's relatively easy to pull information from. *Something's not right about that.*

"Please," the queen translates for me. "I'll tell you anything you want."

It's hard to believe he would betray his own with such little urging, though by the number of welts and bruises, it looks like someone has taken the time to 'pre-urge' him.

I become bored and begin to watch Corrik. Something is off about his body language and I don't like it. Not only is it terrifying, it's clear how little trust he has in whatever Heilren is saying. And something else. Corrik looks like he isn't really here; like his senses are warning him of something unseen.

Suddenly, Corrik's eyes look up at me. "Mother take him out of here, *now!*"

It's amazing how easy it is for the Elven queen to rip me out of the chair and the room, but before she does, the Rogue Elf's head snaps up to look straight at me, his eyes glow dark, blue lightning snaps across the irises and the room builds with thunder. I'm just being pulled out the door, when a dark streak of magic storms down, loud, to where I was sitting, leaving ashes where the chair had been.

The queen pulls me into a hug, one she needs more than I do. "Twice in a handful of days is twice too many. What would your parents say if we had to tell them we lost you after such a short period of time having you?"

Corrik blazes out of the dark. "He's dead."

Corrik says no more about what happened in the room and I don't ask. He's not in a mood to talk to anyone—me at the top of his 'not-talking-to' list. I join Corrik in his silence and listen to Diekin who has lots to say.

I should probably be nervous or concerned. My life's been threatened twice and the Rogue Elf made it clear his mission was to kill me, but this is an adventure Lucca and I couldn't dare to dream—I'm far too excited to be nervous.

When the meal ends, Corrik calls on Diekin.

"Say goodnight Diekin and come with me."

I know that look—Diekin's in trouble. He knows it too—he's known it all night—but he stands with grace and does as told. "And you," Corrik says to me. "You will go with Mother."

"Yes, Corrik," I say, but on the inside I want to throttle

him. It reminds me too much of getting sent to cross-stitch with my mother—I hope the queen doesn't cross-stitch. *I hate cross-stitching.*

To my delight, the queen invites me to her sitting room for tea and I learn that I'm here to be babysat (as I suspected), but also for her own comfort.

"Tell me Tristan, what was it like to grow up in Markaytia?"

"I loved it," I tell her. I expand about me and Lucca, which I imagine she already overheard from some of my conversations with Diekin, but then go on to tell her a bit of Markaytia's history.

"Markaytia is an old province. It used to be ruled by dragons until the last dragon died, but before he did, he passed his blood onto a man and that man became Markaytia's first warlord. It was his duty to name the first king, a title he gave to his brother. It became tradition to do so from then on. He was an ancestor of mine; I'm named for him," I say.

"No wonder your name means so much to you Tristan. You must have an Elvish name for the public, but in private, if you like, I shall call you by your Markaytian name."

"I would like that."

I tell her more stories of Lucca and I tell her more about the history of Tristan the Dragon Warlord. She's fascinated and I find I like the queen a little more. It will be easy to call her Mother.

"I have enjoyed our time, Tristan, but I fear this day has exhausted even me. I'll escort you to your chambers now. Corrik should be there."

Corrik is there. I find him on the bed staring at the ceiling when I enter our bedchamber. He knows I've entered, but he doesn't sit up. I'm not sure what to do—I've never seen him like this, and it's in these moments I realize how much I have to learn about him.

I proceed to get ready for bed not saying a word to him —he can pout all night if he likes, I'm going to bed. Once I've washed up, I return to the bedchamber expecting to find him as I've left him.

He's nothing like I've left him: Corrik is naked with the covers rolled down, reading a book; the main light is out with a small ball of light hovering above him.

I patter to my side of the bed and hope he'll leave me alone for the night.

No such luck.

His book snaps closed and the little ball of light floats to hover above the bed so I can still make out his pale form. He turns on me like a predator would his prey. "You and I need to have a little talk."

I know what his talks are like—I'm sure he just had one with Diekin. I yelp and cocoon the covers around me. *Has he found the other item I've kept hidden?*

"How's Diekin?" I say trying heartily to change the subject.

"Diekin is well, you may see him tomorrow. I don't want to talk about him, I want to talk about you and me."

I swallow. "Yes?"

"Come, here."

"Corrik—"

He gives me a look that says he's had enough belligerence from me for one day; I shimmy over to him keeping plenty of blanket wrapped around me. His icy shell cracks and he chuckles. "You aren't in trouble—we just need to talk, with words," he defines for me. "Come."

When I'm within reach of him, he breaks me out of the blanket and presses my naked body to his—his cock up against my ass. *Maybe I can convince him to skip the impending lecture I feel headed my way...?*

"It took every ounce of my strength not to flay you alive earlier. You can't make such threats to me; that will be the last."

I don't need him to protect me, I've been a member of my father's guard since I was twelve. "Then you must cease to treat me like I'm weak, I'm not your doll."

"That's absurd. I know you're not a doll."

"Diekin had to be the one to tell me about the Rogue Elves before Heilren attacked me."

He doesn't look pleased about that. "You cannot fight an Elf. You're only—"

"—human. I know. You remind me every chance you get."

He holds me awhile like he's simply grateful I'm still alive *to* hold.

"You can't protect me at every turn, Corrik. The world is dangerous. I've faced certain death many times and I'm sure I'll face it many more."

His grip on me gets tighter. "I can protect you and you will not be put in danger like that again. Today wouldn't have happened if you would have let me do my job as your mate."

And that is the crux of the matter. He succumbed his logic to my threat on an emotional whim. He didn't like me forcing his hand in the first place and since it ended badly, he feels justified in never participating in another of my silly tantrums again. I admit that what I did was manipulative, it's not the kind of behavior I'm fond of employing, but I reacted. I'm not good when I feel trapped. "I'm sorry for what I did Corrik, but you wouldn't listen—you never listen."

"I understand things you do not. I don't have to listen to you—you're mine and shall do as I say."

I don't like it. I'm used to being *heard* in the least. Even Father as intractable as he is listened to what I had to say—even if he did not end up taking my advisement on the matter.

"Corrik, I vowed to obey you and I will, but I need to be heard."

"If I had explained everything and still forbid your participation, can you say, with honesty, that you would have left it at that?"

"Fine, no I wouldn't have." And it's true that Corrik isn't unreasonable either; unless my safety is at stake, apparently. I sense there's something else he's not telling me. "But if you're a little more forthcoming with information, I can attempt to understand and even behave myself."

That gets me his signature quarter smile and he nods. "Some Elves can see the future," he says.

"As in prophecy? Some Markaytians used to be prophets, back in the time of wizards, before they all died out."

"Yes, like prophets. Any Elf can have a vision; some Elves will have more visions than others. I have many visions. My first vision told me of you."

"Me?"

"Yes. I dreamt of marrying a dragon, our marriage was written in prophecy—though I haven't yet found out if I ever tame him; he's more misbehaved than I could have fathomed."

I elbow him in the ribs. "Teach you for marrying wild animals, now get back to your story."

"And demanding. It's still not too late for that spanking you know."

"Spank me all you want later, just finish the story," I say, no less demanding.

He knows I'm teasing this time; his hand moves down to massage my cock. "In another vision, you die." His hand squeezes my cock *too* hard.

I moan into his ear. "So, you think if you keep me away from every source of danger, your vision won't come to fruition?"

"Something like that."

"Don't you think me not even *hearing* of danger is going a bit far?"

"With you? No. I've got your number, Tristan Kanes. You look for danger because you think it's an adventure."

I can't argue with that. "What's wrong with liking adventure?"

"Adventure is dangerous. You won't be having much adventure after this trip is over—get used to it. You'll be locked away safe in Mortouge where nothing can harm you."

"Will I have my own tower? Will I have to grow my hair like that girl in the children's fairytale?"

"Do not tempt me," he says with a smile in his voice. He's still massaging my cock. "And I do like your hair long—you are never to cut it."

He's lucky I love my hair too; I'd never cut it. "Are we done talking now? I can put my mouth to far better uses."

"What happened to your Markaytian sensibilities?"

"I'm not Markaytian anymore, am I?"

"Technically, I suppose not, but I'm learning there's no way to take away the dragon in your blood and so a piece of Markaytia you shall always remain." It means a lot to me. It's Corrik's way of apologizing for his fractious nature. "Almost done lecturing you."

"You think I don't know when you're lecturing me, but I always know."

"I didn't think I was making it secret," he says and moves his hand to my nipples, squeezing each one hard as his other hand massages my ass. I don't want him to stop, but I want to look at him more so I turn around. Besides, if he continues like that, I won't be able to concentrate on what he's saying. Suddenly, he pounces on me and towers over top. He nips at my neck sending shivers through my body; I push my hips up trying to join my cock with his. His lips press to mine in a deep kiss. When he pulls away, his eyes are softer and resemble lilac more than their usual dark, cold violet. He's changed—a little and it's because of my near death. Twice.

Tomorrow he will be an over-protective maniac, but today, no matter what I do, he can't find the will to stay angry with me.

He doesn't lecture anymore and our sex that night is tender. The animal in Corrik is barely present, only for a few sharp thrusts at the end, and I *would* call it love making, if I loved Corrik.

But I don't.

CHAPTER 14

"*W*here do you think you're going?"

I thought to get ready for breakfast but Corrik seems to have other plans. His tone, unfortunately, does not suggest anything sexual.

"Nowhere?"

"Precisely. Did you think your behavior yesterday wouldn't cost you?" Corrik manages to sound arid and threatening at the same time.

"C'mon, Corrik. I said I was sorry."

"Yet I'll bet I can make you sorrier."

I sense the ghost of a smile that suggests he's sharing a joke with himself—his own inside joke with 'other Corrik.' In my head, there are two Corriks; right now, it's pernicious Corrik out to play. Pernicious Corrik is hard and unyielding; he likes to watch me squirm—yet he is sarcastically dark and playful. Other Corrik has the ability to be kind, despite what the queen believes; I've seen it. He's not kind in the way other people are, you have to look closely, but it's there. Both Corriks like control, power and each other (especially each other). He and his other half think he's a funny Elf now—but Corrik doesn't do funny—neither Corrik does; someone should tell them that.

"I shall bring you breakfast. You will remain in here the rest of the day and remember this next time you should think to threaten or speak to me the way you did yesterday."

He's grounding me? "You can't cage a dragon, Corrik. I'll go mad in here—you said I could visit Diekin."

"And you shall. *Later*."

Confining me to our room is the worst punishment he could come up with. Even Father saved this for the more egregious acts.

"Spank me, *please*—you'll enjoy that."

"As much as I would enjoy that, I can't. You are just recently healed and as good as you feel, the healing still occurs. You should be resting anyway." He raises both brows toward me because I haven't stopped moving toward the door. He's still on the bed, naked, as the day is long; I have a head start: I could run. He will catch me, but it might soften his stone heart.

A smile splits my face.

"Tristan!"

I run out the door of our bedchamber that leads into the anteroom and catch the movements of the large Elf out of the corner of my eye as he takes up the pursuit. He's quicker than I planned—though I didn't really plan any of this. I make it as far as the outer door. Corrik's frosted, alabaster skin is in my periphery and I feel the ghost of his hand wisp my wrist just as I make it out the door.

That's as far as I get.

I yelp and laugh hysterically as his arm reaches out quick as lightning to curl around my waist. He spins us around so I'm back on the inside of the door, and shuts it with his ass as I writhe and attempt fruitlessly to shimmy out of his iron grip. I still laugh at myself; it was short, but fun. I don't think I've laughed like that since...? Well, I can't remember.

Corrik tosses me on the bed. His face is trackless, but I sense lightness in his posture. "You will stay in your cage, Dragon."

His lips are a rigid line (Corrik's form of a smile) and his dark eyes almost twinkle—he *liked* my game.

Victory for Dragon House.

"All right, but I'm hungry Corrik," I whine.

"Your stomach will be the death of me," he mutters as he pulls on a pair of pants and slings his sword onto his back. He's quite the sight like that. Impenetrable warrior meets Elven farmer. I have to stifle a giggle—Corrik doesn't go anywhere without his sword.

"Couldn't we send someone to fetch us something?"

"Yes, but after yesterday I would prefer to watch them prepare your food with my own eyes."

"Corrik, *seriously*."

"I am serious."

I t seems to take forever, but finally he returns. I attempted to read his book while he was gone, but it's in Elvish of course so I had fun looking at the pictures and pretending what I think the pages might say.

"Any luck with that?" he says putting a plate down on the bed by me. He's making fun again. *Since when did Corrik become 'Mr. Relaxed-Fun-Guy?'*

"Yes. I think I've managed to figure out every time the author swears since I've some experience with that," I tease him back. "What is this, Corrik?" I shake the book.

"It's about magic."

"Don't you know everything about magic?"

"No one can possibly know *everything* about magic. I've many years to go before I reach the level of mastery of some of my siblings."

"What is it?" I say again, still waving the book.

"Geological magic. I'm trying to figure out how the Rogue Elves could have discovered us," he says swiping the book from my hand, and I'm surprised by his offer of information. *Is it possible something I said to Corrik has penetrated his stubbornness?*

"Couldn't you ask someone?"

"Is that how you solve all your problems? Ask everyone else?"

"No," I say, offended. "It just seems rather time sensitive."

His hard features relax. "I could, yes, but Father is already doing something about it and he suggested I attempt to figure this out on my own, since there is no danger in me taking the time to do so."

I'm intrigued by this knowledge: Old as he is, Corrik is a student too. Makes sense though considering Elves live forever.

"So, have you?" I ask.

"Have I what?"

"Figured it out?"

"Not yet, but I think I'm close."

"Maybe I can help."

"Help? What do you know of magic? You can't even read the words."

"Give me that book back, hot shot." I snatch the book back from him, pop a grape into my mouth and flip through the pages thinking on them a moment. "Ah. See this picture here? There are clouds over the sun. I envision—though I know little of magic, some kind of, I don't know, 'geographical magic,' might depend on the sun and clouds to hide our location so we can't be traced?"

"In simple terms, correct."

I flip the page ignoring his jibe at my intellect. "Anyway, that is for day, at night, the same thing must be done somehow involving stars because the stars are a guide. I know that from traveling with Father. The North Star for instance, is a guiding star. The constellations can be used to track someone with magic I'm thinking."

"Correct again, you've done well, but your analysis is of no use to me; I already know all of this information and have a far better understanding. You can't help me." It's a dare; he wants me to keep going. I think I've impressed him.

"Essentially, we are dealing with time too; day and night, makes me think about the time in between day and night. When I was a little boy, Papa would tell me stories and sing me songs of his homeland—he is not of Markaytia, but several provinces over; a province called Nosklac. A particular rhyme, perhaps a ridiculous one, he sang to me, comes to mind when I look at the pictures in this book. *'Day turns to night, night turns to day, but the time in between is ours for play.'* I don't know what the pictures are, I didn't even know what the book was until you told me, but when you did, it clicked into place in my head and that's what I think—whatever they did has got to do with the time in between day and night. A loophole, perhaps."

Corrik is quiet and looks me over like he's never seen me before. "That's what you got from looking at pictures?"

I nod. "Am I close?"

"You are. The time between day and night is called,

twilight. Not a time for children to be playing so you are right, the rhyme is ridiculous."

"I know what twilight is, I was explaining it like that to show you there are more ways to come up with an answer than simply reading about it. I meant the rhyme is ridiculous relative to the answer—not ridiculous to me," I say. The rhyme means a lot, silly as it is. "It was just the thing to trigger my brain to finding what I thought might be a loophole."

"Touché, D'orhai. You are correct—your strange method of derision aside—it's a twilight spell. I just don't know which one or if it's something new."

"New? Can new magic be created?"

"Of course," he says like it should be obvious and is high on himself because he still knows more than I do about magic.

I suppose it should be obvious though. There are always new ways of doing everything else, why not magic too?

I commence eating; I really am starving. Corrik spent a long-time last night showing me how much he cares for me. He likes to demonstrate his feelings with several rounds of sex. I don't mind.

Corrik takes my lead for once and begins eating when I do.

"Thank you, for breakfast."

"You're welcome."

"Do I have to remain in here all day?"

"You do but not to worry. I'll make sure you are kept *occupied*."

Of course, I thought he meant he'd make me (okay, hoped he'd make me) perform sexual acts for him all day, but after breakfast he excused himself saying he had things to get done. He handed me a fat, heavy book.

"This has been written just for you."

"Markaytian to Elvish in three hundred days," I read from the title. "Corrik what is this?"

"A Professor at the University, Cupper Sphir—I had him write this specially for you."

"If he's just written it, why does it look so old?"

"It's old to *you*. I had him write it when I first had my vision of you—it's more than a century old."

I huffed but accepted it. "I want you to work on that today during your confinement—make sure you sit by the window so you can see what a lovely day you're missing out on."

Bastard, Elf!

That was several hours ago, now the sun is at half-mast. I didn't dare take a break—except to eat my lunch earlier—because Corrik warned that if he came in to find me not-working, I would spend tomorrow doing this very thing on a sore ass.

I do want to learn their language, but I have never enjoyed learning from books alone. This Cupper guy, it's like he knew me and wrote the giant tomb with my learning style in mind. His instructions are efficient and engage me, I'm surprised at the headway I've made in the time my husband is gone.

When Corrik returns, he greets me with a simple question in Elvish and despite the complicated accent, I can make out what he says. I try to answer back. Corrik understands me, but his cruel mouth twists in distaste at my poor accent.

I'm happy when I'm dismissed to see Diekin, wanting a break from the stringent taskmaster.

I run away fast before he can change his mind. I've thought of Diekin a time or two over the course of the day. I don't know the reason he merited punishment in the first place, but from his nervous behavior at dinner that night, he expected it.

"Come in," he says.

I enter to Diekin who's pouring over books much like I was moments ago. He doesn't look injured, just annoyed.

"Oh thank, Ylor! It is you and not Corrik—though it would be kind if you didn't tell him I said that."

"What did he do to you, Diekin?" For Diekin to not want to see Corrik, Corrik must have been torturing him all day *somehow*.

"This!" he says disgusted, gesturing to the mountain of books that surround him. "That sadistic maniac has suspended me from the royal guard and instead I must spend my time studying this nonsense! Every hour it seems, he shows up with another stack of books—who knew there were so many books aboard this ship?"

I realize now how easy Corrik went on me. "What would he have you study?"

He sighs. "I suppose I should tell you now. He is angry with me—*extremely angry*—for the way I handled your safety or as he says, lack thereof, when the Rogue Elf attacked us. All of these books are on battle technique and battle history and when we reach Mortouge, if my mate agrees, I will return to the training fields full time."

"That's preposterous, Diekin. You aren't responsible for my injuries; you were almost killed too."

His silence tells me he disagrees with me.

"You can't be serious, Diekin. Is this an Elven thing I'm missing?"

"You almost died because of me."

"We all lose battles, Diekin. Even the best of us." It's something my father used to tell me.

"Yes, but not Elves chosen for the royal guard. Corrik said I might join the palace guard, or even the city guard when we return home, but I am not fit for the royal guard at this time as demonstrated by my lack of skill."

"I distracted you. I should've listened and gone back to my chambers like you said. This isn't your fault." Perhaps I should start listening to what the Elves tell me to do. Now Diekin pays the price for my pig-head.

"I shouldn't have allowed you to distract me. A better swordsman would not have; you know this young Warlord. No. Corrik is right to punish me, and I am ashamed. Of course, I will complain over my punishment to my fellow brats, like you, but I will serve it admirably for whatever amount of time Corrik feels I owe—though between me you, I hope it's sooner rather than later," he says with a wink.

"I'll talk to him. I'll talk with Corrik and make him see it was my fault."

"Please don't. I deserve this and if I don't serve some kind of punishment, it will eat me alive. Corrik knows this too; he is a wise Top, though I did try to bargain a spanking out of him. But *he makes the punishments, not I*," he recites in a mocking voice. "I care about you a lot, Tristan, and I am torn up that the first harm you came by was on my watch. I'm sorry and I swear I'll make it up to you, even if I'm stuck on the palace guard for the next five years."

"It could be that long?"

"It could be longer. Alrik, Corrik's eldest brother, once sentenced Corrik to a ten-year restriction to the palace for an offense far smaller than this."

Right. Elves. Immortality. Ten years is a blink to them; still I couldn't imagine being grounded that long. "A Top can be punished too?"

"Yes," he nods. "By anyone who is elder. No one is free of consequences in Mortouge."

"What was he punished for?"

"Disrespect."

"That's all?"

"You have seen Corrik's temper—it was several times too many and he had been warned. Even the king agreed to that one."

Wow.

Corrik wasn't just lenient with me; he'd barely punished me at all. Maybe I do have him wrapped around my little, Markaytian finger.

"Well, if it's any consolation, Corrik may come spank you yet—I ratted you out for telling me about the Rogue Elves," I say.

He smiles his big Diekin smile. "Thank you, brother, and look at me with no gift for you."

"There's more. Corrik said we could hang out; he was quite vague about it so I'm assuming that means you're released for a time. He also seemed certain we wouldn't have any more problems with Rogue Elves, at least while aboard the ship."

"Yes. It does mean that—you must put him in a good mood for him to be giving rewards so soon. And yes, the king joined the royal guard and Corrik on a hunt into every crevice of the ship today. He and Corrik used their magic; they found no more stowaways."

That was probably the true reason behind the type of punishment he doled out—*get Tristan out of the way; keep him out of danger while we search the ship.*

"What happened after I left with the Rogue Elf? Did you kill him or was it Corrik?"

Diekin shakes his head. "He died, Tristan. He had been buying time by answering our questions and stalling with his begging while he gathered strength enough for one last bout of magic. He didn't give himself away until the end when he became weak, which is ironically the time the magic built up in him was the strongest. It does not offer him any protection, immunity, or personal strength; it's something that once gathered must be released. Once released, it takes with it the essence—the life force—of the Elf. He died the moment he unleashed his power on you."

"A suicide?" *Why do the Rogue Elves want me dead?*

Diekin nods. "But enough of this morose talk. Corrik is giving me a break to hang out with one of my new favorite people—let's get out of here."

CHAPTER 15

There's not a lot to do on a ship—even a large ship —when you're not crew that is. Diekin and I are ready to volunteer as crew by the end of our eventless journey around the ship. I think I might like to get attacked again over this monotony. I enjoy Diekin's company but compared to my everyday life with Lucca in Markaytia, it's dull. We spend some time with our legs over the bow, watching the water as the ship gently cuts through it, tossing us about and even Diekin almost loses his balance several times, a hair's breadth from being tossed overboard. I doubt this is what Corrik would've wanted us to do, but he's not around. We haven't even bumped into him during on our expedition about the ship.

"You look bored, young Warlord."

"Sorry, Diekin. I am."

"I shouldn't do this, if we get caught it will seal my fate as a *village* guard for decades, but I owe you for what's happened, and I can't stand to see you like you are."

I would tell him he doesn't owe me anything, but he insists and drags me to a level of the ship I haven't seen, yet another place Corrik left out of his tour of *my* ship. We walk along the edge of the top deck, until we reach a set of stairs that takes us far below the world. Diekin keeps smiling and looking back at me like we are great co-conspirators on an adventure. I smell trouble, but after hours of boredom, it's hard to turn down the first bit of fun we follow.

The loud, cheering crowd can be heard from a distance, and we must move toward the direction of the bow before we see it. A crowd composed of members of our guard— large, strong male and female elves, who are said to have the quickest hands and smoothest battle technique in all the kingdoms. They stand in an oblong circle with their eyes set to the two Elves in the center. It's a battle. I can't see the details of them from where I stand, but I can see the flash of their mighty, wide-bladed swords as the sun dies behind them, slowly setting into the horizon.

The smaller Elf takes a swing, the crowd takes a collective breath and when his sword comes down, the larger Elf dances out of the way of his blade and the crowd cheers wildly.

I push my way closer; Diekin remains hot on my heels. Other than the other night with Diekin and the Rogue Elf, I've never seen two Elves fight before. The two Elves are shirtless, and both have shimmering blond hair that flows down their backs, swishing and moving with every sharp thrust. When I'm close enough, I recognize his large sword first, the glowing tattoos on his back second. When he circles around, I can see his face and I freeze in place—my Corrik is one of the fighters.

"Sassem, Kiya!" Diekin shout-whispers. "We should go —I didn't realize Corrik would *be* here."

But I can't take my eyes off him.

No amount of Diekin's gentle tugs can tear me away. I

thought him devastatingly beautiful when he prowled on top of me, but that's nothing in comparison to his raw beauty as he handles his sword. The muscles in his back flex, and move like serpents beneath his skin as he retracts his arm and slams into his opponent. He circles back (I don't think he's seen me) and rounds on his combatant; the blade drives straight into the Elf's stomach. The match ends there and Corrik wins; healers are called to tend to the fallen Elf.

"Who dares challenge me next?" There's rage coursing through Corrik. I can sense the violence in the air, even this far away and I know his anger is my fault. He's been trying to hide it from me; my disobedience brings this out in him with his only release to either fuck me or punish me, but he can't do either the way he would like to at the moment. He still treats me delicately because of the attacks—he needs the violence of this.

Diekin is right to try to take us out of here before Corrik sees us. Corrik will be furious if he finds us here, but this is probably the only chance I'll have. I was able to show him earlier today that I'm smarter than he thinks I am I can prove I'm a good fighter too, by giving him the chance to test my skills for himself.

"Diekin. Go," I whisper back. I'd rather suffer Corrik's wrath on my own. I don't want Diekin in any more trouble than he's in. I step forward.

"I challenge you," I say.

Corrik looks down the tunnel of people to see who belongs to the voice that challenged him. He spies me and his look turns from enraged to murderous.

"Hand me your sword," I ask whoever's standing next to me without bothering to see who I'm asking. I long to feel the weight of steel within my grasp again. There was once a time when a sword was an extension of my arm. I practiced every day from sunrise to sunset, but my new husband is going to make sure I never touch a sword again.

"If anyone dares place a sword in his hand, that person's life will be forfeit," he decrees.

The crowd backs away from me as if I'm Death's cold hand, leaving Corrik room to head straight for me. With sword still drawn, he moves to stand in front of me like a guard warding all the others away as if he expects someone else will decide to fight me in his place. He doesn't sheath his sword until the crowd disperses.

Corrik towers over *both* Diekin and I—since Diekin decided not to leave, of course. Corrik is so beautiful, he looks celestial, and it hurts my paltry human eyes to look at him for too long. Now, he is beautiful in a different way, he is the angel fallen that I've seen before; dark, stone, livid and through the calm façade he keeps despite his building rage, I see the part of Corrik that is creature. His lips pull back just enough to reveal his sharp eyeteeth.

"Brother Diekin," he snaps. "I believe you have studies to tend to in your chambers."

"Yes, sir," he says with a small shake in his voice and scampers off.

"And you, will come with me."

I follow behind Corrik with dread. I sense I've done something unforgivable. When we reach our chambers, he grabs my wrist, slams the doors behind us and then slams me into the door. His eyes have tinted to a deep violet, closer to black. His anger crackles around him and his breath is slow, predatory, expanding his ribcage full but deflating it only halfway. It seems to get bigger with every ragged breath. The restraint I've come to recognize is there but it's loosening. It won't hold this time.

I can't fix this or calm him. It's too late.

Corrik yanks his body away from me with great force (though I think he'd rather slam it into me) and turns over the desk I'd worked at earlier, throwing it at the wall. The chair is demolished shortly after that, the oil lamp next and so on and so forth until one by one, the items in our room are destroyed by his temper. What he wants to hurt me.

When he's run out of things to destroy (save the bed, though the bed has not escaped without injury) he turns to me, still plastered against the wall. "I want to hurt you," he admits. "You are disobedient and disrespectful. Not knowing our ways is no excuse for what you've done. I've made my authority on this matter plain."

"Then, hurt me." It hits me in that moment, the impact of seeing his rage, the disappointment; what I need in return of the experience is physical.

"And give you one more reason in your Markaytian sense of morals to hate me? To misbehave? To disrespect me?"

I want to point out that I don't hate him anymore and I've told him so, but I don't think it matters much at this point. Silence seems the best course.

"I love you, Tristan, but I don't want to right now. I'm leaving, and you're staying here. Get on the bed and do not move an inch off of it."

That's all he says and then he's gone. I think my heart just broke a little bit.

Well, it didn't take long for me to fuck everything up. Father was right about me. I push for my way and I don't give in until I've sent everything crumbling to the underworld.

I don't know how long I've been lying here, but I don't even *think* about leaving the bed. I have to pee. If it comes to it, I'll pee in the glass on the bedside table, I'm not moving. I've gone too far this time and I know it. Corrik might decide he's done with me.

I don't expect my chest to hurt this much. I didn't think I would ever care what Corrik felt about me. I told myself I would be nothing more than his concubine. My imagination invented all kind of tales. I would wait in his bed all day until he returned to fuck me, till he had his fill. Maybe some days, I would be chained to his bed like a pet and then made to beg him to fuck me until I was wild with need only to be left for a few more hours, aching and unsatisfied.

"Down boy," I say. My cock likes the images—I think I need help.

But I'm getting away from the point, which is, I thought I'd be meaningless to him, except I'm not. He *loves* me. *Loves me.* Got fucking blindsided by that one. '*I love you Tristan, but I don't want to right now.*' Those words run across my mind over and over.

And he calls me Tristan.

That must cost him every time. He wants to use my Elvish name, most likely because *he* chose it for me. Corrik wants to own me in every way.

Some of the ways he owns me, I can't say I mind. Like sex—I love him owning my body during sex.

I equally love it when he's tender and makes me feel like I'm the most precious thing in the world. No matter which way he takes me, it's bound to leave me breathless and needy. I can never get enough of him being inside me, I can never get enough of having him on top of me.

Afterward, he pulls me to him and declares me 'his' without words and then sings his soft Elvish lullaby.

Is all of that over now?

Time passes. I pee in the glass. I fall asleep.

Corrik doesn't come back.

CHAPTER 16

$\mathcal{I}$ wake up alone.

The bed is cold beside me. Corrik never returned or at least I think that until I see the note. Sitting up, I notice the glass I peed in is gone and in its place, a note written in lovely Elvish script, but thankfully in Markaytian.

Tristan,

I did not mean to be so tyrannical. You may of course relieve yourself as needed. Please attend to your studies.

Corrik

It's impersonal, but it's not a letter of termination and this means he came back to check on me. I take a long, hot bath, contemplating the situation I've weaved myself into. When I enter the front room, I expect to find catastrophe, but the debris has been cleared away and there's new furniture in place of the old. It's not the same furniture, each piece has been replaced down to the oil lamp mounted on the wall above the desk. A fire is burning and there's food left for me. I get to work.

I take this to mean he wants to keep me at least. No point in me continuing to learn Elvish if we are returning to Markaytia, *right*?

For the first part of the morning, I do well and work through three chapters, until I read: *hymwy,* or '*to fight*' in Elvish.

"Hymwyn," I say out loud. *Figures it's easy for me to say.*

Damn it! I close the book. This is hard. I want to obey Corrik, but it's im-bloody-possible. Without a sword, without getting up to practice every day, I don't know who I'll be. The concubine part I can live with, enjoy it even—I'll do whatever he asks of me in bed even if it's to be his bed-chained-love-slave, but the other, being a pampered doll—it's my worst nightmare.

It's nightfall by the time my husband returns and I'm not quite as forgiving as I was last night. Now I feel abandoned, alone, and not so generous to the one Corrik Cyredanthem. The door creaks open and I turn from my desk to glare at him. "Where have you been?"

My voice drops off to nothing as I watch him swarm in, black and menacing. He's dressed like I've never seen him. Corrik always wears white, but now he's wearing a long black coat, black pants and leather boots that reach the underside of his knees and click on the hardwood floors.

"On the ship," he says, like he's not dressed any differently than usual.

I maintain my bravery, like the dragon warrior I am, and throw the book at him. He catches it without exerting any effort. "Do not patronize me," I say.

"Or, what?"

That deflates me. I can't think of anything I'm willing to do at the moment.

"That's what I thought," Corrik says, and smirks circling around me and placing the book on the table. His look is predatory, like he's come to eat me, but not in the way I would prefer. "I was hoping to find you in a better disposition after some time alone."

"You would have done, if you'd returned last night instead of ordering me not to move off the bed and making it so I had to pee in a glass. A glass, Corrik." I didn't care last night, and I don't care that much now but I know he feels somewhat bad about it and I'm using it against him.

"Which is why I've decided you've had enough punishment for this transgression, but I will not be so easy on you in future. I'll not be easy on you in general anymore."

I stare at him for what feels like a long time.

"Fair," I say, but am in no mood to speak with him further. I turn back to my work.

"You do not dismiss me, I dismiss you."

My hands ball into fists; I want to punch his smug face.

"Up," he commands. I obey him without grace, stand and cross my arms trying to recreate on my face the withering look he usually gives me. It doesn't work.

"Kneel."

I don't expect the command and hesitate to look at him sharply.

"Now, Kathir."

I do begrudgingly.

"Uncross your arms."

"Corrik, what is the meaning of this?"

"Now."

I let my arms hang stiffly by my sides, furious.

193

"Sit back on your heels, yes like that, good." He looks over my posture hungrily and I swear I hear him purr. I have no idea what he plans on doing with me and I'm too stunned to ask questions.

"Remove your shirt."

Is this a sex game perhaps? Hoping it will be, I comply with a tiny glimmer of excitement. "Good," he says when I'm half-naked. He takes my shirt from me and then his boots click across the room, muffling when they hit the carpet of our bedchamber. When he returns he's holding a riding crop. *A riding crop?*

Corrik towers above me when we are standing, kneeling, he looks like he's one of the Gods staring down at me. He studies me trying to read my thoughts and I can feel the build of his powerful energy, which he takes with him to sit on the armchair by the fire. I'm left kneeling by my desk.

"Come here, Kathir." I haven't missed that he keeps calling me by my Elvish name; I don't like it, but I'm grateful to rise from this kneeling position—it's already become tiresome. I move to stand.

"Crawl."

"You can't be serious," I sputter.

He turns his head to me in a deadly manner looking all the more fearsome, wielding that long black crop. "*Now.* Do not make me come get you."

I comply feeling ridiculous, and crawl to him, deciding it better to play into his little game—still with hopes of sex—than to anger him when he looks like that. His dominance is in full effect.

"Stop there. Face me," he instructs. His long black, booted calve is crossed over his thigh with his elbows on the armrests, the crop is held in his left hand, the leather tongue flexing and bending against the fingers of his right hand.

My back is to the fire and since I assume I'm to kneel again as before, I do, still wishing for the strength and tools to gut him.

"Good, boy," he says. *I'll kill him for that.* I can't help the growl that escapes. "Enough. You will be silent or I will make you be silent."

I wonder what that means, and I have lots of time to keep wondering. Now that he has me positioned how he wants me, he doesn't say a word and continues to play with the leather tongue of the riding crop. I fix my eyes on him and fume silently. *What is he up to? And how dare he force me to do this?* I am junior warlord of Markaytia—at least I was, *dragon born; dragon blood.*

"Eyes down; bow your head."

I oblige him, hoping if I do, I'll be released as soon as he's had his fill of whatever this is. I wait. I keep waiting for what feels like decades, until I can't take it anymore. *"Corrik."*

"Eyes down," he snaps.

"No. I've—"

Whack! He uses the dreaded riding crop to across my sensitive nipple.

"Ow! Corrik! *By the Gods.*"

Whack again. I get the hint when the riding crop hits my other nipple and clamp my mouth shut. He's standing over me again, this time daring me—hoping—I'll say another word or make another move so he can hit me again. He likes it. Corrik smiles serenely—he's in his element. "Eyes. Down."

I look down at the floor where his boots are, they are as fastidious as he is. I continue to stare at them until his boots click away and he resumes sitting on the armchair. I can't see them, but I can feel his eyes on me. They watch me and savor. Me kneeling before him like this brings him peace.

"Yes Corrik," he says.

"Huh?" I look up and remember too late my eyes are to be on the floor. My nipples are each assaulted with the crop and I have to rub them with my hands to get the sting out.

"Take your hands away. Did I say you could touch yourself?" He waits.

"No?"

"No, Corrik. Say it," he demands.

"No, Corrik."

"Better." That's all he offers, then the bastard sits down again, comfortable as you please, while my knees press against the wood floor and ache. I squirm, uncomfortable and Corrik lets me know he can make it a whole lot more uncomfortable for me by whacking my poor, stinging nipples again. I twist this time and contract my muscles, trying to pull the pain away from them and keep my hands off.

"Thank me for correcting you."

'Fuck that,' I say without words. He hears it loud and clear anyway and uses the crop on my chest this time. My eyes sting with tears. "Corrik that bloody well *hurts.*"

He hits me harder for speaking out of turn; I inhale sharply, but I say nothing more.

"Now, *apologize* and thank me for correcting you."

I don't want to apologize to him, and I don't want to thank him for beating my nipples, but I do want him to hit me less.

"I'm sorry. Thank you for correcting me."

That Gods damn leather tongue of the evil black rod is lashing my nipples again. *What did I do?*

"I'm sorry, *Corrik*. Thank you for correcting me, *Corrik*. *Say* it."

"I'm sorry, Corrik. Thank you for correcting me, Corrik." When I get out of this position, I will hurt him. I don't know how, just that I will—if Diekin survived Corrik's wrath, maybe he'll help me.

"Good, boy. Now remain still and silent. Eyes down," he says again as I eye the black rod with dread. *Why does that thing hurt so much?* It must be imbibed with Elven magic. I can still feel every place he's marked and count each welt without looking.

Now that I know what's in store for me, I'm silent as a mouse. I can guarantee Corrik's not going to hear a peep out of me but remaining stationary is another story. My legs are aching all up my thighs and my shoulders begin to strain after more time has passed.

The whole time, Corrik watches.

I move several more times and earn more chastisement. Each time I'm expected to thank Corrik for correcting me. Each time I do.

Finally, he's decided I've had enough. *He* could never tire of whatever game this is, I'm sure. I accept his action for the mercy it is—I don't think he minds my discomfort, I think he relishes in it.

I hear him rise from his seat and his boots click over to me. He grabs my chin and tilts it up toward him gently, while I gaze at him, too stunned to move. "You have done well, my Tristan," he says, his eyes shine with pride and I get warm all over. His praise melts me instantly and I forget about killing him. Corrik doesn't look at me like that often, but when he does, I feel like the most important thing in the world—I can't tear my eyes away and hope he'll look at me forever.

He didn't call me by my Elvish name, he called me Tristan—my brain searches to find a meaning to all of this.

He releases my chin. "Now press your forehead to the floor while maintaining that position with your arse on your heels."

In a euphoric daze, I don't question his instruction and put my forehead to the floor. Naturally, I stretch my arms above my head. It's like I'm bowing to someone of great royalty and well; I suppose I am.

"Very good, Kathir. Remember all I have taught you tonight. Sleep well." I know he's about to leave so I break my position. "Corrik, wait. Don't leave me alone again, tonight. *Please.*" I might have been a scary junior warlord, but that didn't stop me sleeping in Lucca's bed some nights. I don't care for sleeping alone.

"I don't recall telling you to rise," he says.

"No Corrik," I say as I have all night. It feels like a meditation after kneeling for so long, with nothing to focus on but the floor and the sharp pain on my skin from Corrik's riding crop. I've entered a new state. I like it—it's calming and I'm crazy aroused.

"Apologize, return to your position and I will let it go, *if* I like your apology."

If he likes it? What's that supposed to mean? I'm not sure how to make him like it. I resign to feeling the sting of his evil little stick again. I bow as low as I can, forehead to the floor. "I'm sorry, Corrik. Please forgive me?" I don't look up and leave my back open for whatever he decides to give it. I'm still feeling that slight euphoria, just this side of awareness.

"Acceptable, but I want you to work on that or it will be five lashes next time, in a place of my choosing."

A shiver runs straight to my cock when he says that; I've

gone from anger and resentment, to captivated by his every word and movement. My cock strains and I hope he will say more things like that. Whatever's he's done to me this evening, I like it.

"Yes Corrik," I say without thinking. I can feel pleasure leak off him.

He crouches over me and cards his fingers through my long, black hair like I'm a treasured pet. "Very, good. You were made for this, Tristan. I know you don't understand yet, but in this I can give you the patience you requested. I will enjoy teaching you." He presses a kiss to the back of my neck. "Go to bed, my love. I will see you in the morning."

CHAPTER 17

*C*orrik doesn't return. I miss him and I'm getting serious cabin fever, but once again there is a note.

Tristan.

 Do not leave this room. Be ready for me after dinner.

 Corrik

I crumple it up and toss it into the fire. I'm no fool. I know what *'be ready for me,'* means. he wants me ready and kneeling like last night. I remember how it made me feel. I liked it and I wouldn't mind doing that again.

But I can take no more of this confinement.

Etched into my mind is 'the Corrik' from last night and my body feels inclined to obey him. The only protest I dare is lazing about for the first part of the day, instead of working from Cupper's book. I eat and I stare out the window, but eventually become so bored, I read another seven chapters.

Finally, it's after dinner. I look to the door like he'll come in any moment, but return my eyes to the ground quickly, in case he should catch me with my eyes up. I'm shirtless and kneeling as before, in front of the fire, but facing the armchair he sat in the night before. My head is bowed, and I've picked a spot on the floor to look at. I've made a few extra enhancements to my person, with the hopes of inviting him into sex. I brushed my hair to silk and massaged a lotion onto my body that makes me smell like a summer's day—*a fearsome summer's day*. I may have spent most of my life chaste, but in the short time I've been with Corrik, I've gotten used to being relieved every night. My cock hurts and is already straining at the thought of kneeling while he watches over me with those menacing eyes and hungry teeth.

I hear when he arrives, but I don't look up—I don't need to, his energy surrounds me. I see his black boots stop before me and I catch the hem of the long black jacket he wore last night—I can smell the leather.

"Have you any idea how much I want you? Especially when you kneel like this?"

I hope it's enough to fuck me.

"I intend to have you, but not until we finish the night's lesson."

Lesson? Is that what all this is?

"After that, I intend to ram my cock into your pretty little mouth." He snaps himself away from me and sits in the armchair once again. His words make my cock ache more than before and send a warm buzz to my groin. I can't see if he's brought the riding crop or some other weapon of torture, but I'm sure I'll find out soon enough.

"Your posture is good, but I want your hands behind your back tonight."

I move to do his bidding as he instructs. "Clasp your hands together with fingers interlaced—yes like that—arms straight, no bend in the elbow. Yes. Good."

I feel like a pretty trophy on display and wonder at the point of all this. I don't like being treated as a pampered doll, but this is different. This I like. I like his eyes on me the way they are now, I like being here for his pleasure if he chooses it or as nothing more than something to toy with, if that's all he desires. My cock likes it very much and my breath quickens.

He's quiet again, like he was last night. I know if I say anything, he'll whack me with the crop I know he's hiding somewhere, and my skin is still sore to the touch from last night's administrations. More than that, I'm hoping for some of the same kind of praise I received last night when I complied with his instruction.

I wait patiently in my position, until my muscles ache. This isn't an easy position to hold. My toes feel like they will break from the weight of me, and my thighs burn. All the muscles in my back scream around the same time my shoulders do, and I drops of sweat form at my brow. I think of other things. *What is Lucca doing at this very moment?* I smile thinking that he's most likely entertaining a 'guest' or 'guests' as is the usual case with him. He didn't seem to care —male or female—he's had plenty of both. I sometimes wonder what it would've been like to be with a woman, but I've always held a stronger attraction to men. Lucca hinted on our last day together that he preferred men too. Will he end up with a man? Or will a woman capture his heart? I guess I'll never know.

My thoughts swim in that direction for a while. I don't

feel as sad as I once did about never seeing my family again. I'll always miss them of course, and feel fondly for them, but Papa taught me not to linger in the past for too long. He said it could consume a person, trap them there and never allow them to step foot into their future.

It's high time for me to put his wisdom to good use. My life is in Mortouge as an Elf and as husband to the insane Elf that has me kneeling before him. He mentioned my 'pretty little mouth.' I hope he'll use it soon.

"In moments like these it's hard to believe you've had no training at all. Well, no formal training at least. I'm certain you've absorbed some of your papa's behaviors." He reaches out to stroke my long hair; he seems to be thinking something over.

"Stand up."

I do, keeping my eyes to his polished boots and my arms behind me, fingers interlaced. His long, slender fingers reach to the waistband of my pants and I inhale sharply. He's deliberate, yet primal as he undresses me, releasing my throbbing, bouncing, cock—*no I'm not wearing any underthings.*

When I'm standing naked before him, he gently caresses my cock and fondles my balls—if he doesn't fuck me tonight, I think I'll die.

"You like this very much, don't you? Answer me."

"Yessss, Corrik," I hiss.

His eyes are feral and his posture is taut as a spring; he's holding himself back again. "Kneel."

I stifle a groan, not wanting to get back in the painful position, the short reprieve not enough relief for my tired muscles, but I sense we are on the verge of the things my cock wants and I'll not tarnish the opportunity. I sink down and urge him by nipping at his cock that is barricaded by smooth leather. Corrik almost gives himself away when his hips push minutely toward me, but he refrains and grasps my chin so I look up at him. "Do you want me to fuck your mouth, beautiful boy?"

"Please, Corrik." I hope he'll do much more than that.

He allows me to watch him unzip the leather pants that are a muted, almost grey-black and releases his large Elven member. He's proud of that cock and he should be. It's magnificent. I lean forward to take him in my mouth and he pulls back. "I don't think so. There will be rules."

Rules?

"You will keep your hands behind your back. Do you need me to bind them for you?"

"No, Corrik."

"The punishment for failure will be severe. Are you certain?"

"Yes, Corrik."

He smiles. "My ambitious little Markaytian—you please me." He moves forward so his cock is against my lips; I can smell him, but I don't dare lick him.

"Open your mouth," he says, as he grabs a fist full of my hair in his hand so he can control my head. I do and he slams his cock into me. It reaches the back of my throat. I gag; he keeps going.

"Hold still," he growls when I squirm as I fight for breath, with tears streaming down my cheeks. "Relax, Kathir. I know your limits. I will not harm you."

Harm is different than hurt, I know that. There is pain involved in this, but I will not be damaged. I want to make it through, for him, so I force myself to relax, and it gets easier, but I still gag, and it still elicits tears.

Finally, he's coming down my throat and I drink him in

greedily—his cock doesn't lose its hardness, even once I've sucked his cock dry.

My cock hurts. Corrik is gone and I'm alone with a hard on from the sixth level of the underworld. I'm still naked, but I'm lying in darkness with only the light from the moon to play across my copper skin. He's unhappy, my cock that is. He's thinking of the times from before when I would have to wait for Corrik to send word that I could relieve myself. He would ache and plead with me to touch him. This isn't much different.

Before he left Corrik made it clear that if I so much as looked at my cock, he'd know about it, and he'd make me regret it. Not that I would have touched my cock anyway, I've long since grown used to Corrik controlling what I do and what I don't do with my cock. I try to sleep after that, but no such luck. Instead, I spend close to an hour thinking over this new side of Corrik I've been experiencing.

This is who Corrik really is. He's been withholding this from me. The restraint I saw on our wedding night, his leniency with me, he's been allowing how I might react to decide how much 'Elven lifestyle' he introduces to me.

He's realized that does us no favors and I'm glad for it. This is my life now, to do as Corrik says, and I wish he'd been this way from the beginning.

I love being this for him and I'm enjoying the exploration.

With my thoughts in order, I'm able to drift off to sleep but a noise wakes me. When I open my eyes, a large Elf is sitting there, but it's not Corrik.

I know danger and I can sense it before it happens.

"Calm down, human," a deep voice says. "I will not harm you, *yet*."

The Elf is decidedly a 'he,' though I cannot make out more than his silhouette in the dark and he sits in the armchair in the corner of the room at the end of the bed.

"How did you get in here?" I calm down but remain on edge. I think about the dagger I know is somewhere among Corrik's things, but I doubt I can get to it. I've seen Elves move in battle, they're fast, much faster than any human.

From what I can see of his profile, he's got long hair like most Elves, and a set of wide shoulders. His fingers are steepled with his elbows resting on his knees. He doesn't seem in any rush and I can tell he's thinking about what to do next, like he's making things up as he goes along.

"I can do anything, remember that Junior Warlord," he says my old title mockingly. He's speaking in my home language. I'm not surprised. Not only is Markaytian the most common language throughout all the kingdoms, Diekin said Elves learn many languages. I suppose that extends to Rogue Elves too.

"Fine, you can do anything so either kill me or be gone, I've no wish to speak with you." I sit up and cross my arms. I may not be able to see him, but he can most likely see me.

I don't expect his laughter. "You're brave—I like it."

"I don't know what you know of warlords, but yes, usually we are brave," I say arching my brow. "What do you want?"

"I don't know," he drawls. "I thought I wanted to kill you, but I watched you sleeping—"

"—that's fucking, creepy."

"I watched you sleeping," he snaps over my insult. "And I find I like the look of you."

That's still creepy. One too many Elves are infatuated

with my so-called good looks and watching me sleep. "I'm already a concubine to one Elf, thanks," I say, holding up my ringed hand.

"Yes, but are you happy? Perhaps I can make you happy? What is it you wish for most, Warlord? I will give you your heart's desire."

I don't miss he's dropped the 'junior' from my old title. "Why would I go with you? I don't even know who you are —I can't even see you."

"My apologies. I am Prince Andothair Tar-Jian of the Aldrien Elves or Rogue Elves as we have been dually named. You may call me Ando—that may be easier for you to pronounce. I do not think I could suffer hearing you butcher it."

Are all the Elves who are interested in me this impossibly arrogant?

"Why wouldn't you want to go with me? I know you are unhappy with Corrik; I've promised you something better. It's—what do you Markaytians call it? Oh yes, a no brainer."

"We also have another saying. It's better to trust the evils you know—"

"—than the evils you don't know. Yes, I know that one too. I know quite a lot about your Markaytia and Markaytian culture."

"Then you'll know I couldn't possibly go with you. We've signed a treaty with the Mortougian Elves. Markaytians are nothing if not duty and honor bound."

"Not if I make it look like an abduction."

"Why not just abduct me now, then? We both know you out power me. Why bother asking my permission?"

"Because," he hisses. "I am unable to take you off the ship without your cooperation at this time. If I have your permission however..."

"So, you cannot do everything?" I pretend to be shocked.

He pauses, remembers what he told me a moment ago then laughs a pleasant laugh. "Touché. Most things, then. I could still take you, but I would have to wait, and I do not wish to wait."

"Well, that is how it shall have to be, an abduction, a *real* abduction. I am duty bound; I will not authorize you taking me."

"You will not authorize it, but you do not forbid it. Interesting."

"I—I didn't say that."

"You did not have to."

I glare at him hard because of what he's implying, *but I don't want to leave Corrik, do I?* No, he's playing mind games with me. It must be some kind of Elven Voodoo. I change the subject. "You must be horribly disfigured or why else would you hide in the shadows?" I say to goad him into coming out, but he laughs again, this time trying to restrain himself from laughing loudly.

"I know you are trying to anger me. You also know why I hide in the dark; I do not wish to alert anyone of my presence. So, what say you? I think I could keep you entertained."

"You must think me a grand fool. Your kind has done nothing but try to kill me and now I'm supposed to believe that's over because all the blood has suddenly gone to your cock?"

"Yes. Attempting to have you killed was a mistake. I wish to atone for it. Come with me and I will."

"No."

"Is that your answer then?"

"It is. I won't go with you so kill me."

"Ah. Don't be in such hurry to die, Warlord, you've only just begun to live. I find I cannot kill a creature of such beauty. I have new plans for you," he says suddenly decided.

Elves. Damn them all. I wish I never laid eyes on the Gods forsaken creatures.

"Sleep, now, Tristan. I will come for you."

"If you think I'm going to be 'a good boy' and go to sleep, you're the fool."

"Very, well."

It only takes me an instant to know he's done something because I feel drowsy and can't keep my eyes open. I fight it with everything I have, but it's nothing compared to his powers, and I feel myself fall back to my pillow and my eyes close.

I feel him move close to me now, but I can't see him with my eyes closed and I can't move because the paralysis of sleep has already ensnared me. I can only sense him above me—he could softly slit my throat if he wanted, and I could do nothing.

"Sleep," I hear him repeat. "I will come for you." His lips press to mine. They're soft and full of unleashed mirth; I want to stop him, but I'm nothing but a lamb for slaughter. He doesn't slaughter me though, just kisses me—feasting on me.

"Mmmhmmm," he says. "I like how you taste."

CHAPTER 18

I jump up out of bed ready for battle.

I'm panting and looking around for a weapon —anything. No more talking, I'll try to take a stab at the arrogant prick and maybe that will convince him to kill me or be gone. I won't cry for help. That won't be my dying breath.

I look around wildly, but the room is empty. He's gone.

Wait, not empty—Corrik is beside me. He's up in a flash having heard me stir. He's naked, nothing but his long golden hair to cover his pale flesh.

"Tristan?"

"Huh? Corrik?"

"Yes, it's only me. I'm sorry to have scared you."

I want to tell him he didn't scare me, but him thinking that will work to my advantage.

"It's all right," I say and calm my breath enough to offer him a warm smile. Maybe it was all some bizarre dream. I was pretty horny last night. *Can that affect the brain?*

"You're back," I breathe and realize I'm happy to see him.

He nods. "I'm back."

I pounce him. I've *missed* him. And I'm a closet cuddler. I wrap myself around his body and let him secure me in his arms. "Am I forgiven yet, Corrik?"

"I forgave you days ago," he says. "I can't seem to stay mad at you, you're the antidote to my temper."

I smile and close my eyes again, basking in this moment. I feel content and like maybe I've got a lot to look forward to.

W e shower together, but it's quiet. There's a new tension between us. I'm not sure how to act. In bed, everything makes sense, but outside of that, I'm unsure. Should I be the submissive, kneeling man from the past two evenings? Or am I allowed to be Tristan, as I am?

I tease him by running hands through my hair and down my body, accentuating my hardened appendage by sticking my ass out and grazing my groin, without touching my cock. Corrik is always hard. His hips jump at my seductive little dance and he bites his bottom lip. Aggressively, he turns me around and teases my pucker with his finger before kneeling and jamming his tongue in as far as it will go. I slap the wall with my hand and moan into the sensation.

"You like that?"

"Mmmhmmm, yes, Corrik."

He presses a finger into my wet hole; it's slick with lube —I swear Elves must have the stuff tucked into every crevice they inhabit. *Not that I'm complaining.* The burn feels good and makes me stick my ass out greedy for more. I hope he'll grab my cock, but I don't ask; he'll give me what he chooses and not a thing more.

He nibbles on my ear. "That's it my Tristan, fuck my fingers, ride them until you come."

I do as Corrik says and push back hungry, fucking his fingers until he slaps my ass hard and I do come in hot spurts over the marbled wall without him ever having to touch my cock.

I don't take time to bask in the afterglow of my orgasm, and I don't move without his permission. "May I suck your cock, Corrik?"

"Yessss," he says.

I get on my knees and swallow him whole, the hot spray of the shower washing over the pair of us.

"You are free," he tells me after we're dried and dressed.

"Free?"

"Yes. A dragon can only be caged so long, I know this," he says, giving me a rare smile. Corrik is actually teasing me, which means I'm rubbing off on him. "But you'll remember our lessons during this time, yes?"

I'm not sure what he means by that. Am I to be kneeling by his side from this point forward? I don't want to ask and look stupid, so I don't. "Yes, Corrik. Corrik?" I decide to change the subject.

"Yes?"

"Do the Rogue Elves have a prince?"

His face clouds over. "They have a few princes, and one of them is their warlord. Why do you ask?

"I had a strange dream last night," I tell him, and for a

brief moment I feel the ghost of the Rogue Elf's strong lips on mine. My possessive husband would not like that. It would send him into an angry fit. "I dreamt a Rogue Elf Prince came to visit me."

"As long as his name wasn't Andothair Tar-Jian, you'll be fine," he says.

Except it was. Icy cold shivers run up my arms and down my spine. If it was a dream, how would I know his name? It isn't a name my mind could invent. *I should tell Corrik.*

"What happened in the dream?"

"He said he was going to take me away from you."

I expect him to look vexed, but instead he looks touched. "At least your unconscious wants me," he says pleased.

But it wasn't about him, not really. I allow him to continue thinking it. I shake my head at him, trying to cover what's plaguing my mind: Ando. He's real, he was in my room last night and he's up to something. I'll tell Corrik as soon as I find out what that might be. If I tell him now, he'll be a nightmare to deal with and I can't spend another day confined to this room.

Thankfully, my stomach is my savior, growling loud enough for Corrik to hear. "By Ylor, that stomach of yours," he says.

"Is it an inconvenience, Corrik?"

"Never, love. Never. Come along, I enjoy keeping you fed."

We are alone in the dining room this morning. "Where is everyone, Corrik?"

"I asked them not to be here when we arrived."

"Why would you do such a thing?"

His eyes point meaningfully toward a pillow at the foot of his chair.

"Kneel."

"Corrik."

"I could spank you instead. This room isn't private, maybe we'll put on a show for people, after all?"

I clench my trembling fists and kneel, enraged at him. Kneeling for him when we're alone in our chambers is one thing, but this is entirely another.

"Good, boy." He takes the seat above me and pets my head. *I'm a pet now, am I?* Maybe I'm a pet that bites. I growl when he offers food toward me with his hand.

"Eat," he insists. My stomach groans—I'm too hungry to put up much of a protest, ruled by my hunger as usual. I take the piece of meat from his hand, deciding it will be easier to get through this meal doing as he asks rather than to fight him.

Only fight the battles you can win, Tristan.

Distracted by anger, it's not until halfway through the meal, I realize my cock is hard. Corrik hasn't said to kneel any particular way, but already my body has arranged itself to resemble what he taught me over the past two evenings. My wrists are clasped in each hand behind my back and my toes are tucked beneath me, the toe pads pressing into the ground. Corrik can sense my hard on like a lion senses meat.

The next food from his hand is not easy to come by. He pulls it upward through the air and makes me chase it with my mouth, I feel humiliated—my cock responds by twitching. *Pervy bastard my cock is.* I moan when Corrik rubs behind my ear as I finish chewing my prize: The meat I snatched out of the air.

He bends his head down to kiss me, hot and teasing, then pulls away as I'm left squirming on the pillow, trying to calm my stupid erection. Corrik is smiling. The man never smiles, but he is now, and I can see how beautiful he truly is. I suppose I don't mind eating from a pillow if it can make him that happy, I just wish I didn't like it so much.

He spends the rest of our breakfast feeding me, but not talking, yet stealing glances at me like he must be secretive about it. He hasn't said I'm not supposed to talk, but I understand that I'm not. I decide to anyway—I'm a disobedient 'pet.'

"There's no one here. If you wish to look upon my grand beauty, you may." I pretend I'm the one in charge.

His hand cinches my hair, a physical warning to behave and remind me I'm not the one in charge. "You are a brat, my love. It's fine now, but I'm *practicing*. It's not becoming for one of the royal court to spend too much time staring at his mate, but you fascinate me—I can't seem to stop looking at you. I can already hear my brother's lectures."

It's the first time he's mentioned his brother. I decide to be more insolent and pursue it. Bravery, fueled by the new comfort that has settled between us has hold of me this morning. When his grip on my hair relaxes, I get up and move toward him, he pushes his chair out from the table and I straddle myself across his lap. "And what if we did this? What would your brother say?"

He breathes in my scent and sucks at my ear. "He'd say nothing. This would be okay." His lips smirk against mine. I pull away.

"You can't *look* at me, but I can straddle your lap and fondle you as I please?"

Corrik's glowing with happiness, I've never seen the man smile so much, what is with him this morning?

He nods. "Particular behaviors are expected in each position. Whenever I instruct you to kneel before me, we are both expected to act formally and respect each other accordingly. Once I dismiss you," he says pointedly, because he has yet not dismissed me, "the formal contract is broken. We are free to be open." I'm sure he can see my spinning thoughts. "Do not worry, D'orhai. I will teach you. We'll learn together." He places a soft kiss on my lips.

"Diekin says you and your brother don't get along."

Whatever spell he's under this morning is broken and his smile vanishes. "Diekin often exaggerates," he says shaking his head. "But, yes, my brother is often displeased with me."

"I find that hard to imagine."

"You won't have to imagine for long. We are nearly home. Just a few more weeks north after we dock."

"Home? Corrik, have we reached Mortouge so soon?"

"Soon? We've been traveling weeks."

"Still, it seems like we left yesterday," I say and as soon as the words leave my mouth, I realize what I've said.

"Have I been that entertaining?" Corrik smirks like he's won the prize of all prizes and he knows I won't like it.

I take advantage of the uncharacteristically playful mood I find my Elf in today. "No. It's been quite exhausting looking after your cock day after day."

"Hogwash. You said and I quote, 'it seems like we left yesterday.'" He attempts an impression of me. "I think you like living with me."

"It has its moments," I say.

He looks at me a long time, like he's trying to read my mind and is frustrated because he can't. There is real fear present in what he's about to share. "Tristan, do you think you could ever love me? I've shown you some of who I am, who I really am and what I mean us to be. Could you love a *creature* like me? I know I'll never deserve you. I know I took you away from your family. I know I bar you from the destiny you wanted. I've no right to ask you to love me, but I still want it."

The Elf is in pain and he's babbling. I want to make him feel better, and tell him I love him, but I don't know. I've come to care for him a great deal, but only the Gods know what the future will bring. I brush the shimmery gold hair out of his violet eyes and kiss his forehead. "I shouldn't even like you after what you've done, but I find it harder every day to hold that against you. But love? I'd say that it's not impossible now. I already care for you a great deal, Corrik Cyredanthem."

His smile returns, brighter than I've ever seen it. He sighs, contented. "If that is all you ever give me, I can live with that. I love you, Tristan, no matter what. Never doubt it." He presses his thumb to my lower lip and peels it down, I move toward him and we meet in a wild kiss that sends my groin pressing into his belly.

We're interrupted by a knock at the door.

"Enter."

"Prince Corrik, your father has requested your presence, immediately. There's been another attack on the top deck."

Impossible, the ship was searched, several times over. No. Not impossible—I remember the dream that was maybe not a dream.

The prince and I both look at each other. I wonder if

he'll leave me here with a babysitter and he wonders if I'll argue.

"Have they apprehended the criminal?"

"He is dead, Sire, but we do not yet know if there are others."

"Come along then, Tristan," he says pushing me off his lap. "You're not leaving my sight."

I can barely believe he's going to take me with him. I stay close, grab his hand and together we rush headlong into whatever we're about to meet.

"How do they keep getting on board?" Corrik growls, and slams his hand on the table, at the row of guards before him. They are his royal guard. Diekin is not among them.

"We don't know, Sire," says a large male Elf with black hair.

"Well, find out!"

The Elf scurries out with six others behind him and Corrik is left glaring at the wall, immobile as a statue. I'm the only one brave enough to approach him.

"Corrik—"

He whips around, fury burning through him, his body coiled with restraint.

"Take him away," he shouts, at the remaining guards and it's my turn to glower. I struggle in vain as two guards grab me roughly.

I know better than to say anything in front of everyone, but I make my feelings clear enough without a word. He's locking me up again. *I wonder if Ando would lock me up?* Probably.

"Corrik, wait," the king says. He hasn't spoken in all the time Corrik raged over the events of this morning. At the king's words, the guards freeze, but they still hold me tight.

"I know they have killed Emmery, this is grievous, but we cannot lose our heads. You cannot simply lock up your husband—the time has come for him to be armed."

"No."

"I have been far too lenient if you think you may tell me, no," the king says, letting his words fall upon Corrik, daring him to say more. He doesn't.

"Good then. Tristan. Come before me."

The guards release me, and I go to kneel before the king. Even when Corrik is acting like a bull-headed, ass, I still desire to make him proud of me.

"Purinettira—pass me that over there."

The queen produces something long and wrapped in layers of purple, silken cloth; she hands it to the king. I check in with Corrik; yep he's still burning with unleashed rage, better to keep focused on the king's boots and whatever he's got wrapped in that cloth, although I think if he gave me three guesses, I'd get it on the first try.

"You come from dragon's blood and you have trained all your life to be a warrior. Be that as it may, a Markaytian is defenseless against an Elf and that is why I had this made. This is for you."

Before me, he unveils a sword like I have never seen before. Forged with Elven magic, the blade glistens without the help of sunlight and upon its surface are words written in Elvish.

'He who wields this blade...' I make out but cannot read the rest; I'll have to consult with Cupper's book. The hilt and cross guard are simple in design but made of fine Elven gold and steel. The pommel rounds at the end, carved as

part of the hilt. Without touching it, I can feel a power from within—it is not just forged with magic but imbibed with it.

I look wide eyes up at the king.

"This will protect you, my new son, when others cannot. Take it."

I rise at the king's urging. Corrik growls again but will not dishonor his father by speaking out. I can scarcely believe I'm being given this sword, even as I hold it in my hand and unsheathe it. I can't help but swing it around and circle it in arcs and before I realize it, I'm showing off a bit; my glee is undeniable. The balance is fluid, the weight perfect for my height; I couldn't ask for a better sword and I happily admit it's far better than the one I had back home. I get lost in the dance and I swing around, smack into Corrik. He stops me with one hand firm around my wrist, his nose half an inch from my forehead. I can feel his hot breath.

"Put it away."

I nod carefully and sheathe it, pulling the baldric around my head to allow the sword to rest at my left hip. I keep my eyes to my feet not wanting to challenge him now.

"We will arrive at Port Gilkara in the morning, what do we do until then?" Corrik demands of his father, while his eyes still rest on me. "We don't know where they're coming from and we don't know how to stop them."

"A constant vigil of course, as we've always done, there's not much more we can do than that, Corrik."

I finally look up to catch something passing over Corrik's eyes, a light, like they've been scanned by a sunbeam.

"Something's wrong." He runs out the doors, with me close behind him—I let a few of the guard filter out in front of me and when I exit, I see what he felt.

A massacre: fallen Elves and the strange humans everywhere, Corrik already fighting.

"Tristan!" It's the king; he grabs my arm. "Go. Find Diekin. We need every Elf available." I nod, my sword announcing its arrival with the ring of steel.

I keep hidden as I make my way to the lower deck where Diekin's chambers are. I doubt he's there, but it's the only place I can think to start. The halls of the ship are lit with the natural light of the sun, but feel eerie in their emptiness.

I listen for footsteps, but the chance of me hearing anything is slim—Elves are slippery and able to move silently, beyond the hearing of mere humans. If there are any around, they've most likely heard me already. I press against a wall and hold my breath. I will be strong, I will be brave, I will—

"*Mmmph!*" So much for that plan. With a hand over my mouth, an Elf drags me into a room I don't recognize, fortunately, the voice I do.

"Shhh. It is me Junior Warlord. Don't move, I'll be right back."

He's out the door before I get the chance to say anything else. I hear the clanging of swords and the sound of a body being run through. I close my eyes and hope it's not Diekin.

It's not.

"Come with me—keep your sword out." He looks happy to be able to say that to me; I'm certain Diekin would love to see me fight.

Keeping close to him, I remain quiet until I see the smoke. "Diekin, look over there."

"They've set fire to the ship," he says.

We run now, and Diekin fights through Rogue Elves, as we go, not letting them get at me. It's now that I notice he's only half dressed—he's not wearing a shirt and I can see he's got a surface wound across his broad chest; it's glistening with blood.

When several Elves surround us, Diekin throws me a, worried look: He thinks as Corrik does, that I can't fight Elves and I know from my first experience that they're right. It doesn't mean I won't die trying. I stand back-to-back with him; it reminds me of when Lucca and I fought. I pretend it's the same.

They descend on us and Diekin fights like I've never seen him, but this time, he can't keep them away from me. I bring my sword up in time to prevent one from taking my head.

"No!" one of them yells at the one about to slice me. "He must be alive!"

It gives me the distraction I need, and I run him through, my new sword tastes blood for the first time, the impact of it igniting hits me and I'm thrown back into the circle of Elves. Two of them reach to grab me, but I'm suddenly stronger and faster as I hold the sword in my hand and swing at them with long practiced strokes. They look as surprised as I feel.

It's the sword—it's magic, the king had it made for me knowing I don't have the powers of Elves, knowing I'd need them. I continue to slice through these Elves, confident in the powers of the sword in combination with my own fighting abilities.

Diekin is doing well—he looks like he's having fun. I suppose he wants to amend for failing me earlier. I smile and keep slicing.

We do well and we're left with a pile of Rogue Elf bodies, twelve high.

"Tristan. You fought well." He's trying to hide his surprise.

"The king gave me this sword, it's magic," I explain, and I realize I'm feeling woozy.

"You don't look, so good. C'mon. We must get you back to Corrik. He'll lose it when he finds out you've come down here."

"King's orders."

"King's orders?" he says behind him as we run. "Sassem Ylor, kiya! What's happening up there leaving him with no choice but to send you off on your own?"

"A massacre," I say as we run up to the second deck. We're one floor from the top and from Corrik.

He skids to a halt. "Tristan, I have to get you out of here."

"Out of here? How, exactly?"

"There are lifeboats—if we go back to the lower deck, we can access them."

"No. We're not abandoning everyone."

"That's it," he says to himself. "That's what the king wanted—why he sent you to me. He wants me to get you off the ship, I'm sure of it. You're the most vulnerable."

"Diekin, no. Running away is dishonorable."

"Sack your Markaytian pride. You're coming with me if I have to knock you out and drag you."

"No," says a deep voice from behind. "He is coming with me."

I recognize Ando, immediately.

"Tristan, *run.*"

This time I don't hesitate, and I do run remembering the trouble I got Diekin into for not listening to his orders. I hear them fighting, Diekin and the prince of the Rogue Elves, and the sounds fade into the background as I head down the hallway. This ship is way too bloody huge. I still don't know its every turn, but I know I'm on the floor where Corrik's and my bedchambers are.

Two Elves chase me down a hallway and I turn right then left, hoping to force them into splitting up once they realize that if they do, they could surround me. My plan works better than I hoped, and I lose them completely. It's quiet and I don't know where to go. Should I plan on meeting Diekin at the lifeboats? Or head up to Corrik and the others? What if Diekin is right? What if the king wanted me off the ship? I have no idea so I decide I'll stick with Diekin's plan for now—*where are the damn stairs?* I make it down another hall and realize I'm near my and Corrik's room. I duck inside. Perhaps there are some items Diekin, and I could use for our journey.

My pack is sitting as always, on my side of the bed. I grab it and begin stuffing food inside. There is always a tray of fruit, dried meats and cheeses provided for me and Corrik. I dump as much as I can into my pack. There aren't any other weapons around—except my dagger, I realize. I don't know where Corrik hides it and I don't have a lot of time for looking so I quickly check through his bedside table. Nothing but too much lube, which I grab a bottle of, in the first drawer—who knows what I could use it for. In the second drawer, there's no dagger, but there is Papa's ring. I snatch it and stuff it into the front pocket. There's little time, I must leave, but I can't help feeling that dagger might be handy. I don't know what lies ahead for Diekin and I. I open the armoire, and rifle through more of Corrik's things. Nothing. I'm about to give up when I spy something glinting from beneath a pile of clothes.

"Gotcha," I say as I unearth it—still in its sheath. I tie it to my leg.

Someone falls inside the door, loud and sloppy. "There you are. We must go." Thank the Gods it's Diekin, but he's injured and bleeding worse than before. The surface wound across his chest has been slashed open; he's losing a lot of blood. Medicine! I grab lube, but no medicine. I know Corrik keeps some items in our room that have healing qualities. I run to those cupboards.

"Come! We have little time." His breath is labored.

I swing the pack over my back and give a last regret-filled look to the room and then turn to follow him.

That's when I see something move behind Diekin.

"*Diekin.*"

The Rogue Elf prince is there and runs his sword straight through Diekin's torso. Diekin falls unconscious, but I can see he is still breathing.

Andothair steps over his body like it's nothing more than a log. "Shall we then?"

"Fuck you."

"I thought you would say that."

My eyelids are heavy in an instant; last thing I feel is the ground meeting my body.

CHAPTER 19

*I*f I were to collect a gold coin for the number of times I've been naked on this venture, I would have more gold coins than the Markaytian king, I'm sure of it. And it's ironic you know because I've never actually had to collect gold coins. Of course, there was the time Lucca and I fashioned 'gold coins' out of hunks of bread. We wasted five loaves of fresh baked bread, chopping them up into pieces and painting them with gold paint. Father nearly had me hung for it. He said there were people in the village that starved, while I used food as a toy; I never felt so terrible. He made me bake bread with the chef for five weeks—a week for every loaf—and hand it out at the end of every day to those who needed it.

What I'm trying to say is, I'm naked, yet again and tied to what feels like a chair. I can't tell. Everything's still a bit foggy, I struggle as I come to. The first thing I see is the mirth-filled face of that arrogant prig, Prince Andothair.

I couldn't see him before in the dark, but I see him, now. Like all elves, he looks too beautiful to be real. He is large, but not large like my Corrik; muscular, but lithe like he's meant to sprite amongst the trees. His skin is a dark, copper, more like mine and I know he must be from someplace hot. His hair is black with strands of white and grey, but he's not an old Elf—he's quite young, possibly younger than Corrik. He's got wise black eyes, ones that have had to make many difficult decisions in his short Elven life—but he'll never let onto that.

"Where am I?" I groan. My head is pounding, but he comes into focus as he slowly lifts whatever enchantment he's had me under.

"You are safe, for now."

I'm in a tent, I realize; we are on land. "How long have I been out?"

"Four weeks. It was more difficult than I suspected, getting you off that ship—Cyredanthem fought gallantly as always—but get you off I did. We traveled four weeks after that and now you are here."

"Obviously. Where is here, Andothair?"

"We are camped just outside of one of the smaller of our villages—Hemkilli, the one closest to Port. With the size of our army, there isn't enough room at the Inns."

"And a Prince would stay in a tent when he could be put up at the Inn?"

"This may surprise you, but not all nobles are so super-cilious. I prefer to stay with my warriors."

"How honorable of you. As honorable as abducting a Prince of Mortouge, I wager."

"Don't be silly. You were no more than a concubine to the prince," he says. "Tell me, did Corrik keep you at the foot of his bed?"

I ignore his taunts. "What have you done with Corrik? The royal family?" I can't bear to ask about Diekin because I know the truth: he's dead.

"That is not your concern—I am all that should concern you now."

"I won't be here long, Corrik will come." I want to keep him talking and hope it will taunt him into telling me something of what has become of my party. Otherwise, I'd never say such a thing; I would never depend on someone else to save me.

"He won't be coming."

"He will."

"Think what you like but mark my words: you are mine now, Tristan Kanes. I have plans for you. You are to be a gift for my brother; I wish you to be his servant."

"*Never.*"

He grabs my long hair and tips my head up so my eyes meet his dark ones. "Allow me to make this clear for you. Our kind *hate* humans. To us, you are little more than a fruit fly, to be drowned in a bucket of old wine. You live because you have value to me. I happen to like the look of you, and I think you shall make an excellent present for my brother. Any other Elf would have slit you belly to throat; do not displease me, or perhaps I will find another means of getting what I wish."

What does he wish? I look at him, incredulously. "What happened to your promises of fulfilling my heart's desires? More lies I suppose. You lose more honor by the second."

"I will fulfill your heart's desires. You wish to fight, do you not?"

He would have been right a week ago: All I wanted was to fight, now all I care about is getting back to Corrik.

"How can I manage being your brother's servant, and being a warrior at the same time?" I scoff from my chair. I'm getting tired of being naked before him, even though it's hot in here and sweat is beginning to condensate from my muscles. Hot as I am, I'd still prefer some clothes.

"I shall allow you plenty of time in the training fields. You will train with our warriors, fight with them."

"Fight with them? Aren't you afraid I'll escape?"

"Let me see, how shall I put this delicately without hurting your pathetic, Markaytian pride? No."

"No? I took down eight of your Elves."

"It was three actually and it was with a magical sword, which I might add, you no longer possess."

"I could do it," I say. "Without that sword."

"We shall see, Warlord. But for now, there is something we must take care of," he says as he grabs my hair by the nape, I hear the ring of steel as he draws his sword.

"I thought it wasn't your wish to kill me?"

The tip of his sword is at my neck and he laughs. "No, Warlord. I shan't kill you, not today anyway, but you can thank me for every day you live. I only mean to take this."

In one, clean, slice, he shears off my beloved hair and my head snaps out of his grasp when the hair he holds is no longer attached to my skull. I want to cry like a child when I look at it hanging there from his hand, still shimmering in all its glory.

But I'm not a child, even if I can be a fucking brat sometimes. Instead, I begin to plot my revenge. I struggle in my bonds.

"Will you let me go, now?" My head feels much lighter.

"Aren't you wondering why I did that?"

"What difference does it make?"

"All the difference. It is the mark of your new station. Only royals may have hair as long as you once possessed. Now it will be kept no longer than mid-neck, and no shorter either. You are a *royal concubine* after all."

So now manservant means also acting as concubine? Figures. *Bloody, horny Elves.* "I am not your concubine. I belong to Corrik."

His eyes light up and glow like the blue at the center of a flame. "Corrik is no more—and no, you are not my concubine, you belong to my brother. You will be his concubine now."

I swallow, but I won't be frightened, and I won't put any stock into what he's suggesting. I look away from him. He laughs without mirth.

"No matter, Warlord. It is time for your first lesson."

"Lesson?"

"Yes. It is time for you to learn that you are defenseless. Moreover, you will do as you are told, willingly."

"Is that so?"

He motions wordlessly to one of his guards.

Andothair's warriors are not dressed like the warriors of Mortouge: They've less clothing. I didn't think one could be dressed any less than the warriors of Mortouge, but they are. They wear thick black skirts made from the hides of some kind of animal I don't recognize with leather belts that criss-cross in an 'X' over their torsos. I doubt they wear anything underneath. The women's breasts are in plain site, with the leather of their straps cut to accommodate the weight of them and fashioned to hold them fastidiously in place. Other than that, and their fine weapons, these Elves are naked.

I stop admiring their beautiful warriors, when I see whom they're dragging by his arms, my heart stops—I can scarcely believe what I'm seeing.

"*Diekin.*" He looks terrible and barely alive. He's pale—even for a Mortougian Elf, struggling to breathe, and only just this side of conscious.

"What is it you want, Andothair?"

"I have told you all I am going to for now, the only part you need be interested in, is the part where you are to be my brother's servant. If not, I will kill your friend. However; if you agree to be my brother's and obey him in all things, I shall ensure he lives and that you are taken care of."

"You can still save him, after four weeks of him being in this state?" Diekin is surely between worlds right now: Between the world of the living and the world of the dead.

"It is I that has been keeping him alive until this point—an act of good faith. All I have to do is withdraw my power from him and his life force will be extinguished like a flame."

"I want more than your power holding him vestige if I'm to become your brother's slave," I say calling it like it is, instead of using another one of Andothair's euphemisms like 'manservant'. "You will heal him to full health and keep him that way."

He doesn't even have to think it over. "Bargain, struck, Warlord."

CHAPTER 20

"*T*ristan, come."

Bayaden has only recently begun speaking to me as often as he does now in Markaytian, and I've only recently begun speaking to him in Elvish. The bastard knew what I was saying all along but forced me to learn Elvish claiming the Markaytian language beneath him. I knew he could speak Markaytian, most Elves can, but he'd speak to me in Elvish anyway and the language barrier made us want to rip each other's hair out—what's left of my hair that is. Now he speaks Markaytian whenever when he wants something right away and doesn't desire to go through the hassle of trying to get me to understand his complicated tongue. The Aldrien dialect is far easier to learn than the Mortougian, but it's still difficult.

"I'm coming, I'm coming," I say under my breath. *Bloody, demanding Elves.* In all my life, I've never met a more vainglorious, self-entitled race.

"Suck my cock, now." He's lying on the bed with his hands behind his head looking like the prince he is. His long dark hair mocks me, fanned around him—like mine used to.

"Where *are* your manners?" I say. Bayaden might bring out the brat in me, more than Corrik does.

"You're a servant and a human servant at that. I don't need manners—now get to work. I've had a long, exhausting day, I need to relax."

And I'm responsible for his relaxing. Got it.

Removing my pants as I make my way over to the bed, I crawl from the end of it, up to his spread legs and swallow his cock in one go—I'm quite practiced in the art of fellatio now. I make it good, running my tongue along the shaft, I run my lips down the length and suck hard as I pull back up his body. His hips push forward, his cock hits the back of my throat and instead of gagging, like I used to, I moan. I can't help it. Sucking him like this makes me feel good. I like it, my cock likes it, my body is hot as he continues to push into my mouth with controlled thrusts. His black curls scratch my nose. He spreads his legs wider and I grab the smooth skin of his balls and tug with just enough force as I suck and feel him climb closer to orgasm. His hand is in my hair and he slams his cock into my mouth over and over. This time I do gag, I can't breathe as he chokes me with his cock. I struggle to get away, but I can't; the Elf is much stronger than I am. I can do nothing but be choked by his enormous cock, wondering if I'll ever breathe again.

Maybe this is how I'll die.

I feel the first twitches of his orgasm and then his come shoots down my throat. I'm only just barely able to swallow it all, before I need to take a breath so badly, I have to push at his hips in a desperate attempt to get away. He holds his grip on my head welding it to his cock. I hear him cry above me as I begin to faint. He pulls out of me and I gasp at the air, racking it into my lungs in large gulps. My cock is still rock hard.

I cough and thank the Gods for sweet, sweet air and feel some of the come that I missed, dribbling down my chin as I try to regain my breathing rhythm. His foot reaches out to kick me and I fall off the bed and to my place: *at the side of his bed on the floor.*

"Bayaden!" I scream still coughing. He's laughing.

"What? You're supposed to pat someone on the back when they're choking."

"That wasn't a pat on the back and that's not what you're supposed to do to someone who's choking, you prat!" I say amidst my coughing fit.

"Oh, come here then."

"Is that an order, my Lord?" I never call him that unless I'm being a facetious asshole and I am now—he knows it.

"In fact, it is. Come."

I pull myself up onto the black sheets and stay by his feet. I don't care to be too close to him, the feeling is mutual —we have the same kind of a relationship a cat and a dog living in the same house would. We've chosen to tolerate each other because we are tied to the same master, Andothair. Me, because I've made a promise to Andothair so Diekin will be kept alive and Bayaden because he respects and honors his brother. Andothair is the eldest and will succeed their father as king someday in the distant future, if something ever happens to the Rogue Elf king. Bayaden is Aldrien's warlord. He's in charge of training all of the warriors in their kingdom. I'm certain it's yet another way for Andothair to taunt me. Andothair knew of my wish to fight and now I am the 'manservant' to his warlord and brother, I don't think that's a coincidence. I've not figured out what Andothair has against me, other than my race, but his every action tells me it's something big. Bayaden is of no help on this matter. Either he knows nothing, has no interest, or will not betray his brother—it's more likely all the above. Besides, I'm most certainly not one of Bayaden's confidants.

"That was very good, I feel much more relaxed." His eyes flick to my engorged member. "Does that need seeing to?"

"I'll manage." I can't help but look him over even as I decline his offer. He's a beautiful man, much more so than Andothair who is nothing short of sublime. Bayaden is larger than Andothair despite him being younger. He spends far more time training; his body is strong and I'm sure it's cut from iron. When he moves, he stalks, each limb calculating where the one after it should go for best economic gain. He studies things: the air around him, the light, the people as a good warrior should, but he does so instinctively and with delicate grace. If he were not on the field at war, he would be a dancer. Contrary to the brutal tact he fronts himself with, he's got quite the sense of humor, but unfortunately, he shares his people's dislike for humans and most of the time his jokes have me at the center of them. He does attempt good form on occasion and when his brother is around. All in all, he's not as mean as he could be and he treats me fairly most of the time, well, for a slave. It's more than I expected and more than I wanted.

"You did well at practice today too."

"Is there a reason for all these compliments?"

"No. I just thought, you look unhappy, my brother has noticed."

"Really? And he cares?"

"Apparently."

"Why?"

"I don't know," he says in bored tones as he gets up and

puts on a pair of pants. "But I'm tired of hearing about it so sharpen up, will you?"

I lie back on the bed. My body is bruised and battered. The Elves are hard on me; they don't care that I'm human or if they hurt me, only if I'm damaged irreparably. They'll answer to Andothair for that.

"That lot over there needs to be washed. See to it and bring me some dinner."

"Will that be all?"

I've kept many servants, and in all my life, I've never had to lift a finger for these kinds of chores so I've no gift for it—I'm a terrible manservant. It drives Bayaden crazy.

"No. You'll polish my boots—all of them—and then I wish a bath in my chambers."

"I can't possibly do all of that. I'm exhausted Bayaden."

"Then next time you'll think twice about being insolent."

"I thought I just relaxed you."

"Well now I'm agitated again."

"What happened? Why were you agitated in the first place?"

"Because Andothair breathes down my neck," he hisses. "He wants warriors trained faster than is possible; he's impatient of late."

"Why would that be?" I say to myself getting off the bed and dressing, so I can attempt to do the prince's bidding. It's the first intriguing thing I've heard in all the months I've been here. Maybe I'll ask Andothair if I may visit Diekin—Bayaden hasn't said by what time he'd like these chores completed, perhaps he'll have his knickers by noon tomorrow if he's lucky.

"How am I to know? He doesn't see fit to tell me and even if he did, I wouldn't tell you."

Huh. I didn't think he heard me; I still forget about the superior hearing of Elves from time to time.

"Don't look like that. Shouldn't you be getting on with it?" he says.

"Right, your Majesty—boots to polish and all that."

"And if you're going to take your time with everything else, at least bring my dinner straight away. I'm more likely to be agreeable with food in my stomach."

I move to leave out the door, my mind far away from my aching cock or his dinner preparations.

"Aren't you forgetting something, Tristan?"

"Oh. The laundry. Right."

"I swear. You have got to be the world's *worst* servant."

Not going to argue with that. I duck out the door. Besides, I'm thinking on what he's given away because he considers me a pathetic human, incapable of intelligence. Andothair wants more warriors and just because I'm not warlord anymore, it doesn't mean I've stopped thinking like a warlord. I know the only reason for more warriors is war. It won't take me three guesses to count on that war being with Mortouge. I remember what Diekin said about the Rogue Elves once being of Mortouge and that they were banished long ago.

I decide to seek Andothair.

On my way, I drop the load of washing in the washing queue.

"Hold my place, will you Mary?" I blink at her prettily.

All the Elves are pretty, and I usually forget that amongst them I'm a troll. I was admired by both men and women in Markaytia.

She pretends not to be pleased. "I'm tired of doing favors for you, Tristan, but all right."

Mary is a human, like me, but she speaks fluent Elvish,

unlike me (I'm getting there) but I can understand her now. "Thank you. I'll owe you for this," I say in my best Elvish.

I rush off to Dagenham's Hall. It is a good place to find Andothair before dinner. I tell the guard Andothair is expecting me, which he is not, but I've no consequences to worry about. He lets me in. Andothair is with his father.

The two brothers resemble their father, but Bayaden has a rougher edge to him unlike Andothair, who is more like King Caer Gai that way.

"Warlord? To what do we owe this intrusion?"

"You're planning to attack Mortouge."

"How good of you to notice."

"You can't do that—you'll start a war."

"Don't be stupid. We *want* to start a war, otherwise, why attack?"

"Why?"

"If you knew anything about Elven history, you would know—why don't you go study or something? Quit coming in here to bother us with trivial matters."

"Don't you think I've enough to do with running around after your brother? And I wouldn't call war a trivial matter. I can't let you do this."

The king laughs at me. "And how will you stop us? You are human."

"You both underestimate me." Corrik had too, they all forget I have a dragon running 'round in my blood.

They both laugh at me, now. "Run along and play, Tristan," says the king. King Caer Gai doesn't seem to like or hate me. It's as though he thinks me his son's cute little puppy that is a mere nuisance at times and a fun source of entertainment at others.

"Fine." I'm not going to get through to these two and

I've got the confirmation I wanted. "May I visit with, Diekin?"

"Want to make sure we have not killed your friend, yet?"

Something like that. "You can't be trusted."

"Very, well. You may take him his supper. Now be gone, we have work to do," Andothair says.

Perfect.

After I see to the Prince's laundry and thank Mary for holding my place in line, I'm off to the kitchens. I know they don't feed him well, to keep him weak. Since I'm gathering food for the prince as well, I take liberty and steal some of the prince's heartier food and place it onto Diekin's tray as well as a bowl of stew. It means the prince will get less, but I don't care.

"Food for the prisoner," I say by way of announcing myself. The guards would have me grovel at their feet; it angers them to no end when I don't. I stalk by them, and one reaches out to grab my arm and pull me to him, my tray almost crashes to the ground but I'm able to recover my balance.

"Well look what we have here," he says in a smooth voice. In my first days in Aldrien, they didn't know I was Bayaden's manservant, nor did they care. Even when I made it clear where I was from, some would refuse to speak to me in my home language on principle—like Bayaden.

When Bayaden finally gave me his collar to wear, with his crest on it, they sometimes paid me the 'honor' of speaking to me in my home language. More often, they'd tease me in their own—but I showed them and picked up quite a lot of their language. Unfortunately, and fortunately, their dialect is much easier to learn than Mortouge's—the

Elvish language I would've liked to have mastered so now much of my accent is that way. I've been here far too long.

"Leave me be or I'll tell Andothair of this." The guards fear Andothair. I've long since stopped allowing my pride to interfere and use this excuse to keep them off my back. Protecting my pride only gets me beaten, it's not worth it—usually—though there have been a couple times that were.

The guard releases me but pushes me hard enough to leave a bruise; I just barely catch the tray before the food is lost. "You won't be the Prince's toy forever you know. He'll grow bored then I shall request you."

This is where I would normally insert a snarky comment, or three, but I have a mission in mind.

"Until that time," I say and hold my head high, sticking my hand out for the key. Once I've got it, I move down the dark, cold halls of the dungeon and twist my way to the heart of it where Diekin is kept.

"Diekin? *Pssst.* Diekin?"

"Young Warlord?"

"Yes, it's me," I say as I open the door and move past him. "Here, Diekin. I've brought you good food. *Eat.*"

He smiles at me like I'm incredible. "Thank you, Tristan. Your care of me over these past months will not be forgotten. When I'm out of here ..." He rarely calls me Tristan and he still speaks of getting out of here.

I don't even know if our entourage made it. I assumed I would've heard some word about them being in the area, looking for us, but I haven't. In any case, Diekin doesn't know that I've long stopped looking for a way out because I can never go to Mortouge—not now—I've betrayed Corrik for too long and I'm an embarrassment to his home and mine. Besides, if Corrik is dead, is there any point in me going there? I was to be Corrik's mate; Mortouge has little use for me after that. No. When the time comes, and I will make sure it does, I'll get Diekin free and I'll stay—I'm too much of a disgrace to even consider going back to Mortouge or Markaytia for that matter.

"Diekin, I've learned that they plan to attack Mortouge. I don't know when, but we've got to get you out of here."

"Us."

"What?"

"We've got to get us out of here you mean."

"Right. Us."

"Tristan, I know you mean to get me out and remain, what I don't know is why." His body is cold and his eyes like razors. "What have you done?"

"Eat, Diekin."

"I'm not a fool, young Warlord, c'mon. Try me out." A bit of his old light shines through the bold warrior and it makes me want to tell him. He knows there is something. I can't lie to him anymore, but I can't tell him the truth either, so I go with a little of both. I've hated coming down here all this time and keeping my secret—the one he senses looming over me.

"I've done something unforgivable Diekin. I'm not worthy of Mortouge now and can never look Corrik in the eyes again."

"Whatever has happened isn't your fault and Corrik will understand—he loves you."

"Maybe, but I shall never forgive myself. We don't even know if Corrik is alive, what purpose is there for me in Mortouge then?"

"You are a fool if you think like that."

"I've been companion to the young Prince Bayaden all this time." He's not getting it, so I lay it out for him.

"I know. Andothair told me. You did it to save my life;

he gave you few options. I wish you would have let me die, but I am grateful, Tristan, and I will stand by your side when you tell Corrik because you will one day. I believe he is alive, and he knows how noble you are and that given the choice, you would sooner die than allow a friend to die—and that's exactly what happened. Besides, Elves do not hold the same moral code as humans. All will be well, Tristan."

I nod and keep the other secret to myself. Diekin is an optimist, but even he would think as I do if he knew the other part—Elven morals or lack thereof aside. "Keep up your strength, I'm going to get us out of here; I have a plan."

Diekin eats. "Brave words for a mere human in a valley full of Elves with sharp teeth."

"I have something they do not."

"Dragon's blood."

"It's nice of someone to finally notice."

"Right, but how does this dragon's blood work?"

"You'll see."

"*Warlord.*"

He's suddenly dropped the 'Junior' from my title too; I can't allow that. "Not you too, Diekin. How many times do I have to tell you? I'm not Warlord."

"You are wrong; you are Warlord now. A war is upon us, and you seek to take up the first battle with an army—albeit a small one—at your command. You are my warlord, Tristan, and I am honored to serve you."

I suppose there will be no talking him out of this one. "Let us hope I can prove worthy of those words, Diekin."

"You already have, Warlord," he says with a hearty smile, eating his stew.

I'm glad that by the time he realizes how one is to use the power harnessed by dragon's blood, I will be dead.

"**T**here you are—it's about time," Bayaden says in Elvish, but I understand him perfectly well.

I place the food before him. "Maybe you shouldn't have given me so much to do, my Lord. Now, if you've no further need of me," I say in Markaytian.

"Sit down, Tristan." He switches to Markaytian, not in the mood to play games tonight. He's never invited me to sit with him before. I'm immediately suspicious.

"Have you eaten?"

"No. I'll get something from the kitchens, later," I say when he offers me his bread.

"Why do you take nothing from me?"

Why does he suddenly care? He's never cared before.

"Because it is unnecessary...? Andothair provides me with everything I need."

"Yet I am your master," he says.

"You are."

"Then I will provide for you. Come to me with your needs from now on. That's an order."

"Yes, Bayaden," I lie smoothly. He can think what he likes, but I'll never ask him for a thing and right now I need Andothair.

"Here," he says and holds out the bread again. This time I take it, but don't eat it. "Damn it, Tristan. Must you be so stubborn?"

"My papa used to say I come by it naturally."

He puts his spoon down; he's had enough of me. "The Gods help me; I can't figure you out." Hopefully he never will. "I know one thing, though. I know you will go to my brother tonight. I know what you will ask for and that you are ashamed of it. There are few secrets between us, Tristan."

"What of it?" I say, my dragon's blood beginning to boil. I know Andothair holds no confidence with me, but I am no less enraged to have other people know of my sins.

"Allow me to take his place."

"No."

"I could force the issue, you know."

"Then force it. I will not consent to it."

"Why him and not me?"

"Mostly because he did it first. It makes little difference who does it, but I've already betrayed Corrik with one person, I'll not add to that list." I do not add that I'm possibly only respecting his memory; I like to think as Diekin does, that he's alive, *but then why hasn't he come for me?*

"Betray Corrik? What nonsense, Tristan. Is it not my cock that's up your arse every night? Is it not my bed you sleep beside? You belong to me now and betray *me* by going to Andothair."

I laugh uncomfortably. I don't like where this is headed. Since I've come into his 'care' he's hated the very air I breathe, resented having me in his presence and now he wants to discipline me? "Those are semantics. You know as well as I do that we tolerate each other for Andothair's benefit. Remember what you said to your brother? Remember what you said to me on my first day in your service?"

He shakes his head, but he knows as well as I do, the length of Elven memories. He wants me to say it so he can deny it. Fine. "You said and I quote, *in* Markaytian I might add, *'you can't be serious Andothair. He looks like something the sea washed in.'* You then went on to tell your brother you were insulted by his choice of servant for you, and you warned me to keep my distance lest you are forced to do something only I shall regret."

"I never said any such things," he denies as I knew he would. "I know my brother holds more power than I do with the Elven courts and while it must be terribly exciting for a meager human such as yourself, I will be seen as weak in front of my warriors if you continue to submit to him."

A likely story. "I thought Elves were promiscuous? Isn't it natural for them to have many partners before they mate?"

"Has my brother entered you?" He ignores my questions, his good humor flares to anger.

"No, Bayaden, calm. I only go to Andothair for *discipline*. I promise." I can't believe I have to defend myself in this manner. Honestly, what's gotten into him tonight?

"For a moment I thought he had lied to me, though you have no reason not to lie to me."

"I'm not lying about that—swear on my aunt's grave. Why should you care anyway? I'm a disgusting human."

"I told you already. I care about how it looks to my warriors. I'll not have you embarrass me."

"I shall endeavor not to embarrass you then, Highness." I can only look at my dry piece of bread. Bayaden is as caught up in these games Ando begins as I am, tied to it by his moral duty to his people and his family. *Bayaden and I have much in common.*

"If you're not going to eat, at least leave me to eat in peace."

"I thought you wanted a bath?"

"I did, but I can no longer stand to look at you. I'll go down to the bathing hall to take my bath. Someone far more competent will help me there."

I pretend that I'm insulted by that, when in truth, I'm relieved—one less duty for me to worry about and he's right; the men and women servants in the bathing hall are far more competent than I.

I leave and it's when I'm halfway down the hall I remember I left the bread he gave me on the table.

It's late when I knock on Andothair's chamber doors. "Enter."

He's standing over his desk looking at a large map. "Ahhh, Tristan. I've been expecting you. Sit."

I'm not a fool. I know he isn't inviting me to sit in a chair. I take my place by his feet and kneel properly as Corrik taught me. Sometimes I pretend he's Corrik. "What have you done this time?"

"Do you really want to keep hearing about the things your brother has me do to him?"

"You still feel guilt over that?"

"I shall always. I'm a married man, Andothair, whether you'll believe it or not—whether Corrik is alive or not." I've given up asking him what was done with my Corrik. My ring is gone. It's been gone since I arrived and I assumed Andothair took it and disposed of it before he woke me from my magic-induced slumber, once we arrived at the border of Aldrien, in Hemkilli. I never asked because I knew he wouldn't tell me anyway—there were still some ways to save my pride.

He considers me a long time and for a moment I'm stupid enough to believe he's thinking about what I've said. "You are quite beautiful, for a human. I can almost find what he sees in you when I look hard enough."

"You were intent on killing me, now you hold me captive—why?" I've asked him this every other night and every other night he evades my question, but I have a feeling about tonight—tonight he'll give me a truth.

"Corrik has something I want."

My heart skips a beat. He said 'has' as in *Corrik's still alive*. At least I dare to hope it; I must make sure. "You think by holding me ransom you will get what you want? You don't know Corrik very well, do you?"

"I know Corrik better than you think," he says grabbing my chin hard. "Get out. I cannot look at you tonight."

No one wants to look at me tonight, but Corrik is alive. Corrik is alive. He wouldn't talk like that otherwise. The knowledge does strange things to me; the shame is suffocating. "Andothair, please. I need you."

"I do not care what you need, you are lucky I do not give you to the dungeon guards."

"Ando, I beg you. *Please.*"

"Out."

I storm back to Bayaden's room in a mood that boils my dragon blood. I'll kill him; kill him. How dare he reject me like that? The only counter to my shame has always been rage.

"Problem, Tristan?" Bayaden is naked as usual and sits on his bed reading. He's the most unusual warlord I've ever encountered. Judging by his relaxed demeanor, his anger has cooled from before.

"Your brother, he wouldn't, uh, do the thing." I can't say it.

"Discipline you?"

"Yeah, that."

"What did you do? He isn't easily angered."

"I think it was something I said about, Corrik."

"Ah."

"What do you mean, ah?"

I don't expect an answer, but I get one and I suspect it has to do with whatever his issue was earlier. "He and Corrik used to be a thing, didn't you know?"

"You're lying."

"What reason would I have to lie to you?"

"How is that possible?"

"Before you, it was very possible."

"Like, together—together?"

"Is there another kind?"

"But Mortouge and Aldrien hate each other."

"Corrik and Andothair dreamed of forging an alliance one day. They met in secret—I doubt King Vilsarion knew, but our father knew and encouraged it."

"What happened? Why did they split up?"

"You."

"Me?"

"Corrik had his vision of you and abandoned all thought of my brother—it broke his heart."

"That's why he wanted me killed."

"Yes."

"But that wouldn't have won Corrik back—Corrik would have hated him."

"You'd be surprised what time can heal and the time of an Elf is long. We are immortal, Tristan," he reminds me.

"So why didn't he kill me then?"

"That has me as puzzled as you. He gave you to me though, so you're mine now. Whatever his reasons before, he won't kill you, I won't let him."

"I don't care about him killing me, I care about him killing my friend."

"He won't. I won't let him do that either if that is your wish. Will that make you happy?"

"It will." I don't know why he suddenly wants to make me happy, but if he will protect Diekin, I'll take it.

"I shall see to it then, now, come. I'm in need of my manservant—you've been missing longer than you were meant to be."

"What is it you require, Bayaden? I'm tired." I move over to the bed and take a seat next to his feet as I normally do.

"Too bad. Undress."

I sigh loudly so he'll know how put out I am but remove the light pants that are my only clothes. He motions me toward the headboard. "Lie back."

My cock is already hard at his words, the order soothes me, but it's not enough. I need the discipline Andothair gives me to dissolve my guilt over doing these things with Bayaden, long enough, so I can do these things with Bayaden. It's a fucked up cycle, I know, but here I am.

I watch him pour lubricant onto his long fingers. I hiss when he slathers it onto my cock and my desire takes over. "I didn't take care of you earlier."

"You needn't bother, Highness," I force myself to say, but it feels magnificent. He strokes his hand up and down, rolling the foreskin of my shaft over the head, the lubricant thick and slippery.

"That's it, Tristan. Remain still. I am in control of your cock. Keep your hips down. Yes."

"Please, Baya ... *Please*..." I don't know if I'm begging him to stop or continue. His hand feels itchy in a wonderful way and a burn builds down my groin and up my cock, then his other hand is fondling my balls.

"Do you like that, Tristan?"

"*Yeesss.*" There's no denying I do and the shame I feel because I do is there alongside my impending orgasm, the shame increasing the ache in my cock. I feel a finger at my entrance as his hand releases my balls and spread my legs wider to accommodate whatever thing he'll do. His finger doesn't enter all at once, he slips it in, only to the first knuckle then slips it out again, gathering more lubricant. His other hand is still stroking my cock slowly. If I'd only known the lovely sexual tortures of Elves sooner, I may have begged Corrik to take me with him the first day we laid eyes on each other. Yes, I still think of him, especially during sex, but not too often—it hurts to think of Corrik because it doesn't matter that he is alive, I'll never see him again. I'll never get to tell him what I should have long before now, about how I can no longer dream, but relive the short time we had together, every night as I fall asleep. I fought having any sort of a connection with Corrik, but we did on a level I'm only beginning to understand by being away from him.

I'll die in Bayaden's bed, a human, still dreaming of my days with Corrik.

But I'm not so maudlin as to continue this line of thought while I've got Bayaden's finger inside my arse and one hand on my cock—if this is my life now, I'll enjoy it, whatever it will be.

"I know you want more, Tristan, you have but to ask."

"Please Bayaden."

"That's right—Bayaden. I am your *Master* now. Say it."

"You are my Master now." I'll say whatever he wants me to say, he is the fool if he believes my words.

I don't know if he believes me, but he adds another

finger. I place the soles of my feet flat on the bed and spread wider to give him more room. It's driving me mad not to move and I strain with the effort of keeping my body still. "Gods, Bayaden! Fuck me please."

"As you wish."

He takes his hands away, but I'm only bereft for a short moment and his large cock is slamming into me. Bayaden is a rough lover, always. He enjoys the rawness of sex, the animalistic side. I can see the animal in his eyes as he takes me, his hands become claws down my back, the pain soars to another level and takes me to a greater sexual high. He does the things to me I know Corrik wanted to do, but didn't, afraid it would scare me away from him. Bayaden has no such worry. He simply takes what he wants of me and the Gods help me, I enjoy it.

His lips are on mine and I freeze; he's never kissed me quite like this before. I see little option, but to kiss him back like I don't notice the change and his hand is wild in my hair as his cock continues to fuck into me over and over—I'll be sore tomorrow, I usually am. He's unforgiving, angry, and possessive, yet somehow those feelings have transformed into caring. Bayaden cares about me. *How could that have happened?*

"Come, Tristan. Come for me," he says, as he rakes his nails down my back again, the pain spikes my arousal and I do come in white, hot spurts all over my stomach and his. He still pounds his cock into me with sure, steady strokes and releases his seed into me as he lays me back on the bed and finishes off inside me before he collapses on top of me.

I don't know why I do it, but I bring my arms around him and move the hair from his eyes gently. He's still inside me, his cock still hard—Elves have stamina like I've never seen—come is leaking out from around his cock in my ass as he stares off at the wall, his head on my chest. I continue to run my hands through his hair, and I realize, *fuck*. Somehow, I've come to care about Bayaden too. He may be an arrogant prat, but he's not a terrible creature. He's acting as he thinks he's meant to; he's got a moral duty to his father, brother, and to his kingdom. I understand well and put in his position, I'd do exactly as he has done. I can feel the weight of that duty upon him, and I allow him to let it go for the moment and put it on me.

We spend long moments locked together until he kneels up again, renewed. He slides a hand through my short hair and brings his face close to mine, pulling me into a long, slow kiss. His kisses are unlike how he fucks me—the complete opposite. They're gentle and tender and say what's in his heart.

"I need you again, Tristan."

CHAPTER 21

orrik is alive.

    I wake up tired having got no sleep last night. Bayaden kept me in his bed and when I tried to slide off in the night, he thought I was waking him for more sex and proceeded to put his cock into my sore arse for the seventh time. Or was it the eighth? I don't know, I lost track. Look, it was a lot, okay?

What I do know is that if he approaches me one more time, I'll either slit his throat or die trying. I feel his fingers brushing across my skin and his voice is just as smooth. "Wake up, Tristan."

He is the only one that calls me just Tristan here. "What? I swear to the *Gods* Bayaden."

"Don't worry, I won't take you again. I just want breakfast."

"All right. See you in a bit then." I slump back down on the bed.

"Tristan?"

"Yes?"

"Aren't you forgetting something?"

"Huh?"

"You are *my* manservant."

"And?"

"You're supposed to get the breakfast."

"But I'm so tired. You shouldn't have kept me up all night. *You* get it."

"Now, Tristan."

I sigh heavily, but get my sore arse moving. *Corrik is alive.*

The kitchens are busy; I'm still not used to them. The few times I entered the kitchens back home was when Lucca and I stole pies from the kitchens and then later when I was being punished for stealing said pies.

I'm well received here. Most of the servants in the kitchens are humans of various races, but the kitchens' headmistress is an elder Elven female. I don't know how I managed it, but she likes me.

"Are you here for Prince Bayaden's breakfast?"

"And a breakfast pie for me?"

She gives me a scurrilous look. "Here you are then. You'd better eat it before you return, Bayaden has me under strict instruction not to feed you anymore."

I put on my most charming expression. "You make the best pies, Meren." I eat it quickly and pick up the tray meant for Bayaden; it's filled with a feast fit for a prince. I get little to eat now compared to what I'm used to.

When I've returned, he sits at the table, his black hair is almost camouflaged against his black robe; streaming down it; brushed into waves around him. He's reading again. Bayaden is always reading. I set the tray in front of him.

"Your breakfast. I'm going to have a lie down."

"Tristan."

"What is it?" I almost snap at him. I'm in no mood this morning for him or anyone else.

"Join me and lose your insolent tone. I'm a prince if you'll kindly remember."

"As am I." I stalk past him and lie down on my bed, which is a comfortable mattress with lots of pillows and blankets and is oh so cozy. Just as I'm closing my eyes, a hand whacks my poorly clad ass, hard. I 'get' to wear a pair of thin, beige pants, ones I stole a ways back. Most of the servants don't get to wear anything; I'm lucky I have these, but they do little to protect me—I now have a stinging hand-print on my left cheek.

"The Gods' sake, Bayaden. Let me rest. I'm tired."

"Get up! Get up, now," he says, pulling me and the blanket from the bed.

"All right. All right," I say as I stand up, tangled in the blanket and make my way across the room and to his table. We both take a seat, me begrudgingly and him snidely.

"So, what's on for today?" I ask.

"Practice. You have much to work on."

"Practice," I say. "Why should I bother? They're going to slaughter me like they do every day." I notice he's making up two plates.

"Do you mean you no longer wish to fight? My brother said it's your heart's desire."

"It was. I finally realize it's as Corrik said; I stand no chance against Elves. It's nothing more than a daily beating."

"It's not like you to give up so easily. Come now, what's the matter?"

"What do you know of me?"

"You've lived in my pocket for several months and I'm a warlord. I've watched you."

255

I stare at him astonished. Has he been paying that close attention to me? It didn't seem like it, but I suppose it makes sense; I watch him too. It's good to know your opponent, his strengths, his weaknesses.

"Nothing's the matter. I can't win against an Elf like I've already said—it's humiliating to lose every day. Besides, everyone hates me."

He considers me for a time and takes a bite of food. "Do you want me to tell them to lay off you?"

"Absolutely, not. That you would even ask is an insult. It would make me look all the more a pathetic human. Isn't that how you think of us? Pathetic?" I tug the blanket tight around me for protection against whatever retort he'll have and notice he's put the second plate of food he's made up in front of me. It's filled with the good stuff too—sausage, fresh bread, cheese and fruit.

"I did think you pathetic." He gestures to the food. "Eat."

Did? As in past tense?

"What in the Gods' names is going on with you, Bayaden? Stop this nonsense. You're not supposed to say things like that. You're supposed to call me a filthy, flea-ridden human, not feed me gourmet palace fair," I say pushing the plate of food back to him. "Besides, I've already eaten."

He stands up suddenly. "When could you have eaten?" His voice is dark and angry. I've never seen Bayaden quite like this—it's frightening.

"In the kitchens, it was no big deal."

"Meren. I ordered her not to feed you. Does no one listen to me?" he says to himself and then slams his large hand down before me. "It is a big deal, Tristan. Can you fathom why?"

"No?"

"What did I say only yesterday in regard to whom would provide for you?"

"You said you would."

"Was I somehow unclear as to what 'I will provide for you' means?"

"No, but you say a lot of things—I didn't think you were serious, you don't normally care what I do."

"Well for future, I do care."

"Okay. Sorry."

"No—you're not. You have disobeyed me, come with me."

"Bayaden—I mean it—I really am sorry."

"Now." He will not be swayed so I follow him with great apprehension as he leads me to a room, two rooms down from his chambers—I'm still wrapped in the blanket; it feels like protection.

With a wave of his hand, the dark room illuminates. It's filled with all kinds of odd-looking benches, straps, buckles, and chains. Things hang from the ceiling and the walls are lined with large grey stones and blocks of pink salt. The room is just this side of cold, but there's a warm breeze wafting in through the windows that are way up high so no one can see in or out of the room.

"What is this place?"

"It's a room that can be used for great pleasure or great pain. Do you see where this is headed?"

Now I'm a bit worried. On second look, some of the equipment looks to be painful. "C'mon Bayaden. It was just a breakfast pie."

"You were deliberately defying me—testing me—I'll have no more of it, Tristan Kanes. Don't you know what I am? Your nature practically calls out to me each day with your behavior as it is, but for you to disregard a direct order I've given you? That's a challenge. Not to mention you running to my brother for discipline is like spitting in my face—he isn't even dominant. What do you think that does to me?"

Only half of his words shock me—the half that says Andothair is not a dominant—though I should have figured on it after what Bayaden told me about Corrik and Andothair last night. If Corrik and Andothair were together, Andothair would have to be submissive—Corrik doesn't have a submissive bone in his body.

Bayaden—I realized he was a dominant the first time I laid eyes on him, even with only little knowledge on how it all works. His very essence oozes a presence, dark and authoritative, his nature calls to mine whether I want it to or not, and it hits me like a sledgehammer. It was hard to breathe around him those first weeks until I got to know him, and I still use sarcastic, brat-like humor to ease my unease at being near him.

Nothing eases me now and being near him is like standing next to a thunderstorm.

"I guess you wouldn't know. How could you? You are a human and can't have the slightest clue as to what Elves feel."

No. I don't know, but I've learned from both Corrik and Bayaden, mating with an Elf seems to make that Elf insanely territorial—especially the dominant sorts.

"Do you mean to punish me?" I can barely say it—part of me wants him to with only a small bit of apprehension left.

"Oh, I mean to all right. You will obey me from now on, Tristan Kanes."

"But. No. I told you no yesterday when you asked."

"Does it look like I'm asking now?"

"You can't."

"You keep forgetting: you belong to me. Not to my brother and certainly not to Corrik Cyredanthem. It is my right, a right you gave to me when you became mine. You do remember giving yourself to me, yes?"

I give a jerky nod because I do—he's right. I made a pledge on a bitter evening in exchange for a life. My resistance is moot. I'll never see Corrik again and even if I could; I couldn't face him.

"How do you want me?" Silent tears slide down my cheeks.

A hand runs gentle through my short locks. "Everything off, stand over there," he says softly, pointing to the middle of the room.

I put the blanket down and remove my sad, thin pants, but I take up the blanket again and shroud my naked body in it as I make my way to the center of the room. The tiled floor changes pattern to form a circle here and I stand in the middle.

"Put your arms above your head," he instructs in a serious tone. I can't help but compare him to Corrik. Corrik is hard, when he gives out discipline, but somewhat light-hearted. Bayaden is treating this like it's a grave matter—I fail to see it as such.

The pale blue blanket falls. Pale blue like the blanket Corrik and I had our first 'date' on. The blanket falling is like shedding—shedding what's left of the time I spent with Corrik as I walk into this new life with Bayaden.

I shiver as I look above to see the chains with cuffs at the end. The cuffs are soft suede, and he buckles them tightly around my wrists. I can just touch the floor with my toes; the weight of my body is heavy in my shoulders and I don't like it. I'm already uncomfortable and he hasn't touched me yet. My tears fall faster.

"Don't cry, Tristan. It will be over soon," he says and kisses my lips tenderly. He's quite taciturn and speaks with actions instead of words. His kiss says it all, he cares a great deal for me. This knowledge creates confusion, but one thing I'm not confused about is that I will be all right.

I've come to trust Bayaden, much as I hate to admit that.

"This is what I've chosen. I believe in teaching lessons well, or not at all." He holds a thick, leather strap in front of my face and I take a sharp inhale. Father has used something like it on me in the past—it felt, not very nice. I don't look forward to this, yet I crave the resolution it will bring.

It seems like a formal moment. Should I say something? For the life of me, my lips won't move, and I can only follow that sharp looking strap with my eyes until he moves around me, so I can't see him, or the strap anymore. My breathing is shallow and rigid; I bite my lip in anticipation.

I jump when his hand glides down my back and stops in the middle of my smooth skin. He whispers something in Elvish that I don't understand. I've gotten quite good at Elvish in the months since I've been here, I'm still no expert, but I get by. But he says it too low for me to hear the annunciation. Elvish is like that, a change in inflection and the same word means something entirely different.

After the completion of his strange little ritual, I feel the first taste of his whip on my back. One. "Ahh!" It hisses into my skin and my skin heats up, I tug at the cuffs, lifting myself from the floor in a chin-up motion. It hurts.

Two. "Ahhhmmphh." I attempt to cut off my cries.

"Let go Tristan. This is punishment for your disobedi-ence, I'm disappointed, but I'll not forbid you the release of your emotions. We will reach a point where it will be impossible for you not to cry out." That does not sound promising.

Three, four, *twenty*. His whip is slow, methodic, and consistently timed. The pain is all I am, and I lose count of how many times his strap has licked my back. My shoulders burn from holding my weight and now the twisting and the writhing as I try to get away, but there's nowhere I can escape to. I can only face this. I'm panting and breathing hard, it's intense; my skin feels alive with sensation. He kisses me again slow, soft then more of his strap and more pain.

My face is wet from the sweat and tears that pour in streams. My sinuses clot with liquid as I continue to cry and scream through the pain that will never stop. Lash after lash, down my back, my arse, and thighs—oh Gods the thighs—that's the worst of it. Sensitive, unforgiving—I jump as I feel the air move when he lifts his arm and the skin on my arse quivers, before the strap ever touches it because it knows how much it's going to hurt.

My body is so wrought with pain, I can't feel when he stops and I hang limp, sobbing. "It's over, Tristan—let that be an end to it."

I remember someone saying that to me a long time ago or at least what seems like a long time ago. He kisses me again and wipes the sweat through my short dark hair. When he unshackles me, I can barely stand; my limbs have turned to jelly, and he has to scoop me up after retrieving the pale blue blanket and wraps it loosely around me. I hiss when his arms make contact with my heated skin. I wrap my arms around his neck.

He carries me the short distance to his chambers and places me down on his bed like I'm made of glass. He's gone for a moment and when he returns he has hot, wet towels he uses to wipe my face clean.

"I'm going to roll you over, Tristan—I'm going to apply some salve to your back, it will help the skin heal smooth."

I cry out as he moves me of course, but the smooth salve feels as lovely as I remember, he's used it on me before. I opt to remain on my stomach even after he's finished.

"You feel better now, don't you? You needed that."

I sigh into my pillow. "I do feel better. Thank you Bayaden." I hate that I do; I hate that I, a grown man, would need such a thing—but the Gods curse me, I do.

"It wasn't just for your benefit, I promise you. Get up now. We're going to practice."

Something soft lands on me, my beige pants, I flinch. "You can't be serious? I won't be able to move."

"That's your problem—you shouldn't have defied me. The salve should have eased your pain considerably," he says.

I test the skin by moving, the pants slip off my back and onto the mattress and he's right, it has helped, but I can still feel every mark. I won't admit that to him.

"Bayaden," I whine. All I've wanted this whole morning is sleep; I should've quit while I was ahead.

"Would you like my help?"

I answer by getting up gingerly and slip on the loose pair of pants. The weather is warm here and I suspect we are in the south. It'd been getting colder while we were on the ship and that was months ago, the weather in Mortouge should be cold now. Diekin told me it's their winter. But here, it's summer—I don't know if they get a true winter. Bayaden says that it's summer all the time in Aldrien.

Bayaden wears little; a wide belt, with the emblem of his family crest as big as his abdomen and a baldric strap that runs diagonally across his chest so his sword can rest on his back. He'll wear shoulder armor on one side, his right, that I will help him put on once we arrive at the fields, and wide bands of armor around his wrists. Bayaden has a tattoo like Corrik's on his face, but whereas Corrik's is over his forehead and down his nose, Bayaden's is over his right eye and lights up in yellow tones rather than ultra-violet. He's very beautiful; though that's no surprise, is it? All the Elves are sublime creatures. Where Bayaden is impressive is in the training fields. I've watched him move on the field and command his army so pristine, so flawless. Bayaden moves like a panther but strikes like a dagger; he's quite the sight to watch and sometimes he succeeds in mesmerizing me. When I'm on the field, I strive to be like him; to learn from him.

I know dressed as I am, Bayaden's men will see what he's done to me. I don't care much. It's a common thing in Aldrien and Diekin told me it's equally common in Mortouge. There is little place for embarrassment and it's better I learn to accept this. I've learned that marks are only placed upon those who are meaningful in Aldrien; it's a big deal that I—a lowly human—receive any markings at all. It's going to cause quite the stir at practice today when they see how many new ones I have from their warlord. I smile. I recall the only other time Bayaden marked me where others could see. He chained me to the wall in his bedchamber for almost two days after that and made me apply the magic salve until all the marks not covered by my pants healed. When I finally deciphered the meaning of marks to Elves, I decided that Bayaden must've lost himself in a fit of lust that night and was embarrassed to have marked me in such a meaningful way. Of course, he wouldn't want anyone seeing the marks and getting the wrong idea—that maybe he cared about his human pet. But now, he doesn't seem to care and shows me, *and* his marks off proudly.

We trek the long distance from the palace to the large fields where the barracks are. Sometimes we sleep and eat in the barracks if Bayaden has to be up early—something I'm used to from living with my fathers. Life in Aldrien is quite like Markaytia.

As soon as we approach Bayaden's warriors, I find out how right I am about the throbbing welts on my back. After I've helped Bayaden with his armor and have adorned my own, I'm sent to work with my sword. We've been split off into groups.

"Hello again, human," Siagin says, smirking at me, speaking in Elvish. He doesn't like me, but that's okay, I don't like him either. Without giving me the chance to draw my sword, he grabs my arm and twists it behind my back—I scream; can't help it. My back is on fire and it's not hard for him to take me to the ground and to my knees.

"That's better. You need to learn to always kneel before your betters. If you were mine, you would be on your knees all the time—what's this?" He ghosts his hand along the marks he sees on my back and I picture the surprise on his face. "Oi! Luthern, look at this?"

A large, copper-skinned, blond Elf comes over to inspect me while I try not to show them how much pain I'm in.

"What's the matter, Siagin? Jealous?" I say in perfect Elvish, with as much venom as I can. He releases me, pushing me toward the ground.

"What sorcery is this? How did you fool our warlord into giving you marks like that?"

"Believe me, I didn't ask for them." I glare at him from my knees knowing better than to get up. In past, I was defiant, but it only ever served to get me a beating that wouldn't be as fulfilling as the one I just received from Bayaden. I don't want or need another black eye.

"You most certainly did," says a voice from behind. Bayaden. "What is the meaning of this, Tristan?"

"We know he's tricked you Warlord. You would never honor a human with such marks," Siagin answers for me.

Bayaden studies his two warriors then turns to me still on the ground. He doesn't answer them and that says it all. "Stand up, Tristan."

I do at his command.

"Come with me." I follow behind him like his lost duckling and don't like it. I told him not to save me from his men; I glare at his back.

"Stop, pouting," he says. I swear he's got eyes in the back of his head. "I wasn't saving you; I merely have something else I'd rather you learn."

I don't believe him and when I see where he's taking me, my dragon blood boils. We head away from where his warriors practice with swords and toward where his warriors practice archery.

"This is Deglan, she will teach you how to use an Elven bow. Learn well, Tristan. I will come get you for lunch." He gives me another kiss—he's given me a lot of kisses since yesterday—and leaves me with a lithe looking creature.

She's as proud as she is strong with intelligence shining in her eyes. Her blonde hair swoops up high and down over her shoulder, covering her buttocks and I know immediately she must be royalty. Her hair is undercut on one side giving her a fearsome presence and there is an opaque tattoo above her right, Elven ear. I recognize the royal crest.

"I am Ando and Baya's younger sister—the pretty one,"

she says and winks at me. "My brother is quite taken with you, young Tristan. I've never seen him this way."

I swallow. "Pleased to meet you, though it sounds as if you already know who I am?"

"I've heard nothing but Tristan this and Tristan that for months—though it wasn't always in your favor."

"You have? From whom?"

She laughs a pleasant laugh. "Baya. I told you; he is enchanted with you."

As much as I suspect that as well, it's hard to believe. "I don't understand, I thought he hated humans?"

She runs a smooth finger gently over one of the marks that reach to my shoulder. "No one would give marks like this to someone they hated and most certainly not my brother."

"But, but when I first got here ..."

"He didn't hate you then either. He might have hated his feelings for you, but not you—never you. They drove him insane. He didn't want to care for you, but he did —*does*. I'm glad to see he stopped fighting his heart."

Dear Gods, Bayaden enchanted with me? *What next? Pigs flying? Why do Elves keep falling for me?*

"Enough chatter then. I'm excited to teach you all I know about the bow."

Deglan is a master of the bow, and so was my father. He offered to teach me on many occasions, and I refused, preferring the sword.

Then he made me, much to my dismay. I didn't appreciate the lovely art, but I soon found I inherited his gift. Deglan is far more skilled than my father or I. With her Elven grace and strength, she's quick and flawless.

"All right, your turn."

I expect I'm going to be rusty, but I'm not. Despite my

preference for the sword, Father was relentless, making me practice with the bow at least as much as the sword. After all, I would have to teach and choose archers as acting warlord, I needed some level of mastery.

I end up sinking into the familiarity of it, feeling a pang of longing for my family. Though it was Father who made me practice, Papa fashioned my first bow for me.

Pulling the string back and timing the release with my breath turns into a meditation and I'm relaxed on the inside, even if my muscles are tired on the outside, by the time she calls for me to break so she can give me feedback.

"You have skill, Tristan. We can work with that, but you must improve your speed if you want to match that of an Elf."

"Is that possible?"

"We shall see."

She's a hard taskmaster and makes me work all morning until past noon.

"Look young Warlord, you have an admirer," she whispers in my ear.

She's right. From the corner of my eye, I spy Bayaden. He's pretending to be focused on his warriors, but his mind is far from them. I laugh inside, amazed. I was certain the man hated me only yesterday and he still hasn't stopped referring to me as 'nordo'wa,' the Elvish equivalent of idiot, but now he's watching me in a way that only can be described as admiration.

I'm still not convinced I'm not just a passing fancy and that he's enjoying having a toy in his bed. He might think he loves me today, but tomorrow, I could be a toy for the guards.

In true Tristan style, I decide to play a trick on him. I shoot a few more arrows and make a show of getting a little more intimate with the bow than is necessary. I have no trouble hitting the target.

When I reach the last arrow in my quiver, I check to see if he's still watching me—he is—and pretend to aim for my target. At the last second, I turn and release my arrow; it pierces through the air, landing in the spot I want: in the tree above Bayaden's head.

He frowns at me and I make my way over to him.

"See something you like?" I say running a hand nonchalantly through my short hair as I push my hips toward him.

He blushes. *Blushes*. Ladies and Gentlemen, I've done the impossible. I've caused one of the most indecent creatures of all time to blush. He didn't want me to catch him staring at me.

He clears his throat. "Why would I look at you? And did I say practice was over?"

It's not even his best rejoinder. "Did I say I was stopping? I came to get my arrow. I'm not as good as your sister, my aim is poor," I say tugging my 'stray' arrow from the tree.

"Nonsense," he scowls. "Your aim is good for a human."

"So, you were watching me."

"I was not ... All right, maybe for a short time," he admits. "You're good, Tristan. I thought you would be. Your body is perfect for archery."

"My father is the best bowman in all of Markaytia."

"Why didn't you tell me?"

"I prefer the sword."

"This is your best bet against an Elf. There are less factors to overcome and, of course, you can have the element of surprise."

"True." *Unless I have a magic sword.*

"Are you ready for lunch then?"

"I can't. I'm in the middle of practice. Haven't been dismissed yet, Warlord."

He smiles. "You are dismissed. You must get lunch for your Master, and yourself—go before you anger him."

"Yeah, yeah. I'm going."

"Tristan, wait. Come here."

When I'm closer he pulls me to him pressing a firm kiss to mine with his soft lips. I hate how much I like him kissing me.

CHAPTER 22

*J*ust when I've got used to how things work around here, everything changes. Andothair and I no longer speak as often as we used to. For starters, I've irritated him (husband's ex-boyfriends can be so fickle). Honestly, it's not like I knew he and Corrik were an item, I don't see why I get all the flack.

Bayaden is, well he's still Bayaden, but he's Bayaden infatuated with Tristan and that's different somehow. I can't say he's nice, but he's softer. He still orders me around like a servant because *I am* his servant, but I've become more important to him. I've gained status and am ignored rather than scorned or beaten; no one touches me now. Lutheran and Siagin give me looks that say they would like to have another go at me, but even they steer clear.

"What's wrong with you?" Bayaden says from beside me.

"Nothing, I'm thinking."

"Don't hurt yourself."

I try to push him with my foot; it's like pushing stone, but he takes it as an invitation to roll so he's half on top of me and traces my abs with his finger. He's tender and contemplative. I'm nervous when he gets like this. He tends to admit to the things he's feeling in these moments and I'd rather he didn't. It's less real when he says nothing and easier to pretend our relationship is the same as before.

"Tristan?"

"Yes, m'Lord," I say in a lazy accent, hoping to knock him out of his serious thoughts. It doesn't work. He gives me an annoyed look; I clear my throat. "Sorry."

"I want to say something to you."

I sit up. "Don't. Don't say anything Bayaden, just, take me. Please?" Sex is always a good distraction with Bayaden, with any Elf for that matter.

He stares at me for a long time and if I didn't know him better, I would think I saw a glimmer of sadness in his eyes, but I do know him better and he doesn't get sad. In any case it's gone by the time I've blinked.

"As you wish, Tristan." He buries his face into my neck, kissing it, worshiping it and without words he gets to say what he wanted. *Could I have fallen in love with a man like Bayaden, once upon a time, if I was given the choice?*

I moan when he sucks my navel and arch my back and reach out and pull him closer. He does take me, several times and when he's finished, I can't move. He falls asleep with one hand protectively on my chest like he's afraid I'll leave him in the night.

The morning sun is hot as it rises and wakes me; I'm still in Bayaden's bed. Moving is stiff from three days ago, the pain reminds me of the markings on my back. Bayaden's asleep and rolled off me during the night; he's on the other side of the bed. I slide off, slip into my pants and out the door. They don't wear shoes here, not around the palace at least. They're less polished than the Elves of Mortouge, but I think the no-shoe thing is more to do with the heat.

I begin with the plan to fetch the warlord his breakfast but can't help myself and get pulled outside. It's quiet in the morning, except for the roosters. I sit on the steps and watch the sun finish its ascent and think on what I'll do next. Andothair still plans on attacking Mortouge because of a broken heart. The king allows it because he either desires Mortouge for himself (Andothair's broken heart is convenient for him) or he likes to spoil his children like the Mortougian king does. Diekin is still a prisoner, and I must get him out. I thought I only had one way, using my dragon blood if I had to, but if I do, Tristan the human would be no more.

But now, there's this new thing with Bayaden. Perhaps there's a way of stopping this war without my death. I sit a long time thinking about everything and the sun is well into the sky when I hear a voice.

"Something on your mind, young Warlord?"

"Yes, I was just thinking of you, actually."

"Well, you'd better start thinking of what you are going to say to my brother. He's got his men out looking for you. You are lucky I agreed to join the foray and have found you first," Andothair says.

"Why would he be looking for me? I've only gone to get him his breakfast as I do every morning."

"Breakfast has long passed," he says laughing.

"Long passed? Damn. I've been out here too long." I stand to leave but there's something I've got to say before I miss my chance. "Andothair—I'm sorry. I didn't know about you and Corrik."

"My quarrel is with Corrik. I should not have tried to kill you."

"Or hold me prisoner or give me to your brother as a love slave or start a war with Mortouge. In the least, you should've told me he still lives."

His face hardens. "I regret nothing. And besides, your life is here now, Warlord. It's easier to think of him as dead, is it not?"

I'm not answering that. "Move on. The war is unnecessary; innocent people will die, Andothair, people who have nothing to do our ridiculous love triangle."

"When he's got nothing left, he'll see how I feel."

"It doesn't work like that, Andothair. Let it go."

"It's not so simple, young Warlord."

"Then let Diekin go."

"Bartering for your friend's freedom?"

"Is that on the table?"

"You make my brother happy, and you've upheld your end of the bargain, but Diekin is to ensure you will continue to do so. What would I have if he were gone?"

"You will have my word. I will swear it on the heart of Markaytia. A Markaytian is only as good as his word."

He shakes his head. "I will require something more binding than that. A magical contract."

I'll do it, I'll do anything that gets Diekin out of here, but there's one problem. "I'm already magically bound to Corrik."

"What nonsense are you chattering about?"

"On our wedding night when we consummated our marriage, Corrik said we'd be bonded by flesh and by magic." I no longer bat an eyelash at talking about sex.

Andothair bursts into rancorous laughter, mocking me. "Oh, Warlord, you really had me for a second there."

I wait silently, expecting he'll explain if only he can stop laughing long enough.

"Stop looking at me like that and you sound ridiculous. Bonded by flesh and magic ... that is not a real bonding, not for you anyway—you are a human, you cannot bond to an Elf by flesh."

"Corrik seemed pretty confident about it."

"Corrik is, Corrik. He believes far too much in prophecy and therefore the visions he has had of you—he thinks that since it was written in the stars for the two of you to be together so is everything that goes with that. I know better. Only Elves can bond by flesh, therefore Corrik has bonded with you, but you couldn't possibly bond with him in the way another Elf would."

"I heard thunder in my head when it happened—that's got to mean something. Maybe we can't bond like an Elf and an Elf are meant to, but what about the magic part?"

"Thunder in your head you say? I am sure that was just your shoddy human brain malfunctioning," he says, laughing at this own joke. "A bonding by magic during a wedding consummation is not a real thing, it is more of a, what do you Markaytians call it? Oh yes, an old wife's tale. If only Elves could command sex magic in such a way."

"It's old wives' tale," I correct him. I'm tired of being insulted by him for being human.

"What do you know of magic anyway, Warlord? The magic of humans died well before your time."

"Corrik said new magic can be created."

"Indeed. That much is true, but like I said, Corrik believes far too many outrageous things about magic, figures he would be arrogant enough to think he could command the Sex Gods to do whatever he pleased."

Bloody hypocrite. Corrik is arrogant to be sure, but Andothair talks like he's not. "Well, let's just say he can, and I am bonded to him by flesh in the way Elves are meant to bond and the old wives' tale isn't a tale and so the magic thing has worked too, what then? Won't that interfere with whatever it is you want to do to me?"

Maybe I shouldn't have brought it up, maybe my being bonded to Corrik will null whatever he wants to do to me, but there's also the chance it could rip me apart. Andothair is right on one count, I don't know much about magic, or Elves; my lack of knowledge creates in my mind all the outrageous possibilities of what could happen, things that most likely defy common sense.

"Not to worry Warlord. Elven bonding is a natural thing and is as polyamorous as we can be. Hypothetically, if you did bond with Corrik, you can still bond with another."

"This makes the 'bond' sound meaningless. What's the point of bonding if you can bond with as many people as you like?"

"It is not meaningless. The whole point of bonding is to create some form of unbreakable connection. When Elves mate, they mate for life and it connects them in a way that is above and beyond mere human bonding. An Elf will crave his mate, or mates like no other and can become possessive, especially when the bond is first formed—that is part of mating—I would not expect a human to understand. And while each dominant Elf is different in how he conducts his relationship with his mate, one thing is consistent: They both feel they own each other—something that gets stronger over time."

"Even the submissive mate?"

"Of course, even the submissive mate," he says like I've been living under a rock. "Submissive doesn't mean pushover, submissives feel very possessive over their dominant."

"Your bond to him still exists, doesn't it?"

"You are smart for a human; I'll give you that."

I don't expect that information to cut me like it does. Corrik's lived a long time, I've known he wasn't a virgin since before our wedding day (like he hypocritically expected me to be), but hearing Andothair say they've mated feels different to me; I feel my dragon blood begin to boil, but then I remember this is Andothair I'm talking to and he's probably lying.

"Calm down," he says when he sees I'm about to break something. "I am not Corrik's mate, he has taken you as his mate. Yet my bond with him still exists because *I* have bonded with *him*. He has never bonded with me. This means we have mated in the biological sense of the word, but not in the other sense."

"That can happen?"

"Obviously." He's beginning to get annoyed with my ignorance.

"Well, there must be some consequence for stealing another's mate," I say.

He continues to look at me like I'm the stupidest person alive.

"Let me guess, stealing a mate can result in death." Which is why he said he couldn't help himself wanting to kill me.

"You got it, Warlord. Stealing a mate is not illegal, but it is frowned upon. In most cases, it is almost impossible to break up Elves who have mated, but since you are human, it was no trouble for me at all."

"Good for you. But even if all you say is true, while I may not have the strength or power to fight you, Corrik does and he's going to kill you."

"Do not worry about me, Warlord. I have an offer he can't refuse." His eyes are saying something I can't decipher. Whatever his plan is, he's not concerned with Corrik finding him. "Anyway, the enchantment I have in mind is of a different nature and would not interfere with a bond of flesh or of magic—I am not preposterous enough to think I can command Sex Gods. Humans cannot bond with Elves," he scoffs again in case I didn't heard him the first fifty times.

And I would roll my eyes at him, except, I think that some form of bonding has happened between me and Corrik. No, I'm not as possessive over Corrik as Corrik seems to be of me or Andothair over Corrik, but perhaps that's the part where my being a human comes into play. Maybe the bond simply didn't take as intensely.

But I do have dragon in my blood and that means at least a small inkling of magic, perhaps it even makes me part creature. Maybe the bond was able to take hold in some capacity.

"I'm not convinced, Ando. Tell me more about this old wives' tale."

"You are quite demanding for a little human," Andothair says. "Lucky for you, you amuse me. It is said that once, an Elf long ago, asked the Sex Gods to bind his betrothed to him since, like you, his betrothed was a human. The Elf wasn't content with a simple bonding by flesh, of course; he wanted his intended to fall in love with him. He prayed to the Sex Gods to make it so. When the Gods refused him, he found a way to command their powers on his wedding night. Each time they had sex, his betrothed fell more in love with him," he pauses. "What's the matter, Warlord? You have gone white."

The legend sounds too much like my own story, for my liking, and I can't speak. Corrik wouldn't *make* me fall in love with him, would he?

"It's just a myth, Warlord. The enchantment the Elf wanted is a love spell, which is why the Gods refused to grant his request. No one can evoke a love spell like that. Not even the great, Corrik Cyredanthem."

I'm not so sure. My heart beats faster.

"Bet you wish you could unhear that, eh?"

"Whatever. It's as you said: A myth. It isn't real." I don't want to hear any more of this story.

"It is not real. The enchantment I will use on you; however, is very much real."

"Do you plan for me to become a mindless, sex slave?"

"You are already a mindless sex slave," he says, laughing. "No. This enchantment will not damage your mind— Baya would be extremely displeased if I were to do that. The enchantment will make you feel loyal to him."

That doesn't sound so bad—it's already somewhat true and I seem more compelled to please him each day.

Sadness washes over me. I've fallen in love with Corrik, but not really, only because he performed Elven love voodoo. Andothair may not believe it happened, but I do, I heard the thunder. The sadness is quickly replaced by anger and my dragon blood rages.

"I'll do it Ando. I'll give myself to your brother—gladly."

"All right then. We shall talk details later. You had better go," he says. "You're already in for a decent spanking as it is."

"Ando, can't you talk to him. Tell him I was out here with you?"

"I could, but I'm not going to."

Of all the nerve. I stalk off to get Bayaden his breakfast, which has now become his brunch, figuring it's better not to show up empty handed. I don't make it to the kitchens; I'm accosted by two of Bayaden's men immediately upon entering the palace. They take pleasure in dragging me up to Bayaden's chambers and toss me inside.

"Bayaden told us to tell you to stay here if we should find you," he says. They both delight in my dilemma. They know Bayaden is going to kill me. At least they leave me be, without roughing me up. When I turn toward the room, I see it's a total disaster.

The entire room has been ransacked. Blankets, pillows, even Bayaden's beloved books are scattered all-round the room. Whole wardrobes are turned on their sides with the clothes ripped out of them. The table is not where it's meant to be, and the chairs have been thrust at odd angles throughout his chambers. Stunned, I sit down on my mattress, which is not where it's meant to be either and wait.

Bayaden returns and stands in the doorway, angry. His look alone could boil water and says *explain.*

"Bayaden, I only went to get breakfast, I—"

"—where is this breakfast you speak of?"

I scratch the back of my neck, under his gaze, which reminds me too much of Father when he was displeased with me. "I got distracted. I'm sorry, I didn't mean to worry you."

"You should've told me where you were going."

"You don't usually care." I don't mean to say it; I'm just trying to get myself out of trouble, but now I've gone and thrown down a gauntlet. I run a hand through my hair, frustrated. He takes long, quick strides toward me and wraps me in his large arms. I feel the strength of his embrace, he's grateful I've returned. His head is tucked into my neck and I can feel his hot breath on my ear as he breathes. "I thought you were gone."

"Is that why your room is a disaster?"

He nods into my neck. *Stupid, hot-tempered, Elves.*

I know in that moment it's gone too far with Bayaden. We've said nothing to each other, but we don't need to. I'm forced to admit to myself that there's chemistry between us and it's not just one-sided. I care about Bayaden. Perhaps not to the extent he cares about me, but enough I should be honest with him and with myself.

I try to pull away, but he won't allow it. "Bayaden, I've just made a pledge to your brother."

He rips away from me, a fierce expression on his face like he's about to hunt down his brother.

"Not that kind of pledge, Bayaden, listen."

He doesn't respond, but nods at me to speak, warning me with his eyes to choose my words carefully. "I've told him I'm going to stay with you and to prove my word true, I'm to enter a magically binding contract."

"I don't see why you would need to enter such a contract. You're already mine, of course you're going to stay with me."

I look toward the destruction that is now his room. "Yeah, you seem real secure about things between us."

"Tristan, there is something between us, I can feel it."

"There is." The Gods forgive me, there is.

"Then why would you need to make such a pledge?"

"I want Andothair to release Diekin and send him back to Mortouge. I'm willing to trade my person for that, permanently and remain in your service."

"If that is what you wish, I will participate, but I do not require it."

"I don't wish it either, but your brother requires it. Before anything is done, there's something you must know."

"Yes?"

"I love my Husband." I need to admit it out loud, for myself. I've never said so to Corrik. Even if it's false love forged on our wedding night by sex magic, I feel love for him.

"I'm not worried about your affections for Corrik, Tristan," he laughs. "In time, he will be a memory—I plan to make you forget him quickly."

I hope he can. Thinking about Corrik hurts.

"I must go," he says pulling away. "And you can get to work on all this." He gestures around the room at the complete travesty it is now.

"Me? You're the one who destroyed it."

"Because of you. Clean it up."

"Of all the ... I have a good mind to—"

"—to what?" he says, whipping around.

"Never mind."

When he's gone, I clean. It takes me most of the day until dinner. I leave dinner on the table for Bayaden in no mood to speak with him after a long day cleaning up his mess. I make the trek down to the dungeons to see Diekin instead, not bothering to secure permission from Andothair this time. I've been down here enough I figure I can lie about it; I've gained certain freedoms in my months in Aldrien.

"What business have you here?" one of the polished guards, Emerick, asks me.

"I've permission to seek Diekin."

281

He considers me a moment, but as I expect he does not call my bluff. "Proceed, human."

I take the key and carry on to Diekin's cell. "Diekin?" He doesn't look good; it hasn't been that long since I've last seen him, has it?

"Warlord."

I open the door and hurry to kneel beside him. "Here, I've smuggled you in some food."

"Smuggled?"

"The prince doesn't know I'm here."

"Tristan, what are you up to?"

"He's alive Diekin. *Corrik,*" I say with careful excitement.

"I told you. And the others?"

"I don't know, but there's something else; I've found a way to get you out of here. I don't know when it will happen, but I've bargained for your life and when the time comes you need to go home."

"You're not coming, are you?"

I look at my hands. "I'm not."

"I won't leave without you."

"You're going to die here if you stay, Diekin. Maybe not today, maybe not in a year from now, but you will. I don't know if I'm going to get another chance like this."

"Was this your plan all along?"

"No. Diekin," I say. "I'm not going to use that plan if I can help it." If I can't persuade Andothair to abandon his plans to start war with Mortouge then I will use my dragon's blood.

"You've traded yourself for me once again, haven't you?"

"Yes."

"What have you done?"

"Diekin, listen. My original plan involved my dragon's blood."

"Do you have magic, Warlord?"

"Not in the traditional sense, no. I have one power, but if I use that power I'll die."

"How could you even think of using such a thing just for me? I know you were, Warlord."

"I was."

"What are you up to?"

"Nothing if I can help it. You need to go back and warn Mortouge that the Rogue Elves are coming."

"Corrik is going to kill me anyway when I return without you."

"Then you must explain it to him and make him understand," I say with a look to match my father's. He stares at me a long time.

"I see you are coming into your heritage, Warlord." He sighs as he looks to the ground, resigned to what I'm making him do, but not liking it much. I don't like seeing that look on him. I miss the Diekin I rode carefree on the bow of the ship with.

"Here, Diekin. Eat."

"Only if you will eat with me and tell me another story —one of you and Lucca. This might be the last time I see you."

"Where is your eternal optimism? I might get away yet."

"You have no intention of returning to Mortouge, Warlord. I know this."

I won't lie to him. "No. I already told you. I can never face Corrik or Mortouge again. I only hope I can save Mortouge and that they will still hold alliance with Markaytia."

"I know the man Corrik is he will make sure Mortouge's

end of the bargain is held for no other reason than he loves you."

"I hoped you'd bring him this." I reveal the goal of my secret venture, my wedding ring. I found it scattered amongst the wreckage today and I got the idea to do this.

"Take it and tell him I say... tell him I say, hi."

"Hi?" He laughs and it's worth me looking foolish.

I can hardly tell Corrik I love him—not when he won't see me again and not when I suspect him of sex magic. "Yes, hi. Is there a problem with that?"

"No, Warlord," he still laughs. "It's just, I thought, well it doesn't matter what I thought. I will give him the ring and tell him, *hi*."

"Thank you, Diekin."

"And, Warlord?"

"Yes?"

"You are wrong. You will see Corrik again. I'm going to make sure of it."

I storm into his chambers; my dragon blood still rages. I didn't like the look on Diekin's face, I don't like what I've had to do, I don't like what I'll have to do, and I don't like what I've learned about my and Corrik's union.

Bayaden looks up from his book. He's not pleased with me upon my return, and I don't care. I enter and pretend I don't see him or feel his eyes piercing into me.

"I thought I made it clear you are to tell me where you go?"

"You no longer trust me, m'Lord?"

"You're angry," he observes.

"I'm not angry. I'm but a lowly manservant here to do your bidding," I say.

"Bang up job you do of it." He turns back to his book. I don't know if he intends to leave it at that, but I pass by him and wash my face in the bowl across the room.

"Have you eaten?" he asks when I return. I can't tell him I've dined with Diekin; what I ate was meager anyway.

"No."

"So, you can listen to something I've said? I should take my strap to you more often, uh?" I know he doesn't mean it. It's his attempt to get me to laugh. "Over there, I've left you something." He looks straight into my eyes. "Eat."

Too tired to argue, I move to the table and sit down before a plate covered with a lid. I remove the lid to a fancy plate of fruits and cheeses, but in the center is a familiar, circular band, encrusted with emeralds; I reach out to grab it.

"Allow, me." Bayaden is behind me and picks up the ring; he swings out my chair and pulls me to stand.

"Where did you get that?"

"Your bag. I didn't know I had it until today when I found it amongst my things as I ransacked my quarters. Andothair must've placed it in my rooms. I recognized the Markaytian craftsmanship of the dagger and determined that the gold of that ring comes from far away and is not Elven and so I knew these things must be yours. Tell me, what is this ring?" he says studying it.

"It comes from my papa's homeland. It's his family ring, he gave it to me when I was a boy."

"I can tell by the way you speak of him that you and your papa are close."

"We were." I watch him spin the ring. "I miss him."

"There is an inscription inside. *Submit to the Heart.*"

"Yes. Papa was like me, submissive." I bow my head, still somewhat ashamed of this knowledge.

He lifts my chin with his thumb and pointer finger. "I'd like you to have this back, Tristan. It will be my apology for making you clean up my mess and a thank you for what you're doing. You may not love me as you love him, but that makes your actions all the more meaningful."

"My sacrifice you mean."

"Is it a sacrifice if it's something you give willingly?"

"I ... I'm not sure."

"Look deeper, Tristan. You did it because you value something more than you value yourself."

I can't argue with that.

"Here," he slips the ring on my finger. "I wish I could say I'm sorry for the things I do, but I'm far too selfish. I want you any way I can have you. All I have on offer are apologies you'll find meaningless, and tokens of my affections you'll find insincere."

It's the first time I've let him admit such affections out loud. "Thank you. It means a great deal to have this in my possession again." I run my finger over the band.

"You need not be ashamed of your papa, Tristan. It's a great honor to be submissive. Look at my brother. He commands an entire kingdom alongside my father, and he is submissive. He has no trouble telling me what I must do," he grumbles.

"How does that work, anyway?"

"Submissive does not mean weak. It means great power. Andothair has only ever allowed one to have dominion over him aside from Father."

"Corrik."

"Yes. His need for punishment and rules does not mean he'll allow just anyone to provide that for him."

"How was he able to discipline me?"

"You could discipline someone too if you chose to. You have arms and a brain, haven't you?"

"But shouldn't it go against my nature or his to do so?"

"It will, which is why neither of you would receive much satisfaction in it."

"Which is why he was quick to relinquish the duties. Why didn't he tell me?"

"Because he knew you wouldn't go to him anymore if he told you and he knew you needed it."

"Are you trying to tell me he was doing something for my benefit?"

"Why wouldn't he? Andothair is a good man and would never let a human suffer needlessly. He helped you for as long as he could."

Right. We're the equivalent of animals to these Elves. He makes it sound like Andothair is an anti-human cruelty activist. "He tried to kill me," I remind him.

"He was driven to kill you—he is bonded to Corrik. He didn't kill you—that's what matters. It took great strength to stop himself killing you. Don't you want to do the same to anyone who keeps you from Corrik? Don't you plan my death each night?"

"No. I've no wish to kill you." I reach out to toy with a lock of his hair. *Bayaden is beautiful.*

"I am too magnificent to kill."

He's trying to make me laugh—Bayaden isn't usually this soothing—I cut him a quarter smile, but say no more to that. I'm breathing hard, the room is spinning a little and I have to hold the table to steady myself. Corrik's use of sex magic is irrelevant I realize; what I've done is worse. I had to marry Corrik either way, his use of magic to make me fall in love with him was a kindness, it made everything easier.

As for me, at first, I did the things I have because I was coerced, but what I've been struggling with is how much I enjoy them. I go to Bayaden as willingly as I went to Andothair for punishment. Diekin says Corrik will forgive me, that Elves feel differently than humans, but I am a human and I don't think it's okay. I don't deserve Corrik for that reason and most of all, I don't deserve him because I do have feelings for Bayaden—real feelings. He does something to me, and I crave him.

Corrik will move on or perhaps return to Andothair's side. Diekin will be with his mate and Markaytia will have an important ally. Everything will be good.

So why does the thought of it all make me dizzy?

Bayaden puts a strong hand to the side of me that's not supported by the table. "Especially you with your Markaytian sense of duty must realize you did what you had to in order to save your friend. There is only one reason for all of this guilt."

"I enjoy it, all right? I enjoy when you fuck me."

"There is something more than fucking. It must be more than fucking. If you won't be honest with me, at least be honest with yourself. You care for me. Not like you care for Corrik, but enough."

I've already been honest with myself, but I won't admit it out loud. "Care for you? How could I care for my captor? It's only the fucking I seek, and my body craves you now. I'm tarnished and it's too late. I can't face Corrik ever again."

"You do care for me though," he says again. "Otherwise, it wouldn't matter what your body enjoyed. Rest assured, it isn't your fault, Tristan. I have magic too you know," he says with a beaming smile. "Don't beat yourself up over it, leave that to me."

I say nothing and glare at him.

He sighs. "Am I going to have to deal with your pouting all night? Or could we put all this energy of yours to other things?"

For once, I do not want sex. "I want to sleep, Bayaden, in my own bed and tomorrow I want to shoot things with arrows."

"As you wish, Tristan."

EPILOGUE

I appear calm on the outside as always, but Diekin knows better, he expects I'm going to kill him slowly and painfully. I may just and save him from having to face my sister after such disgrace.

He was returned to us hours ago. I cared little that he was clearly malnourished and paler than is usual for our kind. He is without Tristan—*I want to know why*—but Ditira forced me to wait and allow the healers to do their work. She didn't do more than card her fingers through his pasty hair, never asking a question, knowing I would want to ask the first ones. When he was healed, she kissed him, but left us without a word—that's why I love my sister. She is good to me—too good. I know the anguish she's suffered not knowing what has become of her mate. But she gave me time alone with him I needed. After she left, I listened to him a long time as he told me of Aldrien's plans for war with Mortouge and finally, he forced out the words about my Tristan.

"They are keeping him, Sire. He is alive and well."

"Keeping him? Was there a note? A ransom demand?"

"Nothing. Just this, from Tristan."

In his hand is the wedding ring I gave Tristan long before our wedding day. I snatch it from his hand. "Tristan gave this to you to give to me?" I clarify.

"Yes. And he says ..."

"*Yes?*" I prompt when he stops speaking, the desire to hear any word he might say to me strong and anxious. It's been months without him—at least I now know he's alive. *Tristan is alive.*

"Hi."

"Hi?"

He gives a firm nod.

It means something specific—I know his heart even if he does not know himself.

"Do you know what it could mean, Corrik?"

"I think so. It means, Goodbye."

"Hello, means goodbye?"

"Yes. He accepted it as an act of good faith before our wedding; he's giving it back to tell me to stop having faith because he's lost faith in us. It can only mean one thing: he has betrayed me."

"He bartered to save my life, even if he shouldn't have. He did not betray you, he had little choice." Diekin's eyes narrow, but not at me, I think he's angry with Tristan. I am too.

"I know that Diekin and I agree, but Tristan is a man of great honor, he believes this the honorable thing to do in light of whatever thing he has done. It does not matter that I don't see it as betrayal, he does." I don't care what thing he's done. I should be the one to decide if he may leave me and I'd never decide that. If he won't come home willingly, I'll have to fetch him—somehow. I smolder, growing angrier with him for being so presumptuous over what I might feel that he'd leave me over his own foolishness.

"Corrik?"

Something in the way his voice trembles, I know the accusation that's coming. "Yes?"

"Where were you? Tristan didn't voice it much when he would visit me—he wouldn't, it's not his style, but I know he wondered—why didn't you come?"

The assumption itself is preposterous, if only he knew what we've been through in these past months. "What makes you think I haven't tried?"

"I asked Tristan more than once if he'd heard any word of Elves in the area, he seemed able to discover a lot, he never mentioned having heard anything about other Elves. I'm surprised to find you still in Mortouge."

"I haven't been in Mortouge long, we've been to the place Aldrien lies and it's not there—*it has somehow disappeared!*"

"We've always known where Aldrien is, it's right here," he says pointing at the map. We're in the large War Room, the only place I am these days. I stare at that deficient map repeating the same thing, *but it's right there* because it's the only thing I can do—I have the insatiable need to do something.

"Andothair has figured out a way to hide Aldrien. It's not there, not anymore. We've been in and around the area we know it to be, we remained there for weeks until Father ordered us home when it became nothing more than a camping trip."

"How can it be hidden?" He's staring at the map, barely able to speak, his jaw opening and closing several times trying to make words out of the scattered thoughts flying through his mind. "I believe you, but Corrik, I was there months—it is there I assure you."

"I'm certain it is, but I don't know where it went," I say. "I don't suppose they allowed you to be awake for the journey back?"

He shakes his head. "What do we do about it then? How do we find it?"

"We?"

"Yes. I am going to help, whatever you do."

"How do you know I'm going to do anything? And what makes you think I'd allow you to if I were?"

"Because he means more to you than anything. You'll figure out a way to get him back." Diekin gives me his famous wink. "And I'm not asking for permission. I'm coming. It is my right to redeem myself, we all deserve a shot at redemption, do you not agree?"

I do agree, but I don't say so. Diekin is a cocky little so-and-so and doesn't need any more to feed his ego with. "If I'm to suffer your presence, you will agree to obey me in Ditira's absence."

"Don't I always?" I narrow my brow at him. Diekin isn't behaved at the best of times. "I will, Corrik."

"And if you don't?"

"You'll tan my pretty little hide?"

"Every day for the next millennia," I say and mean it.

"Yes, Sire."

"What's going on in here?" Alrik stands in the doorway tall and foreboding. What does he want? He's the last thing I need to deal with now. Unfortunately, I must answer him. He's owed respect as my brother and elder, even if I want to plough through him with my fist for interfering all the time.

"Diekin and I are going to find Aldrien and rescue Tristan."

"Not without me you're not. The details. Now."

I growl, but I obey him. I relay everything Diekin's told me, including what little I know of their plans for war. I tell him what has become of Tristan.

"Then this is grave, very grave," he says. "Very, well. I will join your search. I have always dealt well with the Aldrien Elves, perhaps I can persuade them otherwise—if we ever find them that is."

He cannot be involved. No one knows of my affair with Prince Andothair; he'll skin me alive. "You will not be able to talk the Aldriens out of war if they've decided they've reason enough—you know how stubborn they are."

"Perhaps, but it is always worth an attempt. In any case, you are too emotionally wrought over that Markaytian, Corrik. I don't trust your judgment in this. Be grateful I allow you to do this at all. I know Father advised you to lay this to rest."

Yes, advised me. He didn't outright forbid it. It's hard to control my tongue, especially when he refers to my husband as 'that Markaytian,' but I do. "I can be trusted, brother. I don't require assistance."

"Nevertheless, you will have assistance, *my assistance*. You have not yet come of age and your youth is yet another thing that blinds you. I do not trust you."

It gets harder to keep my temper at bay; I've never been known to do it long. "I am married."

"You were too young to be married. You know well that is why I did not attend the wedding, in protest of it."

"Father does not agree with you."

"Father dotes upon his youngest son far more than he should. It is up to me to instill the discipline that you lack."

"You've disagreed with the marriage from the start, you don't want me to find him. How can I trust *you*?"

"I have every interest in finding your new husband. It is not his fault that Father is indulgent with you and now we have a treaty with Markaytia that we must uphold. It does not require him living to do so, but I will not have us look irresponsible to the Markaytian royals. I will help you get him back and will invest every skill of mine to do so. How dare you accuse me otherwise?"

It isn't hard to anger my brother, just as it isn't hard to anger me—a trait I must admit I get from him. Our father and mother are not nearly as quick to anger.

"I am sorry, Alrik. I did not mean to insult you," I say, rather than point out how many times he's insulted me during this conversation. Of course, Diekin is witness to this argument and it will further confirm for him the discourse between my brother and I, and he will relay this to Tristan. Normally I'd be upset about that, but it makes me smile with the thought that Tristan is alive and could be home someday to hear Diekin speak of my quarrels with my brother at all. Diekin's return has refueled my hope, the hope that was beginning to wane.

His eyes give me his most disapproving stare and I can only hope he will not punish me in front of Diekin for what I've said.

"Your insolence proves my point; you do not have the wisdom required for such a task. I will join you; that is final."

There is nothing more I can say to that. Once Alrik's mind is made up, there is little one can do to change it. I'll have to accept his help and keep my secret another way. I give him a tacit nod, but make it clear I'm displeased.

He leaves and I'm alone with a smiling Diekin, who is trying hard not to laugh at me. I slam him against the wall, and *that's* the thing that sends him over the edge with laughter.

"You're not yet in my good book as I believe the Markaytian saying goes." I keep trying to practice them for Tristan so he'll feel at home—once he finally is home. "Why are you laughing?"

"Because. The two of you are hilarious. Who needs the theatre?" His laughter reaches uncontrollable so I help him control it by punching him square in the gut. He's only just been healed to full strength, but his behavior is going to earn him a punishment that will rob him of some of that good health.

"Oaf!"

I let him drop to the ground.

"Oh C'mon, Corrik. I'm only teasing." He's still smiling. There are times when Diekin and I are formal and other times when we aren't. I know he acts familiar now, and teases me to ease my tense demeanor, but I'm not in the mood to appreciate it. "Don't tease me—I'm short on patience of late. Go see my sister." I don't possess large amounts of patience to begin with.

I've effectively wiped the smile off Diekin's face. They've seen each other, but he hasn't had to face his mate yet and he knows she will be disappointed in him. Diekin cannot stand her disappointment. Between the two of us, only I know that she won't have the nerve to be hard on him —she was too sick over his absence and is glad to have him back. But I'll let him think he must view her full disappointment; the cheeky bastard needs some form of punishment. He leaves and I am alone.

297

Alone with the true weight of the problem I now face.

I know this war is my fault. *How long will I have to pay for that mistake?* I fell in love with Ando a long time ago, but something always prevented me bonding with him, I like to think it was fate. I do love him still and yet I love Tristan more. I once dreamed of forging an alliance; I would have been the one to finally add the eighth Elven realm to our sphere, but then I saw the vision that told of Tristan and I thought the eighth kingdom could be damned. We already have seven; do we really need an eighth? With seven realms, the Rogue Elves would never dare oppose us. I don't see why they would dare now. It's a fool's errand. They will lose. But one thing shakes me to my core, if Andothair can move an entire kingdom, can sneak Elves onto a boat, defeat my large army, and steal my husband, *what else can he do?*

I look at the ring Tristan returned to me and spin it around in my long fingers. I can feel remnants of his energy still present in the ring and even though it is no longer on his hand, it has energy enough to warm its twin, the one on my finger. The energy is weak, it's been dying awhile now. Too long without the bearer and both rings will go cold—that's how I knew he wore it after our betrothal, that's how I know he hasn't worn it since we lost him—the heat in my ring began to fade instantly. It's why I was beginning to think he was dead.

But he isn't, he's very much alive.

I could sense him through the ring, and I got to know him by it, even better than through the book I left. I felt his essence through the ring; I got to know his beautiful heart. I fell in love with him the first time I saw a vision of him in my dreams, but my love grew deeper as I got to feel his warmth. I tried to send my love to him through the ring. Every night, I pictured him—what I'd seen in my visions of him and what I'd seen of him that first time when Father and I travelled to Markaytia.

I wanted to take him with us that very day, but my father made me wait because of my brother. Alrik was against the marriage from the start and is against it still. He doesn't care that it was foretold by prophecy. Thankfully, he couldn't overrule Father.

It's hard for an Elf to be in the presence of the one they know as their mate and do nothing to assert dominance, even before bonding. I wanted to leave him with a mark and the best I could do was a ring—*this ring.*

He doesn't wear it now, nor my marks, nothing to display that he's mine. This makes me crazy. When he's home, I shall have, *Property of Corrik Cyredanthem, please return if found,* tattooed on his arse—seeing as he's so fond of tattoos—he's mine and someday he'll know it.

When you are back Tristan, I will make sure to impress this upon you.

Taking my sword from its sheath, I bathe the blade in blood, by holding it in my fist and running the blade inside its sharp edges cut through the skin and tendons of my palm and fingers. If I were a human, this would devastate my hand and it would be useless, but I am Elf and my hand will heal in full before the next rising dawn.

I feel the pain as my sword tastes the blood and I say these words, *"Tristan. With this ring I bind you eternally to your one true love."* I place the ring on the table and slam my sword down to imbibe it with the powerful Elven magic I call forth.

It's anti-climactic. There is no flash, but I can feel the power crackling around the ring when I pick it up from the ruin that is now the table.

When he places the ring on his finger, it will give him

faith once again, for it will bind him to his one true love and he'll *know* who that is forever and for certain.

Now, I just have to hope that his one true love is me.

THE END

WHAT'S NEXT?

Wanna see what happens next? Tristan II: A Brat's Tale is available now on Amazon.

OTHER BOOKS LIKE THIS ONE

Did you enjoy the caretaker dynamic in this book? Wanna read it in a non-fantasy setting?

Check out *Xavier's School of Discipline*. Available now on Amazon.

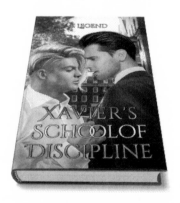

A LETTER FROM MOCK

Hello Dear Reader,

I wanted to personally thank you for purchasing this book. It means a great deal to me to be able to bring these stories to you. They all begin with someone nattering on at me (in my head) with passionate enthusiasm, until I write what they say down. I have little control over what they say and do—I'm just the scribe. I need help. Send help!

I hope you will consider leaving me a review on Amazon and Goodreads. I am but a needle in an elephantine haystack. Reviews and ratings help me show up on the internet so that other people will find my books.

With Love,
Mock
(S. Legend)

ABOUT THE AUTHOR

Mock is the author of the bestselling Tristan series. Tristan became a #1 bestseller in LGBTQ2S+Fantasy on Amazon. All her books have made various bestsellers categories on Amazon.

When she's not writing, she's consuming all the MM fiction she can, lifting, chilling with her family and pretty much refusing to live in the real world. She resides in Vancouver, Canada with her husband.

To read more about S, visit S Legend at:
Website: https://www.mockingbirdpublications.com/

GOODREADS: https://www.goodreads.com/author/show/14493179.S_Legend